FRIENDS

F-BOMB: SEALS LOVE CURVES, BOOK 5

MARY E THOMPSON

Friends

F-BOMB: SEALs Love Curves, book 5

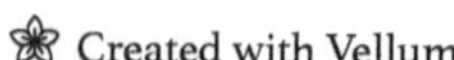 Created with Vellum

F-BOMB: SEALS LOVE CURVES

Welcome to the world of F-BOMB where a group of former SEALs have come together to protect the curvy women they love and the country they call home from the dangers of the world. They have the training and the knowledge, and they have the ability to kick some ass when needed. And it'll be needed.

F-BOMB: SEALs LOVE CURVES
Freedom
Fiancée (subscriber exclusive)
Forgotten
First
Failure
Friends
Family
Forbidden
Future
Finally

SUBSCRIBE NOW AT MARYETHOMPSON.COM

To friends who become so much more...

1

Kyra Cordes cleared her throat and stepped forward in line for the teller. She was in a hurry, and there were not nearly enough people working. She didn't expect it to take so long to cash one check, but if she'd waited until after her interview, the bank would have been closed. And she had to pay her rent tonight.

She tapped her shoe and glanced around. She caught the eye of a guy a few people behind her and rolled her eyes. He smiled and nodded, like he agreed.

Finally, she made it to the front of the line. She cleared her throat again. Her throat was scratchy. Spring was in full bloom, and with it, pollen was everywhere. She dug through her purse to see if she had a cough drop and heard, "Can I help you?"

Kyra looked up and found the teller calling to her. She smiled and stepped forward. She didn't even have to see the woman's stomach behind the counter to know she was pregnant. God, Kyra was surrounded by pregnant women. At work, at the gym, at the damn bank. Rubbing it in that she couldn't get pregnant.

"Hi," Kyra said to the teller.

"Can I help you?" the teller repeated, her smile dipping just a little. There was a line behind Kyra, a long one. The teller eyed it, then brought her focus back to Kyra.

"Yeah, um, I need to cash this check." Kyra handed over the check and the deposit slip and cleared her throat again. "Do you mind if I grab one of these?" She pointed to the hard candy dish next to the window.

"Sure," the teller said, taking the check with a smile.

Kyra unwrapped the candy and popped it in her mouth. She cleared her throat again and turned her neck. Her shoulder was stiff. That didn't usually happen when the pollen started to bother her.

"How did you want this back?" the teller asked, lifting her gaze to Kyra.

Kyra opened her mouth to answer, but her tongue felt thick. She opened her mouth again. Nothing came out. No sound, no words, nothing.

The look in the teller's eyes screamed of concern. Kyra didn't know what was happening to her, but it was obviously not good. This was not pollen, and it was not going to get better with a hard candy.

Kyra panicked at the thought of the candy in her mouth. She couldn't move her tongue to spit it out. Like everything else, it was numb.

The teller stood and got taller and taller and taller. Then a sharp pain hit Kyra's head. She couldn't see the teller anymore, but instead she saw feet. And the front door.

SLADE O'KEEFE WAS BARELY PAYING attention to the other people in line in front of him at the bank. He hated going there. It was almost as bad as the DMV. The people were just as happy to be working there, and just as efficient.

It was his turn to make a cash run for the week for F-BOMB, the company Slade owned and ran with his former SEAL teammates. Their boss, Daniel Dunn, liked to have petty cash on hand in case they bought lunch or dinner or breakfast, or all three, as was the case that week. They'd used the last of their cash buying treats to have on hand for the interviews they were conducting.

With Dunn about to have a kid, the whole team agreed they needed an office manager. Someone who would keep shit together. They all clearly sucked at the job, as evidenced by the fact they ran out of cash and had to tip the last delivery driver in change. Embarrassing.

The group of them were former SEALs who had created a business as private security and investigations consultants. That was the fancy way they talked about it. In reality, they were civilians with the skills of all the bad guys who could work around the letter of the law to get things done. That was how Slade liked to think of it.

The front door opened and closed quickly, drawing Slade's attention. His neck stopped him from turning all the way. Something wasn't right.

In front of him, the teller shouted and the woman on the other side of the counter fell to the floor.

Slade rushed over, more of his body fighting him. He'd definitely been drugged. He didn't know how or when, but something was working its way through his system. Quickly.

He tapped the woman's cheeks and rolled her onto her back. "Ma'am, can you hear me?"

She immediately started choking.

Slade rolled her to her side again and apologized before

he stuck his finger in her mouth to see if she was choking on something.

Something hard touched his finger. He scooped it out, hoping it explained why she fell. Nope, just a piece of candy.

Slade turned her face to his. She looked up at him with hazel eyes, almost green to match her shirt. They were dilated, like she was on something.

"Can you hear me?" he asked, feeling his own body sink deeper and deeper into whatever drug was pulling at him.

She opened her mouth like she was trying to say something, but no sound came out.

Slade reached for his phone to call Rocky, the team's medic, but someone else screamed before he could grab it. Slade turned and froze.

"You aren't going to want to do that," said a man with a gun trained on Slade.

"I'm just trying to help her."

The man shook his head. "No, you're not going to get her help. Because that's why we're here. And besides, you're going to need help soon, anyway."

"What did you do?" Slade choked out. The fight was draining from him. He dropped one hand to the ground, struggling to keep his eyes on the man with the gun.

The man smiled. His blue eyes were like ice. His face was scarred, like he either had a bad case of chicken pox as a kid or serious acne. Slade catalogued everything. The man's short, dark hair with a hint of red. The black hoodie and dark jeans. And the gun that was definitely from a run-of-the-mill gun shop and not something homemade.

Which meant if Slade could get him to fire it, they might have a chance to find him later.

"You're a coward," Slade said. "You don't have the balls to shoot me."

The man shrugged, allowing Slade a moment of relief. Then he lifted his gun to the teller. "You're already on the ground. You're not a threat. Shooting you would be a waste of a bullet. But her?"

Slade struggled to turn his head to the teller. Fear mixed with her tears. Her hands cupped her round belly, protecting her unborn child. She slowly shook her head.

"Are you going to be any trouble?" the man asked her.

"No," she said quickly. "No. Please."

The man looked back at Slade and grinned. His teeth were almost perfect. Everything about the man said he had plenty of money, but he was robbing a bank. That wasn't always about the money, but Slade wasn't going to be able to do anything to stop it.

His arms gave out, and he dropped to the floor. The man lowered his gun so it wasn't pointing at the pregnant teller. He glanced at Slade and grinned.

"See? I told you you weren't a threat." He looked around the rest of the bank and said, "Let's move."

Then he disappeared from Slade's view.

Kyra watched the man who'd tried to help her sink to the ground in front of her. For a moment, she had hope that he would save her and she'd be okay, but then the man she'd smiled at in line pulled a gun on them.

A bank robbery. She could only imagine what her parents would say if she told them about this. Her entire life, she'd been the screw up. The one who let them down. She wasn't thin enough or smart enough or anything enough. Not when her older brother was perfect. He was attractive and athletic and smart and everything a parent wanted in a child.

Kyra? She was as opposite as it could get. She was a disappointment. Which was why she lived on the other side of the country from her family. It was almost far enough.

As she laid there on the ground, the only thing she could think was at least she was wearing clean underwear. Her mother always told her to make sure she wore clean underwear in case she was ever in an accident. Kyra thought it was a weird rule, especially because if she was in an accident that was bad enough that someone would see her underwear, the chances were good that the person also would have no idea they had been clean before the accident.

Kyra hoped she didn't wet herself laying on the ground staring at the sexy man who was giving her looks. Wait, was he trying to say something?

He kept shifting his eyes up like he was trying to look behind himself. Was he having a seizure? No, he kept looking back at her. He was doing it on purpose.

Kyra looked behind him. Not much was going on. The men were getting everyone to lie on the ground.

Oh! He wanted her to watch what was going on.

Kyra tried to nod, but her head wouldn't move. She didn't want to risk making a noise and alerting the men with the guns that they were communicating, so she just blinked and hoped he understood.

He stopped rolling his eyes back in his head, so she assumed he got the message.

Kyra watched the men work. They were clearly in a hurry, which worried her less than if they were taking their time. If they were in a hurry, they were going to try to get out of there before the cops showed up.

Would the cops show up?

Kyra hoped so, but how would she know. Someone had to alert the cops for them to know there was a bank robbery in progress. That usually meant a silent alarm.

She almost laughed at herself. She watched too many cop shows. She didn't know how real life worked.

Two of the men stayed with the other people in the bank. Another man and two women were also on the ground, like Kyra and her companion. Drugged, she assumed. It was the only thing that made sense, although she couldn't figure out how they'd been drugged. It had to be something in the bank that she touched. The door? The pen? Deposit slips! She touched the deposit slips. She tried to look at the man across from her. Yes! He had a deposit slip, too. That had to be how they drugged everyone.

Movement caught Kyra's gaze, and she screamed. The teller she'd been speaking to was being dragged away by the man with the blue eyes. They went to an office. Kyra's noises didn't get far, and she wasn't very loud, but the man across from her noticed.

A tear ran down Kyra's cheek. The woman was pregnant. She didn't deserve to be treated like that.

Kyra stared at the doorway they disappeared through until the two of them walked back out with a third person. A man with keys. The three of them went to another doorway and disappeared again.

They weren't gone long before the man with the gun came back alone. He had a black bag over his shoulder. He nodded to the other two men he was with, now both holding bags of their own, and the three of them went for the front door.

The security guard stepped in front of them. "I'm not going to let you leave here with that," he said.

The man with the blue eyes grinned. It was the kind of

smile Kyra would have found attractive in other situations. God, what kind of men did she like?

"And what are you going to do to stop us?" the man asked.

The guard reached for his side. Before he could even get the gun out, the man lifted his and shot the guard.

Kyra jumped and squeaked. The guard stepped back and fell against the wall. He slid down slowly, his eyes wide, leaving a red streak.

"Anyone else want to stop us?" the man asked. "How about you?" He pointed the gun at a man in his twenties. "No? You?" He chose a woman in her forties. "How about you?" He pointed the gun at Kyra.

Tears slid down her cheeks. She just needed rent money. For an apartment she no longer wanted to live in. And instead, she was going to die.

The man grinned and shook his head. "No one can stop me."

Then he and his friends walked out the door like they were regular customers, if you could overlook the masks the other two had covering the lower half of their faces.

Kyra waited to hear gunshots or sirens or something to tell her the police were there, but there was nothing unusual. Silence. Normal street noise.

The other people started to move. To get up. One went to check the guard for a pulse. One checked the front door. Another pulled out his phone and called the police. Kyra and her companion had no choice but to lay there and let it all happen around them while the drugs worked their way through their systems.

SLADE WATCHED as his companion's eyes scanned the room. He could hear people getting up and moving. His phone buzzed constantly, likely the rest of his team trying to reach him. The word was definitely out about the robbery, and help was arriving.

Feeling returned in his fingers first. Slade itched to grab his phone, but the feeling was slow to filter through the rest of his hand.

The whole time Slade laid on the ground, his anger filled him. Once again, he was defenseless as someone held him captive. This time, he wasn't going to walk away. He wasn't in the middle of a war and had to follow orders. He was going to find the men who did this. He was going to end them.

A firm hand landed on Slade's shoulder, and his entire body jerked. Adrenaline sped through his system as he turned and tried to fight off whoever the hand belonged to.

"Slade, it's me," Rocky said. Adrian Malone, known as Rocky to the team, was the team medic and one of the smartest people Slade knew.

"Oh, God," Slade groaned, the adrenaline forcing the last of the drugs from his system. "Rock."

"What the hell happened?" Rocky asked. He held a light up and shined it right in Slade's eyes.

Slade wanted to fight him, but he knew it would be worse if he didn't let Rocky do a quick exam. "Drugs and guns. I don't know what they gave me or when."

"Deposit," the woman on the ground murmured.

"Deposit?" Rocky asked.

"Deposit slips," Slade said, looking down at the papers still clutched in his hand. "They must have put the drugs on them." He looked down at her. "Good catch."

She tried to smile, but not much of her face moved. Her

hazel eyes still showed fear, but her breathing was steady. Some of her hair had fallen forward into her beautiful face, but she couldn't move it out of her eyes. She was still clearly feeling the effects of the drugs.

Rocky noticed and went to her, brushing her hair back and starting an exam. Slade checked out the scene around them. The guard laid on the ground near the door, not moving. Other people huddled together and walked around. Police officers were taking statements.

"Slade," Rocky said, pulling his attention. "What's her name?"

Slade shrugged. "I don't know. She was the first one to go down. I came over to help her and they pulled the guns."

"You know you need to give a statement," Rocky said.

Slade nodded. "I'll talk to Captain Patrick. Is she going to be okay?"

Rocky leaned back and nodded. "She's going to need to go to St. Nicholas, but she'll be fine. You should go, too. For now, stay put. I'm going to bag those slips."

Slade nodded and watched Rocky walk away. Slade sat back on the floor next to the woman. She tilted her head to look up at him and her hair slid back into her face.

Slade brushed it back from her eyes and smiled. "Hey."

She had beautiful eyes. Hazel with a lot of green in them. Perfect lips with a little bow. Round, soft cheeks. And a curvy, plush body to go with them.

Slade was a sucker for a curvy woman. And damn if the one trying to smile at him didn't make him forget all about the way they met.

2

"HELL, YEAH," BOBBY SAID, SLAPPING THE DASHBOARD. "WHAT a rush! That was awesome! Did you see how they went down?"

Stevie chuckled next to him and nodded. "They never saw it coming. That was smart, putting the drugs on the deposit slips. Genius."

"I told you," Bobby said with a cackle. "I'm gonna make us rich! All of us. Stick with me, boys, and we'll be on a beach, or wherever the hell we want to be, in no time."

Bobby checked the rearview mirror, but no one was following them. His heart was pounding and the blood in his veins was racing. The only thing better than pulling off a score like that was finding a hot woman, or a few, to make use of the hard-on it gave him.

"Why did we have to go there?" Mario mumbled from the backseat. "Of all the banks?"

Bobby rolled his ice-blue eyes at Stevie. They talked about Mario and knew he was going to be a pain in the ass. Bobby'd known Mario most of his life, and he wanted to bring his old friend along, but Mario... Bobby wasn't sure if he was cut out for the life Bobby intended to build for himself. Bobby had big dreams. Dreams that didn't involve regrets or second thoughts or whiny little bitches that made him feel like he shouldn't enjoy what just happened.

"Because we know it. It made the most sense," Bobby said, the frustration in his voice barely held in check.

"You should have told me where we were going," Mario said softly.

"Why? So you could ruin the whole thing for us? No," Bobby spat. He turned to glare at Mario in the seat behind Stevie. His head was down as he studied his fingers, smartly avoiding meeting Bobby's gaze. "That's not what this is about. We brought you in on this because you said you needed some money. Fast money. Easy money. You don't get to be all pissy about the way we got the money. We got the money, so shut the fuck up."

Mario scowled in the backseat, but he didn't say another word. His face was pinched up tight as he turned to look out the window. His neatly trimmed beard and perfectly cropped hair screamed too good. Mario held down a regular job sometimes, but he had bills to pay, so he went to Bobby for help. He knew what he was getting into. Bobby never tried to pretend he was someone he wasn't, but Mario did. He wanted to look like he was all neat and clean and perfect, but he was just a lowlife like Bobby.

No, that wasn't true. Bobby wasn't a lowlife. He was on the top of the damn world. He'd walked away from the person he was growing up. He flipped his parents the bird the day he turned eighteen and never looked back. The assholes didn't get to define him. He defined himself.

The only thing leftover from his childhood was Mario.

Which was why Bobby was so pissed. If he could reach Mario, he'd turn around and slap the little bitch. Mario whining about the bank they hit wasn't what Bobby needed. It killed the boner he had, which meant he wasn't going to be able to enjoy their night as much. It was better when he could walk in showing off what he had and have the women all falling all over themselves for a chance to suck it or fuck it.

And they all wanted to.

Fucking Mario.

Stevie pulled into the garage and closed the door behind them. It was pitch black, shut off from the world. Just the way Bobby liked it. He didn't need anything the outside world could give him. He needed money and women and freedom. Nothing else mattered.

"Are we going out tonight?" Stevie asked when he opened the driver's door. The car lit up, casting a harsh glow over all of them. Stevie pulled off the dark hat he wore in the bank to hide his platinum blond hair and mussed it up.

"I don't know," Bobby muttered. "I'm not in the fucking mood anymore." He shot Mario a glare that had his old friend looking worried.

"Sorry, Bobby," Mario said quietly, averting his dark eyes. He climbed out of the backseat and stood next to the car, away from Bobby. "I just worry we'll get caught. That someone will recognize one of us."

"You need to stop worrying. We're invisible to them. We always are."

"Not to all of them," Mario said, scowling once more. He looked up at Bobby and walked around the car toward the door into the house.

Bobby shook his head and slung his arm around Mario's shoulders just before the garage went dark again. "No one knew who you were. That's why you wore a mask and glasses. Next time, we'll go somewhere else."

Mario nodded and smartly kept his mouth shut. Bobby led them into the house. Home sweet home. Stevie's mom left him the house when she died, and it was the perfect place for the two of them. It was also why Bobby made sure Stevie was in on everything. He was the brains, but Stevie could turn him in in a heartbeat if he ever wanted to. And the son of a bitch was crazy enough that he would totally do it.

The three of them carried their supplies and loot into the house, leaving the bags by the garage door. Mario took off once everything was inside. He trusted Bobby to give him his cut of what they collected. Stupid fucker, Bobby thought with a grin. He and Stevie carried their riches downstairs to where they housed it. They pulled about a tenth of what they collected out and set it aside for Mario, then hid the rest where he'd never know he didn't get his fair share.

After all, what could he do about it? Tell the cops?

Kyra's ride in the ambulance nearly made her sick. Not because of the ride but because of the cost. She had basic health insurance, and it was going to cost her a small fortune.

She asked the EMT what time it was and groaned when she realized she'd missed her interview. There was no way they'd give her another chance. She really wanted the job, too. But no new job and giant bills from the ambulance ride and most likely the hospital meant there was no way she was moving out of her apartment any time soon.

By the time she got to the hospital, she was starting to feel less woozy and numb. The man who'd tried to help her in the bank, Slade, asked if he could ride with her, but the EMTs wouldn't let him since they weren't family.

Kyra figured she'd never see him again, but she'd just gotten settled on a gurney when he strolled into the emergency room looking all big and badass and making every female in the room hope he was looking for her.

Except Kyra.

She didn't do attachments. Not that she didn't enjoy them, but after learning she couldn't have kids, she also learned men had biological clocks that ticked louder than most women. Her boyfriend of six months dumped her for someone who would be able to give him a family someday, and all the dates she'd been on since ended with a similar line.

So, Kyra kept to herself. She was used to relying on herself after a lifetime of being a constant disappointment to her family. Why would she expect anything else from the rest of the world?

"Hey," Slade said, pulling a stool to her bedside and making himself comfortable. "How are you? How is she?" He addressed the nurse with his second question.

"She'll be fine," the nurse said with a kind smile. She was pushing sixty by Kyra's guess, and probably thought Slade looked like one of her children, but it was also impossible not to react to those dark brown eyes when he pointed them at you. The nurse definitely blushed.

"Are you sure? Have you run a tox screen? And checked her nerve function? The drug was definitely powerful. I'm guessing a neurotoxin of some sort. She almost choked on a piece of candy, and she couldn't move."

"She was lucky you were there with her," the nurse said, patting Kyra's arm. "My daughter's boyfriend probably would have left her in the bank and ran if this happened to them. Hold on to this one."

Kyra opened her mouth to argue, but Slade grabbed her hand, startling her into silence.

"I don't plan to let her go," he said.

The nurse grinned brightly. "I'll go talk to the doctor and make sure he tests her for everything. We can't have anything happening to your girl."

"Thanks," Slade said.

He wrapped his other hand around hers and pressed his lips to her knuckles. Sparks shot up Kyra's arm and settled low in her gut. Nope. She could not go there. Not with a man like him. He was way too hot for her to think she had a chance with him. He was just being nice, for some reason. Kyra knew women with as many curves as she had did not get the hot, badass, alpha guy in the end. Not ever.

As soon as the nurse was gone, Slade swung his dark gaze back to hers. He released her hand with one of his and brushed her hair back from her face. He smiled, his eyes full of concern and his face a mask of worry.

"Do we know each other?" Kyra asked. Her own parents hadn't ever given her a look like that. Sure, they loved her, she was pretty sure, but they never worried about her. Maybe it was because she became independent really young, but then again, she became independent because they never really seemed to care what she did.

Slade's face fell. His eyes scanned her head. He stood and gently pressed his hands all around her scalp. She wasn't sure what he was doing, but it had been so long since a man had touched her that her body froze.

He leaned forward, looking at the back of her head and bringing his body close to her, and she inhaled. She told herself she just needed the air, but that was a lie. She needed new fuel to add to her solo fire. If she wasn't ever going to have sex again, at least not with another person, she needed all the help she could get in the fantasy department. And Slade was the stuff fantasies were made of.

Tall, dark, and handsome were only the half of it. She figured she'd barely come up to his shoulder if they stood side-by-side, which was something she loved about a man. Being on the curvy side, she preferred men who could make her feel small. He not only made her feel small, but all the muscles he sported under his black tee made her feel petite. His arms were bulky and his hands were magic on her head. He smelled like a man should smell, spicy, with a hint of musk. He wasn't the kind of man who sat around and did nothing. His jeans were well worn and his boots said he could kick some shit if he needed to. He worked hard. Likely with his hands.

Those strong, steady, heavenly hands.

"I don't feel anything. How hard did you hit your head?"

Kyra remembered she was the only one there and looked up at him. That concern was back in his eyes.

"Do you remember what happened?" he asked.

"At the bank?"

He nodded.

"Um, yeah. Why?"

"Tell me everything that happened."

"Why?"

"Humor me," Slade said. He put a hand on her shoulder and left it there, scorching her skin and making her feel like he cared.

Kyra sighed and went through the whole afternoon from walking in the door to the bank and filling out the deposit slip to collapsing and watching the people around her. Around them. She ended with his arrival at the hospital.

"You pay attention to detail. Wow. Not many people can recall that much about a situation. But I thought you didn't remember me?"

"You were at the bank, but I meant do we know each other from somewhere else?"

He chuckled and shook his head, finally understanding why she asked. He took his seat again and smiled at her. "No. I would definitely know if we'd met before."

Ah. He was one of those men. The kind who took home the hottest woman in a bar and made her wild all night, then walked away the next day without a thought in the world about her.

Kyra knew a few guys like that, but none that were half the man Slade was. But it was clear she wasn't his typical fling. Even if he was looking at her like he was worried. It was more the way a man would look at his sister than the way a man would look at the woman he planned to strip naked. Message received.

"Sorry. The way you were acting with the nurse made me think..."

Slade grinned and reached for her hand again. "I just wanted to make sure they covered all the bases with you. I didn't want them to miss something. We bagged the deposit slips, but if there's something else in your system, something we didn't know about... We want to make sure we have all the information."

"Oh, you're a cop? I didn't realize."

Slade shook his head. "No. I work with the police on special cases, though. I'm familiar with procedure. You're still going to have to make a statement to the police."

Kyra pushed up in her hospital bed and pulled her hand out from under his. "How do I know you aren't one of them? That you weren't in on it?"

Slade leaned back and crossed his arms over his wide chest. Kyra thought he might be offended by the question, not that it stopped her from asking, but he looked as casual as he had the entire time he was there. "You don't, aside from me telling you I'm not. You're going to have to decide if you want to trust me."

"Why aren't you in a bed?" a brown-haired woman asked, her gaze trained on them. She walked up to Slade and threw her arms around his neck. She pulled back and cupped his face in her hands, studying him the way Slade did with Kyra's head. "Are you okay?"

Kyra slinked back on the gurney, feeling like crap for allowing herself to fantasize over another woman's man. She didn't know he was involved with someone else, but cheating was never okay in her world, even if she didn't know she was a part of it. And even if it was only in her head.

"Lily, this is... crap, I'm sorry. I don't know your name."

Kyra smiled and extended her hand to Lily. "Kyra Cordes. I'm sorry. I was in the bank with your boyfriend—" Kyra caught the sparkle of the woman's rings "—sorry, husband when the robbery happened."

Lily snorted and shook Kyra's hand. "He's not my boyfriend or husband. He's an idiot who should be getting checked out. And he's single."

"Lily," Slade growled, shooting her a glare that held no heat.

Lily grinned up at him friend patted his extra large chest. She was clearly a woman who didn't take orders. "You can thank me later. Right now, you're getting checked out. Archer said you were drugged, too."

"You were?" asked the nurse who returned right then and overheard Lily's words. "We definitely need to look at you, too. I can put you right next to your girlfriend, though. Keep the two of you together."

"Thank you," Slade said, ignoring the raised eyebrows from Lily.

Kyra felt like she was watching a comedy sketch unfold in front of her, except she was a part of the show. She had no idea what was going on, but apparently, Slade was sticking by her side a little longer.

"Girlfriend?" Lily whispered when the nurse left to get orders for Slade also. "I always knew you worked fast, but damn. You didn't even know her name a minute ago."

"It was the only way they'd let me see her," Slade grumbled.

Lily smiled the kind of smile a woman with a secret used. She was finding the whole thing endlessly entertaining. Too bad Kyra was ready to get the hell out of there and get far away from the man who was far too tempting.

3
———————

Slade tried to ignore Lily, but he knew she wouldn't be pushed off. She was determined to stick with them. And since Rocky stayed at the scene to help check on others who'd been drugged, and Dunn called Captain Patrick to get permission for the rest of the team to be involved, Slade was at the hospital alone. He knew Archer would call Lily to check on him, but he thought he could handle it. If it weren't for Kyra, he could have.

When he walked in, she looked so alone. On a bed in the corner with no one around to hold her hand. He didn't hesitate when he rushed over to her. And when the nurse assumed they were together, Slade couldn't bear the thought of saying they weren't and being told he had to wait somewhere else.

Lily waited with them until someone came to take blood from each of them. Kyra was still a little groggy. The nurse mentioned keeping her overnight.

"I don't think I can keep you with her overnight, though. We can't allow coed rooms, even for couples."

"I understand. If I'm good to go, I can sleep on a chair or something."

"You don't have to," Kyra said firmly. "I'll be fine."

Slade tucked her hair behind her ear and smiled. "I know, but I'd feel better if I knew you weren't alone tonight."

"Oh, honey, let him spoil you for a night. Too many times we have people in here alone. If he wants to sleep on one of those uncomfortable chairs, hold on tight and don't let go."

Kyra looked like she was going to correct the nurse, so Slade lifted her hand to his lips and kissed her knuckles again. For whatever reason, it seemed to shut her up. And Slade was finding the soft skin of her hand irresistible.

The doctor ordered a CT for Kyra since she fell, but it came back clean. Their toxicology reports showed botulinum toxin, but Slade only had trace amounts. Kyra was exposed to more, so they admitted her for observation overnight.

The ER nurse handed Kyra over to another nurse who was going to take her up to a room. She explained that Slade wanted to stay the night, and the new nurse just smiled and said they had no problem with that.

Lily pulled Slade into the hall while Kyra was getting changed into a gown. It was hospital policy, but they also wanted her out of her clothes in case there was something on them.

Slade didn't like her being out of his sight, but a nurse was in the room helping Kyra get changed. It was already after dinner and quickly heading toward night, but the only thing on Slade's mind was making sure Kyra was safe.

"How do you know her?" Lily asked, tucking her brown hair behind her ear and giving him a curious grin.

"She was at the bank."

"Okay, but do you know her from somewhere else?"

Slade shook his head.

"Why are you so invested in her?"

Slade shrugged. He couldn't explain it, not even to Lily. She'd been kidnapped, but she was set free within twenty-four hours. The fear she felt lingered, but she was able to forget it and move on.

The fear Slade felt after being held as a POW for nearly two weeks followed him everywhere. He always thought he was strong and that nothing could hurt him, but being captured proved that he wasn't as strong as he thought.

He managed to push past the fear and the anger, but being in that bank brought it all back. The helplessness, the frustration, the knowledge that he should have been able to do something. And if all he could do was help Kyra, be there for her so if she had a nightmare she knew she was safe, then he'd do it.

But Lily wouldn't get it. Slade wasn't even sure the rest of his team would. They all knew what happened to him when he was held captive. He knew it could have been so much worse. He'd spent time talking it out with a therapist. The only thing that helped him was getting the hell out of the desert. He was able to move on and trust that he'd never be in that kind of situation again.

Or so he thought.

"She's all set," the nurse said with a smile, leaving Kyra's room.

Lily made sure Kyra got a private room when they admitted her, so it was plenty big enough for the three of them to all be in there. The beige floor and beige walls did nothing to promote healing. Signs on the wall said the nurse's name was Amanda and had instructions on how to use the TV and phone and how to call if Kyra needed help.

"Did you eat?" Lily asked, her gaze going from Slade to Kyra and back.

Slade huffed a laugh and shook his head. "We were a little busy."

"Are you hungry? I can run to the cafeteria, or I can grab something and bring it back."

"That would be great, Lil. Thanks. Kyra, any preferences?"

Kyra shook her head and pulled the blanket up higher. The way her nipples pressed against the thin fabric of her gown, Slade knew she'd removed her bra before she climbed into the hospital bed. He wondered what else she'd removed.

"I eat pretty much anything," Kyra said with a tentative smile.

"There are a ton of places close." Lily's phone beeped. "Hang on." She thumbed a text, then pocketed her phone and looked at them again. "Kyra, would you be okay with a few visitors?"

"No," Slade said. "She doesn't need to be subjected to everyone. I can get us some food. You go... Crap."

"What?" Lily and Kyra both asked.

"Howler," Slade said to Lily.

Lily shook her head. "We'll take him. Actually, we might stay at your house. If that's okay?"

Slade nodded. "Yeah, he'll drive everyone crazy. Or you can ask Kelsea and Jaymes."

Lily shrugged. "We'll figure it out. Why don't you go grab food and I'll stay here with Kyra. That way, they can all see for themselves that you're okay. They're worried about you."

Slade glanced at Kyra. He didn't want to leave her. Walking away was painful to imagine.

"You don't have to come back if you have something else going on. I understand," Kyra said with a forced smile.

Slade shook his head and walked over to her bedside. He couldn't resist leaning down and kissing her forehead. He lingered just a minute, reassuring himself that she was okay. "I'm coming back. Lily will take care of my crazy dog tonight. And I'll be back with dinner."

Kyra nodded and shifted on the bed. Slade waved to Lily and left the room, immediately texting the team that he would meet them in the lobby and not to go up to Kyra's room. The last thing he wanted was all his teammates checking her out.

"It's a good thing Slade was there at the bank," Lily said. She took the seat next to the bed. She was fishing. Kyra could feel it.

"I guess," Kyra replied.

"This whole thing is pretty crazy."

Kyra narrowed her eyes, wondering where Lily was going with it. "Um, yeah. It was."

"Are you feeling any better?"

Kyra nodded.

"Is there someone you want me to call? Sorry, I didn't even think to ask. Family, friends, boyfriend?"

Kyra shook her head. "Nope, I'm all set. I do need to make one call, but it isn't all that important right now. I guess it can wait until tomorrow. Hopefully, I can go home."

"I'm sure you'll be able to. It sounds like botulinum toxin works its way out quickly."

Kyra nodded again. Why was Lily still there?

"So, do you live around here?" Lily asked.

"Um, yeah. Not too far."

"Cool. Slade lives a little north of the city. He has a house with a big yard. His dog, Howler, is the greatest dog in the world. He can't hear or smell and his back legs don't always work, but he's awesome. Slade adopted him from a shelter because no one else wanted him. Our friend, Kelsea, volunteered there."

"Um, okay." If Kyra wasn't mistaken, and it was possible she was since she'd been drugged, Lily was trying to talk up Slade.

"He's a really good guy, Slade. He comes across as kind of an ass at times, but he's sweet and kind and really cares about the people he's close to. My husband works with him. They've known each other for years. They were SEALs together, and they all got out together. Now, they run an elite team that helps protect our borders. You don't usually think about our Canadian border as having a lot of issues, but it's crazy."

"Um, okay," Kyra said again. She had no idea why Lily was telling her all that, but it didn't seem like Lily even knew what she was saying.

"Anyway, Slade never dates. I mean, never. He's the kind of guy who meets a woman and never calls, but he doesn't date. I think he should because I think he'd make a great husband, but I'm taken. I mean, I'm not interested in him like that. He's like a brother to me. But you know, if maybe you were interested, then..."

The drugs were definitely still doing a number on Kyra's system because she was pretty sure Slade's friend was trying to hook them up.

And to think, before she went to the bank, Kyra thought the most exciting part of her day was going to be her interview.

SLADE FOUND the rest of the team in the lobby near the ER. They looked menacing as a group of seven men, all standing together, none of them smiling. They were tall men, and strong, all former military, and all tough as hell.

Archer saw Slade before the others and broke from the group first. "You have a girlfriend?" he asked.

Slade rolled his eyes. "Your wife needs to keep her damn mouth shut."

"So you do?" Archer asked again, his eyes lighting with humor.

"She's not my girlfriend. I don't even know her. It was the only way the nurses would let me see her."

"You were pretty concerned with her at the bank," Rocky added, his own smirk curling his lips.

The others joined them and asked Slade how he was.

"Doing okay. The drugs were powerful as fuck. They're gone now. I feel better," Slade said, looking to Rocky for confirmation.

"Botulinum toxin. Definitely powerful, but also fast acting. Enough to knock you out but not something that usually leaves any permanent issues," Rocky explained. "You should still get checked out in a few weeks to make sure everything is okay."

Dunn nodded. He was the leader of the group and technically the boss of the rest of them. Daniel Dunn was their second in command when they were stationed in the desert. As their XO, he was a damn good leader behind their commanding officer, a man who betrayed them all and almost killed them. Slade considered the group of them his brothers, even their two newest members, Jaymes and Mason.

"You okay?" Dunn asked.

Slade nodded. "I'll be fine. How was the interview?"

Dunn shook his head.

"Not a good fit?"

Dunn shrugged. "Never showed up. Kind of disappointing. She had the best resume of all the people who applied."

"We'll find someone."

Dunn snorted. "Ashleigh's due in five weeks. I'm running out of time to find someone and train them before I'm off for a month."

"We can handle training someone," Dex said. Ryker 'Dex' Hamilton was the new second in command. He was smart as all hell and lethal. If there was a man Slade wanted at his back, he'd pick Dex. He'd take any of them, but Dex topped his list. Dex made interrogations look easy and lethal force even easier. He was not the man Slade would ever want to face off against and was happy he was on their side.

"I know," Dunn said. "None of that matters now. What are you doing down here?"

"I need to get food and head back up. She doesn't need all of you invading her space."

Dex raised an eyebrow. "You mean you don't want all of us around her. You're settling down?"

"Jesus. You're all ridiculous. Archer, Lily said you could stay with Howler. I'm staying here tonight." Slade headed for the door, not caring if the others followed him or not.

"Yeah, we'll stay. We might mess up your sheets, though," Archer called out.

Slade snickered. "You might want to change them first."

Archer doubled over like he was going to vomit. Slade wasn't about to tell him to change the sheets because they smelled like Howler. He knew Archer and the others thought it was because Slade shared his bed with more than a few women.

He did that, too, but not in a long time. After their former CO and friend tried to kill them all and ended up dead in the process, Slade struggled to sleep. He woke up more than a few nights a week in a cold sweat or screaming. The first time he was with a woman and she freaked out, rightfully so. Slade decided until he got the nightmares under control, he needed to keep his distance from the opposite sex.

Slade walked outside into the warm May evening and stopped short at the crowd behind him. He turned and glared at them. "You're not going to follow me."

"We don't want you alone," Rocky said. He liked to mother-hen the rest of them.

"I won't be alone. I'll be in a hospital surrounded by trained medical professionals. I'm sure none of them are as good as you, but they're capable of saving my life if something happens. Any word on what was taken or who they were?" Slade asked Dunn, needing to change the subject.

Dunn shook his head. "They took a bunch of cash, but no clue who they were."

"Was there an inside person?" Slade asked.

"Hard to imagine there wasn't. They're still going through footage. You know it'll be awhile before they have anything." Dunn said. He looked as disappointed as Slade felt.

"One guy didn't wear a mask," Slade told them.

Dunn nodded. "Patrick knows. The others told them. Trying to get a good description. Someone will probably come here tonight to talk to you if you're okay with that. And to your girlfriend."

Slade rolled his eyes and walked away, showing them all

his finger as he left. He loved them, but he wasn't in the mood for them to choose him as the butt of their jokes.

Slade got in his truck and sat there for a minute. His adrenaline was finally slowing down, and he was going to crash soon. He'd been amped up all evening, on alert because of Kyra. Being alone in his truck and knowing she was safe meant his body could finally relax.

Slade drove through a burger place and got two meals with fries and a couple of milkshakes. He was back at the hospital in less than ten minutes and on his way up to Kyra's room.

He heard Archer's voice as soon as he stepped off the elevator. He was at the nurse's station, watching the elevator. When he saw Slade, he thanked the nurse he was talking to and headed toward him.

"I thought I told you not to bother her," Slade growled.

"I'm here to get my wife. She wouldn't leave until you got back. I stayed outside so they could talk," Archer said.

"What are they talking about?"

Archer snorted. "You. You know how Lily is."

Slade rolled his eyes and groaned. He pushed the door to Kyra's room opened and glared at Lily before looking at Kyra.

Lily looked at him and grinned, but her gaze immediately slid past Slade. Her whole face lit up before she rose from her seat and bypassed Slade for Archer.

Slade walked toward Kyra as Lily kissed Archer. Kyra cleared her throat and shifted on her bed, then tugged the thin sheet covering her up higher.

"I hope burgers are okay," Slade said, feeling uncomfortable again.

Kyra nodded and forced a smile for him. "Yeah, that's great. Thanks. Um, you can give me your address and I'll send you a check. I was at the bank to deposit a check and I'm out of cash. Crap. I need to call my roommate. She's going to kill me if I don't pay her tonight."

"We can go over there if you want," Lily said. "We can give her cash for you."

Kyra shook her head and chewed on her lip. "No, it's fine. Hopefully she'll understand."

"Seriously?" Slade asked. "Why would she not?"

Kyra snorted. "She's not the most reasonable person. I'll just explain everything and let her know I'll get the money to her tomorrow. I mean, I hope I can. I don't even know where my check is. I gave it to the teller."

"We'll find out," Archer said. "I'm Archer, by the way."

Kyra blushed when Archer moved closer to shake her hand. "I've heard a lot about you."

Archer's lips curled up, and he looked back at Lily. Lily had a guilty look on her face that said exactly what kind of things she told Kyra.

"Well, we should go," Lily said quickly. "Let them eat and get some rest. We're going to stay with Howler tonight. We'll come by in the morning to check on you guys. Let us know if you need anything."

Kyra nodded. "Thanks, Lily. It was nice to meet you both."

"You, too. See you tomorrow," Lily said as she dragged Archer from the room.

4

———

Slade gestured to the tray table, and Kyra nodded for him to set their food there. He put the bag and drink tray down and pulled out the burgers and fries. "Chocolate or vanilla shake?"

"Vanilla please," Kyra said. "Thank you. And you really do need to give me your address. I'll send you money."

"You don't need to worry about it. Just get better. The least I can do is buy you dinner."

"Thank you," Kyra said with a smile.

She unwrapped her burger and took a bite. She groaned and sank back against the bed. The sheet she'd clutched so tightly before slid down, exposing her neck.

Slade got lost for a second, staring at her skin. It wasn't erotic in the slightest, but it had him thinking of all the ways he wanted to make her feel good. He let his mind wander to where that little bit of skin could lead and how it would taste.

"Aren't you hungry?" she asked, nodding to the burger clutched in his hand.

Slade nodded and shoved it into his mouth. He was

starving, but the burger only satisfied one part of his hunger.

They ate in silence, both of them devouring their burgers before turning to the fries and milkshakes. Kyra dipped her fries into her milkshake and Slade made a face.

"You've never tried it?" Kyra asked.

"Uh, no. Because it's gross."

She shook her head. "You haven't lived until you've tried fries dipped in a milkshake."

"Oh, really?"

She laughed. "Absolutely. Better than sex."

Slade's brows shot up, and Kyra's cheeks turned bright red. So did that patch of skin at her throat. Slade wanted to see how far that red went, but first, he had to try her better-than-sex fries dipped in milkshake.

He chose a fry and pulled the plastic top off his milkshake. He dunked the fry in and swirled it around like she had done. Then he put it in his mouth.

Kyra watched with an expectant grin.

Slade shrugged. "I don't think it's better than sex, but it's not bad."

"Well, when you're not having any sex, you take what you can get," Kyra said. She immediately clamped her hand over her mouth, and the red that was fading on her neck deepened.

Slade chuckled. "Well, that's a fair argument."

Kyra pulled her hand away and nodded but didn't say anything else. They ate their fries and milkshakes, then Slade threw their trash in the bin near the door.

"Do you need to call your roommate? Or anyone else?"

Kyra looked at her phone and nodded. "I should. Sorry. I feel so rude."

Slade shook his head. "It's not rude. You have people in your life and I'm invading your space. I can step out."

"No, you're fine," Kyra said. "This will be quick."

KYRA FELT awkward with Slade hovering, but he made her feel safe. She had gotten so used to being alone and taking care of herself that when fear kicked in, she didn't think about having someone to lean on. But Slade was there. He was big and strong enough that maybe she could lean on him, just a little bit.

She decided to call Autumn first and let her know she would bring her the rent money the next day.

"Hey, Autumn," Kyra said when her roommate answered.

"Where are you? I told you I needed the rent money today."

"I know, and I'm sorry. I was at the bank when it was robbed. I'm in the hospital," Kyra said.

"Oh. Um, sorry. Are you okay?"

"Yeah, I think so, but they wanted to keep me for observation. Is it okay if I bring you the rent money tomorrow?"

"Yeah. I'm sorry, Kyra. I'll tell the landlord, too. He knows I usually pay him a little early. Do you need anything?"

Kyra shook her head, surprised Autumn was being even a little bit nice. "No, I'm fine. Thank you, though. I'll be home tomorrow."

"Okay. Have a good night."

"Thanks. You, too."

Kyra hung up the phone and looked at it for a minute. "That was weird," she said.

"What was weird?"

"She's not usually that nice to me. I figured she'd get mad."

"Maybe she's not as bad as you thought. How long have you been friends?"

Kyra shook her head. "We're not friends. We met through a mutual friend online. She was willing to have a roommate, and I needed a place to live. It was always meant to be temporary, but we've lived together for almost three years. I'm hoping to move out soon. Which brings me to my next call."

"Are you sure you don't want me to leave?" Slade asked.

Kyra shrugged. "It's up to you. If you have calls you need to make or something you need to do, you don't have to stay here."

"There's nowhere else I need to be."

Kyra nodded, feeling a little like he actually wanted to be there with her. She couldn't imagine why, but it didn't matter. After the night was over, she was sure she'd never see him again.

She dialed the number she'd used to connect with the guy she was supposed to interview with and listened to his voicemail say he wasn't available until it beeped.

"Hi, this is Kyra Cordes. I was supposed to come in for an interview this afternoon, but I was held up unexpectedly and unable to let you know I couldn't be there. I don't know if you're still conducting interviews or willing to speak to me, but if so, I'm still very much interested in the position. If not, I completely understand. Thank you for the opportunity."

Kyra hung up and sighed.

"Why didn't you tell them what happened?" Slade asked.

Kyra huffed a laugh. "I think that's the adult version of

the dog ate my homework. I mean, really? They're not going to believe I was in a bank robbery."

"They might. What kind of job was it?"

"It's an admin job. I don't know much about the company, but it sounded interesting."

"Is that what you do? Admin type work?" Slade asked, his brows pulling together.

"I've been an administrative assistant for the last three years. I've done office manager work and stuff like that. It's regular hours and decent enough money. It lets me have a life outside of work. Although, I don't really do anything so I don't really know why it matters."

Slade opened his mouth to say something, but there was a knock on the door. He turned and nodded to the police officer standing in Kyra's doorway. She sat up straighter in bed and pulled the sheet up again, wishing she could have kept her own clothes on. They wanted to make sure the neurotoxin wasn't on them and insisted she take everything off. Nothing like meeting a man and immediately removing all your clothes.

Too bad it wasn't for a much more exciting reason.

"We'd like to ask both of you a few questions," the officer said.

Slade extended his hand and introduced himself. The officer clearly knew who he was. "Nice to meet you, sir."

The officer was young and cute, but when his partner walked in, it was clear who was in charge.

"Slade, good to see you," the second officer said.

"You, too, Captain. It's not often we get you out of your office."

"Yeah, yeah. When something like this happens, I have no choice. I figured we should talk since you were there."

Slade nodded. "I was, but I didn't see much. I could

describe the one guy to you, but I didn't see any of the others. I... it knocked me on my ass and I was facing the wrong way."

"Yeah, I heard. It was some powerful shit, that's for sure. Why don't you and I head out into the hallway and these two can chat in here?"

Slade nodded, then turned to Kyra. She smiled at him. He walked over and bent down. He kissed her forehead and whispered, "Are you okay with that?"

She nodded, his lips moving against her skin.

"Okay," he said. He squeezed her hand and walked out with the captain.

The young cop stood at the foot of Kyra's bed. "Ms. Cordes, can you please tell me what happened at the bank?"

Kyra smiled and told him the whole story, a story she was sure he'd heard from every other person in the bank.

"Would you be willing to sit with a sketch artist to describe the man you saw?"

Kyra shrugged. "I can, or I can just draw him for you if you'll give me something to draw with."

"Um, I'm not sure..."

"Here, I'll draw it right here. He had dark hair with some red in it and light blue eyes. They reminded me of ice. They were unusual. He was wearing a dark sweatshirt and jeans. Nothing descriptive. Clean and nice, though. Like they were expensive." Kyra drew as she spoke to the officer, knowing he was recording what she said.

When she finished, she turned her sketch around. "That's him."

"I thought you said you needed to come back with an artist," Slade said, walking back into the room with the captain.

"We do. What the heck, Montgomery?"

The young cop shook his head and pointed at Kyra. "She did it."

"Is that him?" the captain asked Slade.

"I thought he had scars on his face, like from chicken pox or something."

Kyra shook her head. "I saw him when I was still in line. When he was talking to you, it almost looked like he'd put something on to disguise himself. This was what he looked like before everyone else started looking at him."

"Well, that should help us narrow things down. The privacy glasses they wore blocked out most of their facial features from the cameras, and the other people didn't get as good of a look at him. Thank you, Ms. Cordes."

"Happy to help, sir. I figured if I could draw him it would be better than trying to explain what he looks like."

"And you did a damn fine job. Hell, we might need to hire you."

Kyra chuckled. "In another lifetime I wanted to be a police officer."

"What stopped you?"

Kyra smiled sadly. "A lot of things."

Slade talked to the officers for a few more minutes while Kyra tried not to let her imagination run wild. It wouldn't do her any good to think about the things that would be different in her life if she'd made other choices. Or had a different family. She was happy with her life, and she wasn't going to bitch about it. She was going to spend her night in the hospital and enjoy the company of an attractive man, and then move on and pretend everything was okay.

She'd gotten really good at that. No reason to stop now.

SLADE SETTLED in the chair next to Kyra and tried to figure out what to say to her. He rarely had trouble speaking to a woman, but that was when he was trying to get her naked. The one in front of him... well, he wouldn't mind getting her naked, but she was in the hospital, and he wasn't that big of an asshole.

The only thing Slade could think to ask was about her art. "Where did you learn to draw like that?"

Kyra shrugged. "I've always enjoyed it."

"Did you go to art school?"

She snorted. "Um, no. That wasn't an option."

"Why not?"

"Because you can't make any money being an artist."

He got the feeling the words weren't hers, so he let it go. "You're truly talented."

"Thanks. Um, do you want to watch something on TV?"

She was changing the subject. Good to know. She didn't like to talk about her talents as an artist. "Sure," Slade said, if for no other reason than she might relax.

Kyra tried to hand him the remote, but it was attached to the bed and didn't go far. When she saw how close he needed to get to control the TV, panic filled her gaze before desire slid in.

Slade leaned back in his seat and said, "You pick. I'll watch anything."

She nodded, slumping back against the bed in relief, and flipped through the limited selection of channels. When she settled on a cooking competition, Slade grinned.

"I love these. You have to pick a favorite. Who do you think is going to win?"

She scoffed. "First, I need to watch the show for longer than five seconds."

He chuckled and nodded. "Fair enough. I think it's going to be the woman."

"Why?" Kyra asked, her voice ruffled and annoyed. "Because she's fat?"

Slade glanced at her and saw the death glare she was giving him. "She's not fat, and her weight has nothing to do with my opinion. I think she's going to win because her chopping skills are the best and she's not running around. She has a plan. She's organized and settled. She's just cooking, not competing. She's doing something she loves."

Kyra opened her mouth, then snapped it shut. She stared at the TV for a long minute before she said, "You're right. I'm sorry."

"You don't need to be sorry. I imagine there are people who would think that way. And you don't know me very well. I think we should share a few things about ourselves. I'll start. I have a dog named Howler who barks so loudly I need earplugs sometimes. I'm a former SEAL. And I live alone with my crazy dog."

Kyra narrowed her eyes at him. "That told me absolutely nothing about you."

Slade chuckled and tried not to let his shock show. Most women didn't care anything about who he really was. They didn't want to know what made him tick or what made him happy. They wanted to know how quickly he could make them come, and if he knew how to use what was in his pants.

"If that's all you want to share," Kyra continued, "then I'll say I live in an apartment with a roommate. I work as an administrative assistant, and I'm from California."

Slade grinned. "Where in California?"

"Southern California."

"Near San Diego? I spent some time there."

Kyra rolled her eyes. "Are you back to telling me you were a SEAL, because I know. You're supposed to share something real, not something surface."

Slade grinned and shook his head. "Fine, you want real? I don't know what to say to you."

Kyra snorted. "Anything. Your favorite color, your favorite food, if you sleep on one side of the bed or in the middle..."

Slade lifted his gaze, and it collided with Kyra's at her last statement. Heat filled the space between them with a healthy dose of desire.

Slade leaned forward, unable to stop himself.

Kyra grabbed the remote and jerked back. "Look," she said, cranking up the volume, "the woman won."

Slade was more than a little disappointed Kyra pulled away from him, but he tried not to take it too personally. She didn't know him, and she didn't seem like the type of woman he usually met. She was solid, stable, and had commitment written all over her. Slade usually kept far away from women like her, but he couldn't seem to resist this one.

He settled back in his chair and watched the show with her. And the next one. A nurse came in around eleven to check Kyra's vitals and draw more blood, then turned off the lights and closed the door on her way out.

Kyra's eyes started drooping in the darkened room. Slade's back was already hurting from the chair he was in, but he wasn't going to complain. He stretched out the best he could and let the sound of the TV and the subtle scent of Kyra lull him to sleep.

The rapid beat of gunfire woke Slade. He looked around and couldn't remember where he was. Everything was dark, and the smells... he thought he was going to be sick. He tried to move, but he couldn't. The drugs. He remembered the drugs they gave him, so he could see everything but not do anything.

More gun shots pierced through the air outside. Someone raced toward him. The door stopped them, but not for long. The wood splintered before it slammed open.

"They're not going to get you back alive," the man said in broken English. He lifted his gun and pointed it at Slade's head.

Slade wanted to duck or run or fight, but he couldn't do any of it. All he could do was lie there and watch death come and steal him away. He thought of his parents finding out he was gone, learning whatever lies the military would tell them because they couldn't know the truth. His sister would be crushed. She made him promise he would come home. Megan would never forgive him.

There was another woman, but he couldn't think of who she was. Someone Slade knew mattered, but her name was just outside his reach.

Then there was more gunfire. Slade's gaze slid to the door where someone else walked in. Help. Someone to save him. He was going to be rescued.

The person lifted their gun at Slade, and all hope drained from him. He screamed. If nothing else, his team would find his body and be able to take him home. A closed casket was better than an empty one.

"Wake up!" Slade heard from behind him. He still couldn't turn.

"Slade, wake up. Justin!"

That did the trick. No one in the military called him Justin. Even when he was in deep shit, they called him by his rank and last name. He was never Justin.

But that voice called him Justin. And told him to wake up.

He jerked back and pried his eyes open. The room was still dark, but there was enough light to see he was in the hospital. Was this part of his dream?

"Justin?"

That voice again. He looked around until he found it. "Kyra," he sighed.

She nodded, but her eyes said she was terrified.

"Did I hurt you?"

She hesitated and shook her head.

"I did. I'm sorry. Are you okay?"

She hesitated again and nodded. Slade let his gaze slide over her, looking for injuries she didn't have the night before.

"I'm sorry," Slade said, feeling like the lowest scum of the earth. The last thing he wanted was to hurt her.

"I'm okay," she said softly. "You just scared me."

"Did I touch you? Did I hurt you?"

She shook her head. "No. You were restless, then you started hitting the bed. And you were yelling."

Slade sighed and pushed his chair back, giving her space. He stood and walked to the foot of the bed. "I'm sorry. I didn't know it would happen. I haven't had a nightmare in a while."

"Want to talk about it?"

"No," Slade said, then walked out of the room.

5

———————

KYRA WATCHED HIM GO AND KNEW SHE'D NEVER SEE THE SEXY, wounded man again. She didn't know what made him so terrified, but she could only imagine the kind of thing that would scare a badass former SEAL like him.

She tried to go back to sleep, but sleep was impossible at that point. The sun was starting to come up and the soft glow through the shades outside her window said it was going to be a beautiful day.

Funny, since to her it felt like a day to lie in bed and never leave her apartment again.

Kyra grabbed her phone and checked her messages, but there weren't any. She hoped she didn't screw up her chances with that job, but it was hard to imagine the guy she was supposed to interview with would be understanding about her not showing up and not calling in advance. It wasn't the sort of thing that screamed reliable to a potential employer.

A nurse came in an hour later and told Kyra she would likely be discharged. Everything from overnight looked good, so there was no reason to keep her any longer. Kyra asked if the nurse knew anything about her car, but she didn't, so Kyra had to wait.

When the doctor came in with discharge papers for her to sign, Kyra thanked him and changed into the scrubs they offered her since her clothes were turned over to the police as evidence. She knew calling Autumn for a ride wasn't a good idea. She ordered an Uber and asked the nurse for directions to the front of the hospital where she needed to meet her ride.

She was almost there when she spotted Slade in the distance. He was talking to someone, and Kyra felt awkward facing him the morning after. She turned into the bathroom to wait a few minutes until they left so she could escape the hospital without running into him.

She washed her hands, then checked her phone again, sure he'd be gone when she left the bathroom. If she didn't get outside soon, she would miss her ride, so she took a breath and walked out.

He was leaning against the wall next to the door.

Kyra jumped back.

Slade dangled her keys in front of her.

"Where did you get those?"

"Your purse. We brought your car here so you don't have to take a cab or whatever home. I would have given you a ride, but I didn't think you'd want to be locked in a confined space with me."

Kyra smiled softly. Her hand itched to reach up and cup his jaw. He smelled amazing, like he'd showered since he left her room early that morning. And he had a cup of coffee. For her.

She was definitely in love with him.

"Is that for me?" she asked hopefully.

He nodded.

"Oh, my God, thank you."

Slade grinned as she inhaled the coffee. "Usually that kind of thank you is for something other than coffee."

Kyra smiled and shook her head. "I'm in love with coffee. Especially good coffee. This is amazing."

Slade nodded and turned toward the exit. "Are you ready to go?"

"Yep, discharged and free."

"Good. So, I, uh..."

"Thank you for staying with me. And for being there in the bank. And for dinner last night. And coffee. It was nice to meet you, even considering the circumstances," Kyra said, extending her hand to shake his.

He stared at her hand for a long moment before he slid his rough one into hers and shook it. The scratchy feel of his palm went through her body and settled between her thighs. Kyra was never going to forget him.

She smiled once more, then released his hand and walked out the front door, leaving Slade behind.

It was better that way. Even if it meant she had to search twenty minutes for her car in the hospital parking garage.

THE REST of the team was in a meeting when Slade made it into work. Archer knew he was heading back to the hospital after he went home early that morning. Howler was happy to see him and almost knocked Slade over when he let himself in the door. He sat on the floor and loved on his dog, needing the affection as much as Howler did to settle his raw nerves.

Sleeping next to Kyra was a mistake. He never should have put her in that position. Especially when he was feeling unsettled. Just like he should have seen something coming and helped her before she went down at the bank. So many times he let her down. He had to make it up to her, and he knew exactly how.

"...not sure if I should call her back or not," Dunn was saying when Slade walked in.

"Call who?" Slade asked.

"Morning. You okay?" Dunn asked.

Slade nodded and knew that would be the end of it. They weren't emotional men. They got the job done, and if the job involved crazy shit, they were expected to know themselves and if they were okay.

Slade was as okay as he was going to get.

"Call who?" Slade repeated.

"The interview from yesterday never showed up. She left me a message last night that she was held up unexpectedly and hoped we could reschedule. I was debating calling her back and giving her another chance. She has a great resume, but I'm not sure."

"Well, if you decide not to call her, I have someone I think you should call. The woman from the bank," Slade said.

"Your girlfriend?" Jack teased him.

Slade ignored Jack and focused on Dunn. "She has experience as an administrative assistant and she's looking for a new job. She's smart and talented and creative. She can do it, Dunn. We should call her."

"Do you have her number?" Dunn asked.

Slade shook his head. "I figured we could get it off the police report. Her name is Kyra Cordes."

Dunn tilted his head to the side and raised an eyebrow. "Are you fucking with me?"

Slade shook his head, giving Dunn a questioning look.

"You're serious? Your girl is Kyra Cordes?"

"Do you know her?"

Dunn nodded. "She was the no-show yesterday. She was our interview. And getting 'held up unexpectedly' wasn't an excuse. It was literal."

"Call her, dammit. She should have this job," Slade said.

"Why? How do you know she's so good?" Dunn asked, leaning back in his chair with his arms crossed.

"I don't, but I owe her. I should have been able to protect her in the bank, and I scared her last night."

"Whipped it out?" Jack asked with a laugh.

Slade flipped him off and kept his focus on Dunn. "I owe her. And you said yourself she has a great resume. We should hire her."

Dunn unfolded his arms and leaned forward again. "I'll tell you what. I'll reschedule her interview. I'll ask her to come in. If she's as good as I thought she would be, we'll hire her, but we're not giving someone a job because you feel guilty. It wouldn't be fair to her or to us."

Slade knew Dunn was right and nodded in agreement. "I want to be in the interview," Slade said.

Dunn laughed. "Not gonna happen."

"Why not?"

"You're too close. And if you're sitting here, it might make her uncomfortable. We need to judge her on her merits, just like we did the others, not on how much you want to sleep with her," Dunn said.

Slade flipped him off. "That has nothing to do with it."

"You weren't interested in being here for the other interviews. You weren't planning to be here last night when she was originally scheduled. Why the change?" Dunn asked pointedly.

Slade grumbled, but Dunn was right. Slade wanted to

see Kyra again. It wasn't fair to her or the other candidates if he sat in just because he couldn't stand the thought of being in the same building as her and not being able to talk to her.

He sat back while Dunn called Kyra. She was clearly shocked to be getting a call about rescheduling her interview and agreed to come in after lunch to meet with him and Dex.

On to the next order of business. "Any word on the bank robbery?" Slade asked when Dunn was off the phone.

Dunn shook his head. "You know that's not the kind of thing we usually deal with."

"Yeah, but I was there. I was hoping we could help. Or at least find out what the hell is going on."

"We can ask, but there's no guarantee they'll tell us."

"Ask. Please."

At Slade's *please*, Dunn picked up the phone in the conference room and dialed Captain Patrick. He put the phone on speaker while it rang.

"Patrick."

"Captain, this is Daniel Dunn and the rest of the team. We were wondering if there is any news about yesterday or anything we can do to help."

"I guess I should have expected your call. Unfortunately, we don't have much. The deposit slips were definitely how the drugs were administered. And we found out the wrapper from the candy Ms. Cordes ate had some of it also. That's why she had such a severe reaction. The cameras were tricked. They had privacy glasses on that obscured their faces and rendered the footage all but useless. We know where they went within the bank and who they spoke to, but we don't have pictures of any of them. The only thing we have is the drawing Ms. Cordes did, and that's already out to the media," Captain Patrick said.

Dunn looked at Slade and raised an eyebrow. "That's good news. Listen, we obviously have a vested interest in this case. If there's anything we can do to help, or any information you can share with us, we'd appreciate it. Do you think they had an inside contact?"

"Hard to imagine they didn't," Patrick said. "They walked into the bank with their privacy glasses on. They knew what type of cameras the bank had so they had everything dialed in to the right frequency. And they seemed to know what they were looking for. The teller said one guy wanted money from the drawer, but the leader of the whole thing was after the vault. He asked the manager to let him in, but the manager said two of them were needed to open it up."

"What did he do?"

"Nothing," Patrick said. "The guy acted like it was no big deal. He took some money but all together, they got about two hundred grand."

"Does that make sense? They knew all about the cameras but didn't know they needed two people to let them into the vault? And then they walked without worrying about it?" Dunn asked.

"The only thing we can figure is this might have been a test run. They might be trying to hit a few banks or building up to one big one. As for the keys, sometimes it's policy and sometimes it's mechanical, like two keys or something. If their inside person didn't know, they wouldn't have been able to warn them," Patrick explained.

"So, we're looking for someone other than the bank manager?" Dunn clarified.

"Seems that way," Patrick said. "That would be my guess at least."

"All right. Thanks, Marcus. Be in touch."

"Yep," Patrick said before he hung up.

Dunn looked around the table before settling his gaze on Slade. "These fuckers were smart."

Slade nodded once. "We're smarter."

KYRA WAITED in the elevator for the doors to open and told herself not to be nervous. They called her back. They wanted her. If they didn't, they wouldn't have agreed to reschedule her interview. It had to be a good sign.

Kyra wore her favorite sleek, black suit with a teal camisole beneath it. She looked professional and pulled together, but the camisole gave her a little bit of comfort. She wasn't the type to wear a suit, but when she got home and stripped off her blazer and bra, she was the type to dance around in her cami and panties with her headphones on in her room.

The elevator door opened, and two men stood in front of it. The man with the darker skin stepped forward and extended his hand. "I'm Daniel Dunn. It's nice to meet you, Kyra."

"Thank you, Mr. Dunn. It's nice to meet you as well. I really appreciate you rescheduling my interview."

"We're glad you could make it. This is Ryker Hamilton. He'll be joining us today for your interview."

Kyra shook his hand and said it was nice to meet him. She wondered how many men worked there and if all of them were as attractive as these two. She was going to have fun if she had so much eye candy to look at every day.

Of course, she would do her job, too.

"Let's head into the conference room," Daniel said. "We can get to know you a little better in there."

Kyra nodded and followed him into a small room off the

foyer. There were no signs on the outside saying what the company was. No one else appeared to use the floor. For a moment, she thought maybe the whole thing was a setup. Maybe the job was a front for human trafficking and she was about to be taken.

For whatever reason, she continued into the conference room and sat down on one side of the table. Daniel and Ryker sat opposite her, both facing the door. Kyra figured she might be able to get out if they tried to grab her, but she wasn't sure.

The robbery was doing a number on her, making her paranoid. She'd been on countless job interviews. There was no reason to think this one would be any different.

"Ms. Cordes, why don't you tell us about yourself," Ryker said once they sat down.

Kyra smiled at him. "Of course. Aside from yesterday, I'm typically very dependable. I am organized and smart. I have worked in a lot of offices and am familiar with different computer systems and office equipment. But even with all the experience I have, I'm always open to learning new skills and expanding my knowledge."

"We'd be remiss if we didn't ask about your employment history," Daniel began. "In the last five years, you appear to have changed jobs eight times. Is there a reason for that?"

Kyra expected the question and nodded. "Some of the positions I left for personal reasons. Most of them were temporary jobs. I've filled in for women on maternity leave, I've taken over for people who went out for surgery. I worked for a temporary agency for two years and most of the job changes were when I was with them. In the last three years, I've only had two jobs."

"Two jobs in three years is still movement. And you're looking for a third job. We're hoping to fill this position with someone who plans to stick around. What about this job makes you think you might stick?" Daniel asked.

The scenery. Kyra smiled to herself and said, "I've been looking for something different. To be perfectly honest, a part of what attracted me to this job is the pay. Another part is the title. I'm still called a secretary at some places, even though that term was phased out when I was in elementary school. Office manager makes me feel like I won't be dismissed here."

"Are you at your current job?" Ryker asked.

The way he questioned her made Kyra wonder if he would take it out on someone if she said yes. She shook her head. "Not directly, but I'm not involved in a lot. I don't know... well, anything really about what you do here, but the description made it sound like you're doing important work. Growing up, I wanted to be a police officer. I want to know what I'm doing is helping people."

Ryker and Daniel exchanged a brief glance that Kyra couldn't interpret. They both wrote something down, then looked up at her again.

"What do you feel is your greatest strength?" Ryker asked.

The rest of the interview last almost an hour. They sprinkled in questions with discussion about her and her previous employment. Kyra felt more and more comfortable with the two of them the longer they all talked. By the end, she was almost positive they were going to offer her the job right then.

"Do you have any questions for us?" Daniel asked her. He flipped his notepad back to the front so she couldn't see what he'd written and folded his hands on the top.

Kyra was prepared for that question, too. "Can you tell me what a typical day will look like for me, if I get this job?"

Daniel and Ryker glanced at each other and grinned.

Ryker said, "First of all, this is a new position we've created, so right now, we don't know what typical will be. Secondly, there's not really a typical around here. You will be expected to be self-directed. There will be days you're working here alone. As far as the tasks we expect of you, we will have you answering phones and talking to potential clients. You will be working with local agencies to understand where they need our help if they call on us. You might be asked to run interference at times. But you will have downtime. We all take time off. This place is like a family business. We all work hard, but we play hard. We spend time together outside of work. If you work here, we will get to know you. Trust is crucial here, and if we can't trust you, you won't last."

Kyra was even more curious about the position after Ryker's cryptic response. "Have you interviewed other people for the job?"

"Yes, we have," Daniel said simply.

"Do you have a timeline for when you will be making a decision?"

"Today," Daniel said. "We are meeting with the rest of the company right after this to discuss our options. We'd intended to meet earlier in the day, but we wanted the opportunity to speak to you before we made a final decision."

Kyra nodded, knowing her cancellation had cost her the job. She could tell them the truth and hope it garnered her some sympathy, but that wasn't who she was. If she couldn't get the job based on her skill set and her interview, then she wasn't the right fit. "I appreciate you rescheduling and taking the time to meet with me today. I look forward to hearing from you soon."

The three of them stood and shook hands. Daniel stayed in the conference room while Ryker walked her to the elevator. He thanked her again and asked if there was anything else they needed to know to help them make their decision.

Kyra smiled. "Not that is relevant to the job. Thank you for your consideration."

The elevator arrived as Rocky nodded. Kyra got on and waited until the doors closed to let her disappointment sink in.

"Dammit!" She really wanted that job. Better luck next time.

6

───────

Slade was pacing the hallway the entire time Dunn and Dex interviewed Kyra. He really hoped they liked her. He owed her, and pushing for her to get the job would help her.

It would help him, too, because he wanted to see her again. Dunn told him to stay out of sight while she was in the building. He didn't want Kyra to see Slade and think something was going on. Slade wanted to be the one who greeted her, but Dunn refused.

"Well?" Slade asked the moment Dunn walked into the hall.

"Let's all sit and talk," Dunn said calmly. He nodded to the conference room they used for meetings inside the office. It was bigger than the small one at the front. That one was only for people who weren't let through the secured door, and since Kyra didn't yet know exactly who they were and what they did, she wasn't allowed inside.

"Meeting!" Dunn called down the hall.

The rest of the team expected it. They were supposed to talk earlier, but the interview with Kyra pushed their schedule back. Slade took his usual seat on the far side of the table where he could watch the door. He wasn't going to let anyone sneak up on him.

The rest of the team filtered into the conference room. They all settled into seats before Dunn started talking.

"We have three candidates we think would be good for the job. They each have strengths and weaknesses," Dunn explained.

"How bad are the weaknesses?" Jack asked.

"Candidate one has a spotty job history. She hasn't stayed at one job longer than eighteen months," Dex said.

"Does she have an explanation?" Archer asked.

"Temp work for part of it, the rest is personal," Dunn said

"So, she didn't tell you?" Mason asked.

"Personal is a reasonable response," English chimed in.

"It is. And it's fine. It's more the jumping ship that worries us," Dex clarified.

"What about candidate two?" Slade asked. He wanted to get to Kyra. That way, he could convince them all to hire her.

"Candidate two is inexperienced. Her work history is not bad, but she's only worked for her family's business. We think she could have been sheltered being there and aren't sure she can make the leap."

Not Kyra. She didn't mention family the night before so she likely didn't work for her family's business. "And three?" Slade pressed on.

"Three lacks confidence. She barely looked us in the eyes. She seemed like she was worried we were judging her every word. Her resume was good, not great, but her interview was almost painful," Dex said.

"Maybe she just has trouble being around people she doesn't know," Rocky suggested.

"We thought so, too, but if she's afraid of all of us, that's not going to make the job easy," Dunn said.

"Candidate one is my vote," Archer said. "She could be looking for the right fit. She knows she hasn't found it yet."

"And are you willing to gamble that she'll find it here?" Jack asked. "I think I'd vote for number two. People need a chance at some point."

"I'm with Archer," English said.

"What about their strengths?" Mason said. "We know where they suck. What about where they shine?"

"One has lots of knowledge. She's smart and personable, professional. Two is curious and eager to learn. Three is loyal and talented."

"One," English and Archer said together.

"I'm with them," Rocky said.

"I think I'm with Jack," Mason said. "Eager to learn and looking to stretch her wings from her family sounds good to me."

Slade wasn't positive which of the candidates was Kyra, but he was pretty sure it was candidate one.

"Slade?" Dunn asked, meeting his gaze.

"Which one is Kyra?" Slade asked.

"We're not telling you that," Dex answered. "We need to know who the best candidate is, whether it's her or not."

"Don't you two get votes?" Slade barked.

Dunn nodded. "We do. And since we know more about these candidates, our votes will count more, but if majority agrees with us, it's an easier choice."

Slade glared at them. He wanted to pick Kyra, but candidate one was the one he liked most from the choices. She could be three. If he chose two, it would be a tie and Dunn and Dex would choose the candidate they liked the most, and both said they thought Kyra was the top candidate even after interviewing the other two.

He had to trust his gut. There was no way Kyra was Two, and he doubted she was quiet enough to be Three, so she had to be, "One," he said.

Dunn and Dex nodded. "She was our pick, too. For the record," Dunn said, holding Slade's gaze, "she didn't say anything about the bank. We kept waiting for her to say that was why she couldn't be here, but she never did."

"She said it was the adult version of my dog ate my homework," Slade told them with a chuckle.

"It kind of is," Jack agreed. "Maybe I should use that excuse next time I'm late."

Archer snorted. "You're the one who's always early. It's built into you to be the first one everywhere."

"Then maybe you can use it," Jack told Archer.

"I'll make good use of that time," Archer said with a grin.

"No one is using the excuse unless you're actually in a bank robbery," Dunn growled. He focused on Slade. "I'm going to call her now. Stay out of my office."

Slade nodded. "I want to be involved with training her."

"I bet you do," Jack teased.

Slade flipped him off without even looking at him.

"Fine. I was going to ask for a volunteer anyway," Dunn said.

"I'll volunteer," Jack said.

"Fuck you. You're practically married," Slade growled.

"Yeah, but it's so much fun to mess with you," Jack said with a wide grin.

Slade glared at him, but Jack just laughed his way out of the conference room. The rest of them filtered out behind him.

Slade returned to his office. He was trying to figure out

anything he could about the bank robbery. Aside from the cameras inside the bank giving them nothing to help find the men, all the cameras outside had just as little. He saw them leave the bank and walk off in different directions. He followed each of them until they disappeared into shops. A coffee shop, a retail store, and a grocery store. It would take time to get access to the footage inside each of those places, but Slade watched and the men never walked back out from the places they went into.

He searched the other cameras in the area until Dunn knocked on his door just before he went home. "She starts next Monday. She wanted to give notice at her current job. Didn't feel right leaving them high and dry."

Slade nodded once. "Thank you."

"She was the best candidate. Even if you didn't vote for her, Dex and I were going to. She's smart and talented. She wanted to be a cop. Did you know that?"

Slade nodded. "She's a talented artist. She's the one who drew the sketch that's on the news."

Dunn's dark brows went sky high. "No shit? That's what Patrick was talking about? That's a damn valuable skill."

Slade nodded again.

"Are you going to be able to show her everything when she starts?"

"Definitely. Does she know what we do?"

Dunn shook his head. "She doesn't know much of anything. Even though we went into her interview thinking she was the best fit, we didn't know for sure until she refused to explain away her absence yesterday. She's the kind of person we need. She doesn't make excuses. She gets shit done."

"She'll be a good fit," Slade said, not doubting his words for a minute.

"I think so. But for tonight, I need to focus on my woman, not yours. Don't stay too late."

Slade nodded and waved as Dunn walked off. Slade stared at the screens for a few more minutes before accepting that he was too tired to focus and needed to get some sleep.

Howler whimpered at the door when Slade opened it. As soon as he saw who it was, he howled and licked Slade's boots. Slade closed and locked the door, then dropped to the floor.

"I missed you, buddy. You doing okay?"

Howler farted in response.

"Yep, you're good," Slade said, choking back his breath. "Damn, dude."

Slade stood up and headed for his room. Howler followed him, close enough that Slade nearly kicked the dog.

"Be careful," Slade said softly. Howler didn't back off at all.

Slade stripped out of his work clothes and tossed them in his hamper. He pulled on a pair of shorts and a tank and went back to the kitchen. The two steaks he'd left in his fridge for dinner the night before were still there, so he grabbed the plate and headed outside to the grill. Howler followed him, wandering onto the grass to use the bathroom before walking back and flopping down on Slade's foot.

"We hired Kyra," Slade told Howler.

Howler looked up at him, his head tilted to the side and his tongue hanging out. He looked like he was listening and actually understood Slade.

"She starts a week from Monday. I'm going to train her."

Howler barked once, like he approved.

"I think it's a good thing, too," Slade said. "I owe her. I can help her. And she can get out of her apartment."

Howler whimpered and leaned against Slade's leg.

"I'm sure she'd love you. You'll meet her soon. You'll love her, I know that."

Howler harrumphed and dropped onto his belly. Slade chuckled and pulled the steaks off the grill. Howler jumped back up and followed Slade inside. He heated up some vegetables from a few days earlier as he cut up the steaks.

Half of one of them went into Howler's bowl. Slade carried the rest to the couch and turned on the TV. He let his mind stop while he watched a comedy that made him feel like maybe there was still good in the world.

After all, Kyra was out there, so there had to be some good in the world.

Bobby pulled his microwave dinner out and dropped it on the counter. "Fuck," he mumbled to himself. He sucked on his finger and shook it to stop the burn.

While he let the food cool, he grabbed a beer from the fridge and twisted the top off. He chugged half of it, then grabbed a second beer and stuck it in his pocket. He took his dinner and went to the living room.

The house was quiet, which wasn't usual. Most of the time Stevie was home, and half the time other people were around. They lived in an old neighborhood where the houses were on top of each other and the neighbors minded their own business. As long as you didn't rat them out for the shit they did, you could trust they wouldn't rat you out.

Bobby set his dinner on the tray in front of his chair and

put both beers down. He dug the remote out of the chair where Stevie sat and flopped into his chair.

They stole cable from one of their neighbors so they got every channel out there. Bobby was hoping he could catch something with naked women in it, but for some reason, Stevie left it on the local channel.

And Bobby was looking at himself.

He spewed his beer all over the room and swore. "What the actual fuck!"

He jammed the button to turn the volume up. The reporter said, "The man you see on your screen is the man believed to have orchestrated the bank robbery last Thursday. At this point, the police are looking for any information about who this man is or where he lives. He's about five-eleven with short, dark hair. He had two accomplices with him, but both were wearing masks. Call the police tip line if you know anything about this man. There is currently a reward for any information leading to his arrest."

Bobby threw the remote at the TV. It missed and hit the wall next to it, shattering. His breath heaved out of him, his dinner and beer forgotten as his life filtered out of his reach.

He dug in his pocket as the reporters continued talking about shit Bobby didn't care about. He scrolled through his phone and stopped at Stevie's name.

"Yo," Stevie answered. Music thumped in the background and a woman's voice called to him.

"Get here. Now," Bobby demanded.

"What's up? I'm, uh, kinda busy." Stevie chuckled.

"Yeah, and my fucking face is all over the goddamn news."

"What?" Stevie gasped. More quietly, he said, "Move. Stop. Back up. Get the fuck off me, bitch."

"You done?" Bobby growled.

"I'll be there in ten," Stevie answered, sounding almost as mad as Bobby.

Bobby hung up and called Mario.

"Hey, Bobby," Mario answered, his smile evident in his voice.

That just pissed Bobby off even more. If he was in a bad mood, everyone needed to be in a bad mood. "Get over to the house. Right now."

"Why? We were about to have dinner."

"Yeah, and my face just popped up on the fucking news. We need to figure out why."

"Um, shit. Okay, sorry. I'll be there soon."

"Ten fucking minutes. Or I make sure mine isn't the only face on the news."

"I'll be there," Mario said, finally taking the whole fucking thing seriously.

Bobby stared at the TV, not listening to the hot reporter talk about some stupid shit happening. He wouldn't mind meeting up with her one night. She was sweet. Maybe he should watch the news more.

Stevie burst into the house as soon as a commercial came on. "What the fuck happened?"

Bobby shook his head. "I wish I knew."

"Do you think you were recognized?"

Bobby shrugged. "Mario is on the way."

"He called you?"

Bobby shook his head again.

"He can tell us if anyone at the bank knew who we were."

"I'm sure I could be identified, but not if they know what's fucking good for them," Bobby growled. Angry didn't even begin to cover it.

A knock on the door told them Mario was there. They

didn't give him a key and never let him just walk in. They didn't trust him.

Stevie glanced at Bobby and they both waited. When Mario knocked a second time, Bobby jerked his head toward the door for Stevie to let him in.

"Oh, uh, hey, Stevie," Mario stammered. Bobby's new friend and roommate made Mario anxious. It was one of the things Bobby liked about Stevie.

"Mario. Any idea how a picture of Bobby made it onto the goddamn news?"

Mario shook his head. "No. I thought those glasses hid our faces. That was the whole point."

"The whole point was so they couldn't put our pictures on the fucking news. Me walking in without a mask on meant I could get things in place without people knowing what I was doing. I was supposed to be invisible," Bobby said. He already explained it to Mario. Why he couldn't understand was beyond him.

"Well, yeah, but all those people saw you," Mario continued, digging the hole deeper.

"Yes, they did," Bobby said. "But they shouldn't have been able to describe me that well. By the time I was someone to pay attention to, I changed what I looked like."

"Well, someone recognized you," Mario said.

"Yes, that's clear to me. It's funny how you were worried about being recognized and then I was. Isn't that ironic?" Bobby said.

"You don't honestly think..."

"It's hard not to draw that conclusion," Stevie said. The two of them advanced on Mario.

"No. I promise you. No."

Bobby stopped and looked at Stevie. "He promises. So, I guess we just have to make sure we're keeping a low profile."

Stevie nodded. "Yeah. I mean, if you were recognized by someone who knew you, then your name would probably be out there, too."

"Good point," Bobby said. He tilted his head to the side and stared down Mario. "I wonder why it isn't."

"It... it must have been one of the customers," Mario said quickly.

Bobby nodded. "Maybe. If only there was a way to find out who all the customers were."

Mario sucked in a breath and nodded. "I'll see if I can find out."

"Good. Don't let me down."

Mario nodded and backed toward the door. "I'll let you know when I have the list."

"You do that."

Mario nodded and let himself out.

Bobby and Stevie waited until Mario's car sped away, the deafening exhaust ensuring he was gone.

"Do you think it was them?" Stevie asked.

"I don't know, but it's pretty damn convenient."

"We'll keep an eye on them."

"We have to. And we need to know who else was there."

7

―――――

Kyra rode the elevator up to her new job with a smile on her face. She actually got the job. A part of her couldn't believe they were willing to overlook her no-show, but maybe something was finally working out for her.

She was trying to move past the bank robbery and put it all behind her. She gave her notice at her other job, and they barely blinked. She told her roommate she was moving out by the end of the month, and Autumn agreed it was for the best. All Kyra had to do was hold on to her new job, and everything would be okay.

She hoped.

The elevator doors opened, but this time, no one was there to greet her. She didn't expect them to be, and it gave her a chance to look around the lobby area. The elevator slid away quietly while Kyra took in the nondescript space she was in. The walls were a soft gray color, and the doors were a dark black, standing out in the otherwise plain space. No plants or tables, chairs, or decorations were in the space. It was a hallway, except the only place you could go was into the conference room door where Kyra was interviewed or the other door, where Daniel told her employees were to enter.

Kyra walked up to the second door and pulled on the handle. It didn't budge. Not even a little bit. She looked for a button to push to release the door or something that would tell her how to open it, but all she found was a pad where you could scan a card.

She didn't have a card.

"You're here early," a voice said from behind her.

Kyra turned with a grin and froze. "Slade? What are you doing here? How did you find me?"

He grinned. "I didn't. This is where I work."

Kyra turned to look at the door she couldn't get into, then back to him. "What?"

"The interview you missed was with my boss and coworker. They liked you enough they were willing to give you another chance. I asked them to interview you and when I told them your name, we realized you were the same person."

"You told them to hire me?"

Slade shook his head and scanned his card. The door beeped and a loud click said they could go in. Slade opened the door for them and said, "We'll get you a card today. And no, I told them to interview you for the job. You were the best candidate."

Kyra kept staring at Slade, unable to believe anything that was happening. She'd wondered about him since she left him at the hospital, but she... yes, she googled him. And she found absolutely nothing about him. No social media, no personal history, not even a mention in an old newspaper.

She figured she'd never see him again, not that she'd end up working for him.

At least with that line between them, she wouldn't do something stupid and let how attracted she was to him spill out. He'd fueled more than a couple of fantasies over the ten days since she walked away from him at the hospital, fantasies that were making her thighs ache and her whole body hot while she stood inches from the man.

Kyra finally let her brain take over instead of her vagina and she walked through the door. The hallway was far too narrow for the two of them. Between her wide hips and oversized breasts and his... everything, they could barely stand next to each other in the small hallway.

Slade smiled down at her and jerked his head. "This way. I'll show you your new office."

Kyra nodded and followed him. She barely noticed everything as they passed. Offices and a large conference room, some included other people, some vacant. Mostly, the space was empty except for her and Slade.

He walked past a door and stopped on the other side of the frame. He gestured for her to go in first. She squeezed by him, being careful not to touch the man, and got her first look at her new office.

It was plain also, but well equipped. It looked like someone went to a big box office store and bought out everything there. Maybe they did. She had a large white desk that faced the door. A file cabinet was next to it, and a bookshelf was behind the desk. The chair looked brand new, unlike the chairs she usually inherited.

Kyra ran her hand along the surface of the desk and sat in the chair. It spun and slid back when she sat down, making her laugh. She grabbed the edge of the desk and looked at Slade.

He was watching her with a crooked grin. He was even more attractive than she remembered. There was a part of her that wondered if she'd made up how hot he was, but sitting in front of him, she knew she'd downplayed it by a long shot. Him standing there, his shoulder against the door frame, his black tee stretched tight across his chest and barely containing his arms, those low-slung jeans that looked like they would fall without much encouragement, and that smile... If she was going to draw him, she'd title it *Badass Smirking*.

"Is it okay?" Slade finally asked.

Kyra nodded. "It's great. Thank you."

"Good. Let me show you around the rest of the office and introduce you to everyone. They're not all here yet, but you can meet whoever is."

Kyra nodded and followed him, her purse still slung over her shoulder. She wasn't sure what she should do with her stuff, so she kept it with her as they walked to the break room, fully stocked with everything from coffee and tea to fruit and other snacks.

"We like to eat," Slade explained. "And first one in usually starts the coffee. You're welcome to a cup. I know you love your coffee. It's a weakness for most of us after spending so long in the desert. Kind of like a reminder that the little things like coffee are still available."

Slade poured himself a cup and took a sip. Kyra wrinkled her nose. "You drink it black?"

Slade nodded.

"Like his soul," another man said from the doorway. "Hi, Kyra. I'm Mason. It's nice to meet you."

"You, too," Kyra said, shaking his hand. Mason was almost the same size as Slade, with a shaved head and the same wide frame. There was a sadness in his eyes that made Kyra wonder what happened to him. Then again, she probably didn't want to know what happened to any of them.

"Meeting in five," Mason said to Slade.

Slade checked his phone and nodded. "Thanks." He looked at Kyra again. "Want a coffee while we walk? We also have water and tea and energy drinks. You're welcome to anything you want."

Kyra nodded and said she was okay. Her stomach was in knots before she got there, and seeing Slade didn't ease her tension. Starting a new job was always a bit stressful, but starting a new job with the man she'd been fantasizing about brought a whole different level of anxiety into it.

She followed Slade out of the break room and back down the hall. He stopped at the offices where people were sitting. All men. All hot men. If Kyra was the type to date at work, she'd never get anything done. Of course, none of them compared to Slade in her mind. But it didn't matter.

Slade stopped at Kyra's office and told her to grab a pad of paper from the bookshelf and a pen from the top desk drawer. Kyra wondered how he knew where everything was in her new office, but she just did as she was told.

She followed him into the conference room they passed earlier, not the one she had her interview in, and stopped short when she saw so many men in one room. Daniel stood when he saw her and welcomed her to the team.

"For those of you who haven't met Kyra, she's going to be working with us." Daniel went around the room and introduced everyone.

Kyra was surprised to see a few familiar faces. She remembered Rocky and Archer from the bank and hospital. And Ryker from her interview. "Um, hi, everyone."

They all smiled at her, then smirked at Slade. Kyra turned back to see what he was doing, but he wasn't doing anything. Her cheeks burned at the thought of him making fun of her behind her back. She'd had it happen enough to know being the butt of any joke sucked.

She didn't expect Slade to say anything, but he stepped forward and said, "These assholes think it's fucking funny that we hired you after I told half the hospital you were my girlfriend. They razzed me about it all last week. When we hired you, it was all they could talk about. They find it hilarious. And I'm sorry on their behalf that you are in the middle of their harassment of me. Hey, Dunn? The next person we hire should be an HR manager so I have someone to complain to."

"You can complain to me anytime you want," Dunn said. "I just don't care."

"Real nice thing to say to our new hire," Slade grumbled.

Dunn shook his head. "I wasn't talking to Kyra. That was just for you. If Kyra has an issue, I'll listen and deal with it. It's just you who doesn't matter."

Slade flipped Dunn off. Kyra's eyebrows shot up. Dunn shrugged and grinned at her. "Slade is jealous because my wife is about to have a baby, and it's made her very affectionate toward me, and Slade isn't getting any at all. So, he threatens me, or maybe it's a proposition."

Slade growled and moved to the other side of the room before he sat. Kyra chuckled at the dynamic. She'd never worked somewhere where it was acceptable to speak to your boss the way Slade did. She wasn't going to push her luck and do the same, but it was interesting that Dunn didn't think twice about Slade flipping him off.

"We have a new case," Dunn said, turning back to the room. "Kyra, you can sit in and take notes for us, but don't worry if you don't get everything. For this week, we want you to mostly observe, get a feel for what we do, and start to figure everything out. Most of your work will be more admin stuff, managing the office instead of the ops, but I wanted you in here so you have an understanding of the kind of work we do. Everyone who works here is under a strict NDA, which you've already signed. Most of our clients are private citizens, but we do work with the government and local officials. Where possible, we stay within the guidelines of the law, but we aren't afraid to stretch those guidelines to save a life."

Kyra nodded, trying to wrap her head around everything. What Lily mentioned at the hospital about the work they did was coming back. They were real life heroes, and she worked for them.

She grinned. She was going to like her new job.

SLADE WALKED out of the conference room with the others after Dunn gave them the rundown on their latest client. A scared father who thought his daughter had been kidnapped. Dex was working with the FBI, since kidnapping was their jurisdiction, but if the team needed to step in when the FBI wasn't willing to, they wouldn't hesitate to do so.

Slade saw Kyra walk into her office and followed her. She sat in her chair, staring at the surface of her desk, eyes wide and fearful.

"Is it always like that?" she asked.

"Like what?"

"Someone is in danger and you have to figure out why and save them?"

Slade nodded slowly.

Tears welled up in Kyra's eyes. "I can't imagine how

scared that woman must be. She's only a year younger than I am. I just turned thirty-one last month."

Slade wasn't sure if he was supposed to comfort her or not, but he ached to hold her. Whenever his little sister would get upset, Slade was always the first one to wipe her tears and make her laugh.

He crossed the room in three steps and pulled Kyra out of her chair and into his arms. She sagged against him, like she hoped he would hold her and was happy he did. Slade pressed his nose to her head and breathed her in.

Holding his sister was nothing like holding Kyra. Holding Kyra was heaven. He could stand there forever with her in his arms, listening to her breathe and feeling her curvy body tight against his. Her trembles softened, and she started to pull away, but Slade wasn't quite ready to let go of her yet.

He tightened his grip on her and whispered, "Are you okay?"

She nodded against his chest and squirmed again.

He didn't want to risk sending her running, so he finally stepped back. She didn't look at him as she returned to her seat.

"Why don't I show you how to get into all the systems?" Slade suggested.

Kyra nodded, still not meeting his gaze. She moved the mouse, bringing the computer to life.

"We wrote your login and password down for you in the top drawer. Actually, Lily did. She helped me set up your office over the weekend."

Kyra opened the drawer. "You set this up?"

"With Lily's help."

"It's really nice. Thank you." She looked up and smiled.

Slade couldn't speak for a minute. That current he felt

before was there, in the room with them. Even when she turned away and put in her password, he felt it arcing around them.

Kyra went through the password reset and made a note on her phone, then looked up at him. "What do I need to know?"

Slade's mind immediately went to all the things his body wanted to teach her, but he didn't come out and say any of it. Instead, he focused on the work.

He showed her their email program and the communication program English set up for them to chat without leaving their offices. "It's housed on the internal server so no one outside this building can see it. It doesn't have an app or anything, so if you aren't here, you're not connected. We do have another one that we use when we're in the field."

"How often are you in the field? And what exactly is the field?"

"That just means out of the office. If we're meeting with clients, we bring them here. In the field is usually recon, surveillance, interviews with suspects, meetings with local PD or other agencies, stuff like that."

"Do you do that a lot?"

Slade nodded. "I'd say someone is out every day. Sometimes we're all involved in something, but sometimes it's just one or two of us."

"Wow. I feel so sheltered. I didn't realize so much happened here. I thought it was safe."

Slade shrugged. "It is safe, but there are always shitty people. People who think they don't have to do what everyone else has to do. Those are the people we deal with. Like with the missing woman. We'll find her and deal with whoever took her."

Kyra looked up at him again and smiled. "She's lucky to have you looking for her."

Slade wasn't sure what to say, so he just stayed quiet. He kept showing Kyra the different programs they used, and when he mentioned the police scanner they had linked to their network, she perked up.

"You can listen to a police scanner? Right from your desk?"

Slade nodded. "Yep. At least one of us has it on at all times so we know what's going on. It's rare we react, but it's good to know just in case."

"Can I listen?"

Slade nodded. "If you want."

"I do. Where do I go?"

Slade leaned over her chair to show her which button to push, but he got too close and got a whiff of her hair. Strawberries? No, raspberries. He leaned in closer and inhaled deep, drawing her scent inside him.

He told himself he should pull back, should take it slow, but there was no such thing as slow when she tilted her head and met his gaze. That fiery green he saw in the bank rushed back to him when their eyes locked.

Yeah, she felt the same as him. There was a shared experience that brought them together, but good sex was going to keep them that way.

He tilted her chin up and claimed her lips, instantly feeling her pull drag him under. He groaned and pried her lips apart with his tongue.

She dueled with him, chasing his tongue around her mouth and sucking his back in when he retreated. Oh, yeah, she was going to be fun to play with. Slade loved a woman who teased and taunted but always delivered. Kyra was the type who always delivered.

He shifted his head and deepened the kiss, his cock growing hard behind his zipper while he debated where they could go to get their first time out of the way. It was going to be quick and dirty, but he would make it up to her.

Her hand planted on his chest and twisted, yanking a few chest hairs as she dragged him closer. He needed to feel her, to touch her.

He pulled back and trailed his lips down her throat. She tasted as good as she smelled. He pressed the flat of his tongue to her racing pulse and moaned softly. The other guys in the office would be pissed if they caught him, but Slade couldn't hold back.

Not until Kyra whispered, "I think maybe we should just be friends."

8

____

Kyra licked her lips and looked up at the man in front of her. She wanted nothing more than to keep kissing him, but she knew better. He wasn't kissing her because he thought she was the hottest woman around, he was kissing her because of some misguided sense of obligation.

He felt guilty about the bank. He stayed the night in the hospital, bought her dinner and coffee, and then got her a job and kissed her. If it weren't for the bank robbery where they met, Kyra could almost think of it as normal, but there was nothing normal about meeting a man during a bank robbery.

Slade backed up. Kyra could still feel the cool spot on her throat where his tongue just was. She wanted to wrap her arms around him again and let him continue. Slade stared at her, and she stared right back. The two of them were locked in, the air between them pulsing with sexual tension and desire and desperation.

Kyra never should have let herself fantasize about him.

A knock on the door drew Kyra's attention. Dunn stood

there, looking at a folder in his hands. "Can I steal Slade for a minute?" he asked without looking up.

When neither of them answered, Dunn finally lifted his head from the folder.

"Everything okay in here?"

"All good," Slade said.

"Kyra?" Dunn prodded.

"I'm fine. Slade was just showing me the different programs you guys have."

Dunn slid his gaze back to Slade and nodded. "Sounds good. You got a minute?"

Slade nodded and followed Dunn out of the room.

Kyra sagged against the back of her chair and touched her lips. It was a good kiss. No, it was a spectacular kiss. It was the kind of kiss that made her forget everything. Where she was, what she was thinking, her whole world before the kiss. All that was left was after, and after was terrifying because all she could think was she wanted to kiss him again.

Slade walked back into the room while Kyra was leaning back. She jerked forward and plastered on a smile.

"Sorry about that. Uh, it's almost time to call it a night."

"Okay," Kyra said carefully.

"Uh, so, listen, I'm sorry about," he waved his hand toward her, "you know. And this has nothing to do with that, but everyone is coming to my place tonight. We get together a lot. And Dunn wanted me to make sure you're invited."

"To your house?"

Slade nodded. "Yeah. This is my address. If you can't make it, I get it, but it's a good chance to get to know every-one. Dinner is around seven."

Kyra picked up the slip of paper he set on her desk and smiled at him. "Thanks. Daniel... Dunn?"

Slade nodded.

"Dunn said you guys get together a lot. I'll be there. Anything I can bring?"

Slade shook his head. "No. We're all set."

"Okay, sounds good. As long as you're okay with it."

"Yep," Slade said with a pop.

"Um, okay. Thanks."

Slade nodded and left her office. Kyra hated changing things between them, but it was better if they were coworkers and friends instead of something else. He would run the minute he found out she couldn't have kids, and if she was going to work there, she couldn't be hung up on him. It would hurt too much to watch him fall for someone else because Slade was the kind of man who snuck under your skin and built a home inside you. He was already doing it with Kyra, and she needed to find a way to evict him.

Fast.

Slade was laughing at something Kelsea said when the bell rang. Of course, that set Howler off as he rushed toward the door, sliding on his way and slamming into the wall.

"It's a good damn thing you don't have brittle bones," he told his dog on his way to the door. He scooped up Howler and groaned when the dog licked his face. "Come in," Slade yelled toward the door since Howler was quiet. "It's always open."

The door opened just wide enough for Kyra to slip her head through and peek inside. "Hey," she said with a grin that lit up her face. "Did you say to come in?"

Slade nodded. "Yeah. When everyone is coming over I just leave the door unlocked. Glad you could make it."

Kyra grinned and stepped inside. She closed the door behind herself, then focused on Howler. "Is this Howler?"

At his name, Howler let out a deafening howl. Slade turned his head so he had some hearing left, and Kyra jumped back.

"Yep," Slade said when his dog finally quieted down. Howler was practically leaping at Kyra. Slade set him on the ground and whispered, "I know the feeling."

Kyra chuckled and bent down to pet him. Some women were funny about his dog, but not Kyra. She just rubbed his belly and talked to him like he was the best dog she'd ever seen. Slade thought he was, but how long he sat at the shelter made it clear most people didn't agree.

Most people also sucked, so Slade didn't mind not being lumped in with them.

"He's so sweet," Kyra said with a grin.

Slade nodded. "He likes attention. He's a little bit of a man whore."

"That's why he's the perfect dog for you," Mason said, throwing a meaty arm around Slade's shoulders.

"You're so damn funny," Slade growled back. He liked Mason, although at first he was definitely opposed to him having anything to do with their team. Over time, Mason grew on him and they'd become friends, but that would change if he started moving in on Kyra.

"I love dogs. I really want to get one when I move into my own place," Kyra said.

"I have the perfect place for you to go. I volunteer at a shelter. It's where Howler came from. I can take you there sometime, show you around," Mason said.

Kyra nodded. "That sounds great. Thank you."

"Any time," Mason said with a wink for Slade. "Why

don't you come in and get a drink? If Slade had any manners at all, he would have offered the same."

Slade glared at his former friend when he offered Kyra his hand to help her up. She slid her hand into his and let him lead her to the kitchen with a hand on her lower back. Even his dog followed behind Kyra, like she was his human now.

Slade grabbed a beer and headed out to the patio. It was a nice night, and with the grill going and people outside, he could pretend it didn't bother him that Kyra told him that afternoon they should be friends but was cozying up to Mason in Slade's own fucking kitchen.

"You gonna help with this?" Dunn asked when Slade walked outside.

Dunn's wife of six months, Ashleigh, was sitting in a chair, her round belly taking up space. Dunn was watching her, clearly worried about her sitting there alone.

Slade nodded and took the spatula from Dunn so he could check on Ashleigh. It wasn't until Slade heard Kyra's laugh that he turned around again.

"That did not happen," Kyra said.

"Hand to God, it did," Mason said. "It was just as funny then, too."

Kyra shook her head and reached down to pet Howler. He was sitting on her foot, looking up at her like he'd finally found the thing he'd been looking for.

Slade focused on the food instead of the people, trying to tell himself if she'd rather date Mason, he wouldn't say anything. But he knew he would. He knew he'd be a jealous ass because he could already feel it. The words *he killed his wife* were on the tip of Slade's tongue. If he said them out loud to Kyra, she'd run the other way from Mason.

"Don't," Rocky said, stepping up next to him at the grill.

"Don't what?" Slade growled.

"Don't do whatever it is you're thinking about doing to get Kyra away from Mason. You know it'll make you look like the asshole," Rocky said low and firm.

"I wasn't going to do anything."

"And you're a fucking liar. What is it with this woman? I've never seen you like this?" Rocky asked.

Slade shook his head. "I don't know what you're talking about."

"Please see my previous statement."

"Here," Slade said, handing over the spatula, "finish this for me."

He turned and walked back into the house, ignoring Rocky and everyone else outside. Slade went right to his bedroom at the end of the hall. Almost everyone was outside, so he was alone, but he wanted to get rid of all of them. They got together a few times a week, almost every week. Normally, he enjoyed the time with his team. They were his brothers, and their women were women he loved like they were family. Slade always pictured having a family one day, but the one he created wasn't exactly like he thought it would be. He wanted kids and a wife and someone who was just his.

His parents were crazy in love, even after more than forty years. Growing up, Slade thought he'd have the same thing, but his duty won out and he joined the Navy. He left his first love behind and left home, choosing a life he never pictured for himself.

He wouldn't trade what he had, but looking back almost twenty years from his current thirty-seven to the eighteen year old who made the choice to leave, he wondered if he would have made the same decision if he knew it would lead to a life alone.

He definitely wasn't the same person who walked away from love and a happy, small town life, but he couldn't handle regrets either. Jessie was better off without him, and Slade knew his life was exactly how it was meant to be.

But once in a while, he wondered if he would ever have what his brothers had found.

Slade finished his beer and left the bottle on the bathroom counter. He'd grab another one before he joined the group outside. If the noise he heard was any indication, the food was done, and he'd miss out if he didn't get out there.

He opened his door and the unmistakable sound of a woman drawing a breath made him stop. In the fading late day sun, the hallway was dark. Slade stood still, letting his eyes adjust to the darkness, then he saw her.

She'd just walked out of the bathroom, or it looked like she had. He hadn't heard her in there, so maybe she was on her way in. No matter what, she was there, staring up at him.

"Slade," she whispered, her voice both needy and tentative.

"Hey," he said, unable to stop himself from taking a small step toward her.

"I, um... I don't like Mason," she blurted out.

Slade closed his eyes, hating himself for the relief he felt. "He's a good man."

"Do you want me to like him?"

"Fuck no," Slade breathed before he could stop himself. "But we're friends, right? That's what you said. I'm not going to stop you from being happy."

"Oh, yeah. Um, okay."

Slade moved closer, and her breath hitched. She drew in a breath, like she was trying to take him with her. Her chest rose and brushed against his. His fingers itched to pull her close and never let go, but he wasn't the kind of man who didn't listen to the word no. She told him they were friends, and he would honor that until she told him something else.

Slade moved past her, his body brushing hers in the too small hallway. She leaned into him, but he kept going. If she wanted him, and he could tell she did, she was going to have to do something about it. Until then, Slade would have his own kind of fun teasing her.

KYRA'S entire body felt like it was on fire. She leaned against the sink in the bathroom and tried to breathe.

She knew waiting for Slade in the hallway was a bad idea, but she wanted to make sure he knew she wasn't trying to make him jealous by talking to Mason. What she meant to say and what actually came out were two very different things.

Kyra waited in the bathroom until she was able to breathe without panting and her thighs stopped shaking. The hallway was empty when she left, and so was the house. The back doors were slid all the way open, letting the outside air in. Kyra liked the group she was a part of, even though she didn't really feel like she was a part of the group yet.

"Kyra, come sit with us," Lily said, calling Kyra over.

Lily was sitting next to Kelsea and Pilar, two of the women Mason introduced Kyra to earlier. They were both really nice, and so was Ashleigh, the fourth woman of the group. Kyra was sure the women would be skinny and perfect and not at all welcoming, but all four of them were very real. They were different ages, from close to Kyra's age to maybe ten years older, if she was to guess, and all of them were curvy women who wore their bodies like badges of honor. Their men weren't shy at all about how much it turned them on that their women were plus sized.

Kyra took the open seat between Pilar and Ashleigh and smiled. She wasn't sure what to say to them, but she didn't have to worry.

"How in the world did you manage to get Slade turned inside out?" Kelsea asked.

"I didn't... what do you mean?"

"I told them he said you were his girlfriend at the hospital," Lily supplied.

"Oh, that was just so he could see me. He wasn't serious about it or anything," Kyra said dismissively.

"He seemed pretty serious," Lily said. "I think Slade might be a little in love."

Kyra's cheeks heated, but it was Ashleigh who scoffed. "I'm all for love, as evidenced by the basketball under my shirt, but I don't see Slade falling that quickly."

"Archer told me he had a serious girlfriend growing up," Lily said.

"Jack said he's always wanted a family," Pilar added.

"He's great with Howler. What kind of man adopts a dog no one else wants and then buys a house just so the dog can be loud? He's built for forever," Kelsea said.

"I just think you're all setting Kyra up for disappointment," Ashleigh said. "Slade is a serial man whore. I mean, I love him, and I'd trust him with my life, but not with a friend." Ashleigh smiled sadly at Kyra. "Sorry."

Kyra shook her head. "It's fine. Nothing is going on with us. I told him today it's best if we're just friends."

All four of them leaned in.

"You told him that?" Ashleigh asked.

Kyra nodded.

"What prompted that?" Kelsea asked.

"Oh, um, we..."

"Oh, my God, ladies, she's already gone," Lily said with a wide grin. She shook her head, her brown hair shifting. Her eyes were kind but definitely amused.

"What did he do?" Kelsea asked, leaning forward and grinning wider.

"It was nothing. I mean, it was all the emotions and being close, and I shouldn't have turned my head. Our lips almost touched before he even kissed me," Kyra blurted.

"I knew it!" Lily shouted. "I knew it. He's gone, and so is she."

"No one's gone," Kyra argued. "We're just friends."

"I thought the same thing," Pilar said.

"Me, too," Lily said.

"Absolutely," Kelsea agreed.

"We weren't even friends, and look what happened," Ashleigh dead-panned, pointing to her stomach.

Kyra looked at the women around her. They were all so sure she and Slade would end up together, but they didn't know the reason it would never happen. She wasn't quite ready to tell them all, but it would definitely make them stop pushing her.

"I can't have kids," Kyra said quietly. "I found out a few years ago. I know you all mean well, but you keep talking about how perfect Slade is and how he's meant for a family. He'll never have that with me. So, I really appreciate it, it's just not an option."

"I'm so sorry," Lily said. "I didn't mean..."

Kyra smiled. "I know. And it's okay. I've been down this road a few times with other guys. Even guys who aren't sure if they want kids at least want the option one day. If Slade is the man you're all telling me he is, then he'll definitely want kids. It's better if we're just friends. It's better if we don't get involved. I like him, but I know where it'll end up, and I can't do it."

Kyra got up, happy she never grabbed a plate of food. All of a sudden, she wasn't quite so hungry. She headed into the house, ready to make a quick escape. If she didn't tell anyone she was leaving, she could leave and tell them all she didn't feel well and didn't want to ruin the party.

She was almost to the front door, her escape secure, when she heard his voice.

"Why are you sneaking out?"

9

"I'm really tired," Kyra lied. She wouldn't even look at him.

"You're tired?" Slade repeated.

She nodded. "Yep. It's been a long day."

"I don't believe you."

She did meet his gaze then, and with fire in her own she said, "You don't know anything about me."

He stepped closer so they were both in the shadows. Someone could walk by and not see either of them. Slade got close enough that she gasped and took a step back. Another one and she'd hit the door and have nowhere to go.

"I don't know much about you, no. I'm not going to make up some things that I've guessed because that wouldn't be fair to you. What I do know is I want to know you. I haven't hidden that. I want to know you. We all do. Dunn asked me to set this up last week so we could all have a chance to get to know you."

Kyra shook her head and stared unfocused toward the back. The group of them could be heard from where Kyra and Slade stood. "They think we're going to end up together."

That made Slade take a step back. "Who?"

"Lily and Kelsea and Pilar. Ashleigh basically warned me not to get too close to you."

Slade wasn't sure if he should be upset because they were trying to fix him up or because Ashleigh wasn't. "They're in love. They think everyone else should be. And Ashleigh is cranky since she's pregnant."

"Must be nice," Kyra muttered.

"What?" Slade asked.

Kyra shook her head again. "Nothing. I'm sorry I caused a problem for you. I don't want you to think I'm trying to... I don't know, trick you or something into dating me."

"I don't think that. We're friends, right?"

Her gaze snapped to his. She nodded, but her eyes said she wasn't as sure as she was in her office earlier. He liked that look.

Slade tucked a strand of hair behind her ear and lingered. He tugged the hair and let his fingers trail down her neck. Kyra's eyes slid closed, and she swayed toward him.

She tilted her jaw upward and parted her lips. Vulnerability was painted on her face, from her closed eyes to the cautious tilt of her head. If he didn't kiss her, she could tell herself it wasn't a rejection.

But Slade wanted to kiss her. He wanted another taste of her more than he wanted to go back out and tell his friends she left. More than he wanted to walk into his bathroom and take himself in his hand. More than anything.

So he closed the distance between them, sealing her little sigh in their joined mouths. Just like the first time, she gasped and leaned closer, like she was shocked he kissed her but also wanted more.

Slade wasn't one to shy away from what a woman wanted. He took a step closer, one that forced her back. Then another. Her back hit his front door and ensured they were hidden from the prying eyes outside.

Slade slid his hand down her side and grabbed a handful of her thigh. She lifted it for him, allowing him to step between her legs. He licked his way into her mouth, and she rewarded him with a greedy groan that definitely said she didn't want him to stop.

He pressed himself against her, making sure she knew exactly how much he wanted her. He didn't know if he'd get another chance, and he had to make sure she thought twice before she said no to him again.

Kyra wrapped her arms around his neck and pulled him closer, reducing the distance between their bodies. Slade kept the hand on her thigh in place and slid his other one behind her back. She moaned and tilted her head to the side, allowing him deeper access to her mouth.

Slade fucked her mouth with his tongue, pressing his cock against her core in the same rhythm. She moaned again and went liquid in his arms.

Then she pushed him away.

Slade took a step back and released her. They both panted for air, staring at each other. Slade wasn't about to let her get away again. She was going to have to explain why she was hot one minute and cold the next.

"I can't have my first orgasm with you against the door where all my new coworkers could walk in and see us," Kyra breathed.

Slade's lip curled up. "First?"

Her brilliant eyes widened. Her breath hitched. She nodded and bit her lip.

"I like the sound of that. Although, I think I'd like the sound of the actual orgasm even better."

Kyra chuckled and shook her head. "You're intoxicating."

"I've been told," Slade said.

"Do I even want to know how many women you've seduced?"

Slade stepped closer and told her the truth. "None have ever been like you, Kyra."

"Wow," she breathed. "I... wow. You're good."

"It wasn't a line."

She chuckled. "Oh, it was totally a line. And it worked. And I need to go before I burst into flames."

"I thought you wanted your first orgasm. I was hoping we could get to at least ten today."

"Ten?" she squeaked.

"Fifteen," he said with a shrug.

Kyra shook her head. "We're going to stay at zero for right now."

"Why? You could just stick around after everyone leaves."

"And have them all know why? No. I don't want this to affect my job."

"It won't," Slade growled. He took a step back, giving them both space. "Nothing that happens between us will ever have anything to do with your job."

"You're one of my bosses," Kyra said softly.

"Do you feel like I'm forcing you into this?" he asked.

"No," she said quickly. Too quickly.

"But you think I'll have you fired if you refuse me?"

"I... no, but—"

"Wow. Okay. Well, I'm sorry I made you feel that way. I will let Dunn know someone else needs to train you for the rest of the week. I don't want you to feel like your employment is conditional on how many orgasms I give you, so I'll keep my distance. Thanks for coming. Be safe getting home."

Slade turned and walked back outside to the party, feeling like he needed to take a shower instead. He wasn't that man. He would never let anything that happened between them dictate her employment. But she didn't know him.

It was better if they were friends, like she said. Then she wouldn't worry about her job, and he wouldn't think she was with him so she didn't lose it.

But it still gutted him when he heard his front door open and close and he knew she was gone.

KYRA HELD BACK her tears until she made it to her room. Autumn wasn't home, so it didn't matter if she was crying before then, but Kyra wasn't about to let appearances get away from her. She'd held her shit together longer than a twenty minute drive and walk up to her apartment many times before.

She stripped off all her clothes and immediately went to her bathroom. While the hot water ran to fill the tub, Kyra took deep breaths and told herself staying away from Slade was for the best. One kiss and she was ready to let him past all her defenses.

Before the tub was even full, Kyra climbed in. She cursed herself for not thinking ahead and pouring a glass of wine to bring with her, but she could get that after her bath. She needed to relax.

She laid back in the hot water, letting the steam fill her head and replace Slade's scent. She had to erase him before she gave in and asked him... She didn't know what. She wanted him. She liked him. He was sweet and funny and holy hell, was he gorgeous. If she ever let herself dream of a man, she couldn't have come up with a man as perfect as Slade was.

Except for the fact that he was her boss and he wanted a family.

Kyra understood, but it wasn't the first time she was disappointed by her diagnosis. No, disappointed was walking into the donut shop and seeing your favorite kind was sold out. This was rip your heart out, trash your world, never be the same kind of pain.

Kyra finally gave up on her bath since she couldn't stop thinking about Slade. She climbed out and dried off, then wrapped herself in a bathrobe and stood at her door. She didn't hear Autumn, so she stuck her head out and listened again. Definitely no Autumn.

Kyra went to the kitchen and made herself a sandwich. She poured a large glass of wine. Before she left, she grabbed a candy bar from her stash, the one with her name on it because Autumn insisted they label everything, and headed back to her room.

People kept telling her she wouldn't like living alone, but she already was. She had a roommate, but she was never home. Kyra was always trying to make sure she wasn't in Autumn's way, so she ate alone in her room, watched TV in her room, and did everything in her room.

She settled on her bed and turned on the TV. She flipped until she found a rerun of an old sitcom and ate her peanut butter and jelly. She was only half paying attention to the show, wondering if the food Slade grilled was any good. The way everyone was devouring it, she assumed it was.

She tried to replay the conversations she had through the night, but all it did was make her head hurt. It didn't matter how great Slade was. They weren't going to be together. She needed to get that through her head.

When Kyra was done with her dinner, she set the plate and wineglass to the side and slid her AirPods into her ears. She found one of her dance mixes and pressed play. She closed her eyes and let the music flow through her.

Then she danced.

She threw her hands up and shook her butt. She tossed her head back and stomped her feet. She let go, forgetting all about how she looked to the outside world while she danced all alone in her room.

It was her escape. Her whole life, Kyra was told to be quiet. She was too loud when she was little, she was too bold when she was a teenager, she was too fat all the time. When she went to college, she thought her parents would stop seeing her as too much and be proud of her, but it was too late by then.

Kyra didn't hate her brother. She was jealous of him. With his perfect job and perfect family and perfect every-thing. He was her big brother, but he realized if he wasn't her buddy, he got more from their parents, so Kyra was alone. Always alone.

Moving away was an easy decision, especially once her parents left the small town she grew up in to live closer to her brother. Her mom told Kyra that since she'd never have a family, it made sense. But they started making plans before Kyra's diagnosis. That was just the excuse they needed.

So Kyra got really good at being alone. There was no reason it needed to change. She didn't have to like it, but she had no choice but to accept it. She could be herself that way. She could dance in her underwear and not wear makeup and fill her home with bright colors and sketches and everything she wanted.

Kyra collapsed onto her bed, exhausted from dancing. Her skin was damp with sweat and her chest heaved from the effort. But she felt amazing. It was what she needed.

She let the next song finish, then Kyra sat up and turned off the music. She opened the notebook she used at work and reviewed all the notes she took that day. She liked to go over things and refresh her memory so she was good for the next day.

When she got to the last page, she had incomplete notes. She knew why. Slade. Damn him. He distracted her when she was trying to take notes.

She turned the page and let her pencil work. She drew his face, tilted to the side. That look in his eyes... the one that said he liked to tease, but he would always deliver. She had no doubt he would deliver.

Her entire body shivered with need at the thought. The way he kissed her and commanded her body had her wet without even trying. She'd never been with a man like him. Most of her dates were men who would pee themselves if faced with someone like Slade as competition.

But he was only competition in Kyra's mind. He wasn't real competition. For one, there wouldn't be a competition if he was really into her, and for two, he wasn't.

He was damn good for solo fun, though. Kyra leaned back on her bed and slid her hand into her panties. She was already soaked. She let her robe fall to the side and grazed her fingers over her taut nipple. She slid her eyes closed and replayed the kisses she shared with Slade.

She teased herself the way she knew he would. One finger dipped into her opening, then slid away to tease her clit. Back and forth until she couldn't take it anymore.

She pressed her fingers inside, then drew the slickness up to her clit and rubbed fast. She pinched her nipple, needing to release. Fast.

Her body twitched, then tightened, then released. She kept going, unable to stop at one. He said he'd give her ten, but Kyra couldn't do that. Her arm was already sore, but Slade's voice inside her head was making her greedy for more. She had to keep going.

Thankfully, it didn't take long for her to come again. Every cell in her body screamed his name, but she kept the sound inside. Living with a roommate taught her to be very, very quiet. Growing up with her parents taught her the same.

One day, she'd be able to have an orgasm without worrying about who heard her, but not yet.

Kyra was exhausted but felt amazing after her two silent orgasms. She should have kept her mouth shut when she was with Slade. Her mouth seemed to keep getting her in trouble with him.

Nope, she couldn't think that. It was for the best that he didn't want her. She wasn't strong enough to resist him. And that wasn't okay. He was too much for her.

And as much as she wished they could be too much together, she knew she would never be enough.

KYRA WOKE up to the sound of Autumn slamming cabinets. Autumn was always loud in the mornings, something Kyra wouldn't miss. She loved to sleep in on the weekends, but it was nearly impossible with a roommate who was always making noise.

Kyra turned over and groaned. She passed out thinking about Slade and had dreams about him all night. Slade. Wait, Slade. Kyra grabbed her phone. It wasn't the weekend. It was Tuesday. Her second day of work. And she was going to be late.

"Shit, shit, shit," she hissed as she yanked off her sweaty clothes and jerked the handle to turn on the shower. She jumped in, yelping when the cold water hit her skin. She didn't have time to wait for it to warm up. She made a mental note to check how long it took for the water to heat up when she started looking for new places to live.

She raced through her shower and got dressed in the first thing she saw. She pulled her hair back into a ponytail and shoved her notebook into her oversized purse. She prayed the food in the break room was still there from the day before and sped through the city to work.

She parked under the building in the garage and half-ran to the elevator. She grabbed her boobs to stop them from bouncing as she ran and breathed a sigh of relief when the elevator was on the ground floor, waiting for her. And blessedly empty.

Kyra pulled out her compact and checked her reflection. She managed to put on eye shadow and blush on the drive. She uncapped her lip stain and carefully applied a coat while the elevator silently lifted her to her floor.

The doors opened as she stuffed her things back into her purse. She still needed mascara, but she would take care of that in the bathroom.

Kyra swiped herself through the door and rushed to her office. No one saw her, so she figured everything was okay. First order of business was finishing her makeup, second was coffee and breakfast.

She was in the break room pouring a cup of coffee when Rocky walked in.

"Hey," he said, waiting for her to finish with the pot.

"Hey," Kyra said with a smile.

"Are you feeling better?"

"Um, what?"

"Slade said you weren't feeling well last night. That's why you left early. Are you better?"

Kyra nodded and forced a grin. "All good. I think it was just all the excitement of starting a new job."

Rocky nodded like he didn't believe her at all but wasn't going to question her. "I guess I'm going to be working with you for a few days. Showing you around. Let me know when you're ready to get started."

Kyra froze. Slade said he was going to pass her off to someone else, but she didn't think he was actually going to do it. Knowing he had hurt. Not that she had a right to be hurt, but it did. "Um thanks. I'm ready whenever you are." Breakfast was definitely not an option with that news.

"Okay, then let's head to your office and get started. Did you get the email last night that we have a meeting in an hour?" Rocky held the door open for Kyra and smiled when she walked by.

Kyra shook her head. "I didn't check. I think that might be something I need to get set up today."

"I'll see when English is free and you can talk to him about it."

"Thanks," Kyra said. She took a seat at her desk and pulled out her stuff.

She flopped her notebook on the surface without even thinking about it until Rocky said, "Is that Slade?"

"Is what me?" the man in question said, pausing in front of Kyra's door.

Well, fuck.

10

———

Slade watched Kyra's eyes go wide, then lift to Rocky for help. Rocky's lips curled up and his eyes danced with humor.

Slade looked at the notebook in his hand, but he couldn't see what Rocky was looking at.

"Just thought I heard you coming in," Rocky said.

Slade glared at him. He didn't like the idea of Rocky working closely with Kyra, but he, Dex, Dunn, and English were the best ones for it. They were the ones who needed the most help. They all agreed the night before, after Kyra left, that they were all more than happy to take a turn showing her what they needed.

The only one who wasn't getting a turn was Slade. He fucked that up good and hard.

"You guys okay?" Slade asked, trying to catch Kyra's gaze.

"We're good," Rocky answered for both of them.

Slade lifted his eyes to his teammate's. Rocky gave him a subtle nod that meant get the hell out. Slade nodded once, getting the message. He passed on Kyra, so Rocky was going to take a shot.

"Got it," Slade growled, then left the room.

He walked down the hall to the break room and poured himself a cup of coffee, wishing he had whiskey to go with it. He swallowed the hot, black liquid and poured another cup. He barely slept all night, and it was already a shitty damn day. He was going to need all the help he could get.

"THANK YOU," Kyra breathed when Slade continued past her doorway without seeing the drawing she did of him the night before. "I really appreciate you covering for me."

Rocky set the book down and turned to her, crossing his arms and leaning back. "You're into him."

It wasn't a question, but it definitely required a response. "I have no intention of getting involved with someone from work."

"That wasn't what I asked," Rocky said.

Kyra sighed. "Fine, yes. I like him. He's a nice guy. He watched out for me and stayed with me at the bank and after. He's kind and considerate. I find those qualities hard to resist."

"Damn. I don't think I've ever heard a woman talk about Slade's personality. Sometimes I think he doesn't really have one when women are around."

Kyra chuckled. "I guess it's easier to see his personality when I'm trapped in a hospital bed instead of sitting at a bar."

Rocky laughed with her. "Probably true." His face grew serious. "Why did he say he couldn't work with you? He made it sound like you requested someone else to train you."

Kyra's cheeks flamed hot. "I... he... we kissed. I told him I thought it was a bad idea, and that I didn't want us being involved to affect my job."

"Ah," Rocky said. "You think you're going to get fired if you say no to him."

"No, I... it's happened before."

"Are you kidding me?"

Kyra shook her head. "I had a boss tell me I should smile more. He said I had such a pretty face, and when I smiled, people would respond to me. I did, and then he asked me out. When I said no, he fired me and said it was because I wasn't friendly enough with the clients and some had complained that they felt like I was rude."

"What a dick."

"Yeah, well, women who look like me get that all the time."

"Where does he live? Give me his address and Slade can line his house with explosives. He'll never see it coming."

"Are... are you serious right now?" Kyra asked, more than a little afraid.

Rocky chuckled and shook his head. "No. I mean, Slade could, and probably would if I told him, but we don't do that kind of stuff. Not without cause at least."

Kyra breathed a laugh and shook her head. "I was worried there for a minute."

Rocky flashed a sideways grin at her. He was cute, too. Jeez, they all were. But Rocky didn't make her pulse race. None of them did the way Slade did.

"So, why are you still single?" Kyra asked.

Rocky shook his head. "Haven't met the right one. What about you?"

"Same."

Rocky's gaze drifted to the empty doorway. "Think maybe that's changed?"

Kyra's cheeks burned with the hope that maybe Slade was, but she knew better than to hope. Hope only led to heartbreak. "There are a lot of steps between a few kisses and finding The One."

Rocky shrugged. "Maybe, but you gotta start with step one, right? I'd say a kiss that makes your cheeks that red is a hell of a step in the right direction." He sat on the edge of her desk and nodded to the drawing. "He's a good man. You talk about the person he is, not what he looks like. Men are objectified, too. Yeah, we like it most of the time, but that's not someone you're going to settle down with. Slade has an awesome family. His parents are still together and his little sister adores him. He is a good guy. I think you could be really good for him."

Kyra forced a smile. It always came back to family. Time after time, the men she was with wanted a family, and she couldn't give them one. Which was why she needed to stay away from Slade before she got in too deep.

"What else do I need to work on?" Kyra asked, turning back to her computer. She didn't need to think about Slade any longer. She needed to do what she was there to do. Work.

SLADE WAS GOING to destroy something. He really had no choice. As a man who was used to having an outlet for his anger, he needed to get it all out or he would end up destroying himself.

Or one of his closest friendships.

Rocky and Kyra spent every moment of three days together. Her laughter filtered out of her office and down to

Slade's daily, treating him to a torture filled week of imagining Kyra and Rocky doing more than just working.

Hell, she kissed him the first day they met. Why wouldn't she kiss Rocky, too?

He shook his head to clear the thoughts. He wasn't being fair to her. He kissed her, she didn't kiss him.

But maybe that was the point. Maybe she never wanted him. Her body said she did, but her words kept cutting off everything.

Slade had never been happier that he bought the large piece of land he had. When he saw it, he knew it was right for him. Plenty of space for Howler to run and play, but also enough room for Slade to do what he did best.

Blow shit up.

He'd only taken advantage of the space once, but the first week he lived there, he went deep into the woods and built an explosives range. A place where he could detonate whatever he wanted and not worry about the neighbors, because there weren't any.

He and Howler needed to take a long walk out there when he got home. Three days of torture was enough. Especially when it included two nights of wondering if Rocky and Kyra were together.

Kyra's laugh pierced the air again, and Slade clenched his fists. The two of them ate breakfast and lunch together in the break room. Rocky refilled her coffee mug. They were all chummy and friendly and Slade fucking hated it.

But he couldn't do a damn thing about it.

Except leave.

He was almost done for the day. There was no reason for him to stick around. He could go out and blow up whatever he wanted and maybe he'd feel better.

He locked his computer and cringed when Kyra laughed

again. He closed his eyes and counted to ten, but before he made it, she laughed once more.

Then she said *his* name. Nope, not Slade's.

Yep, he was fucking done.

Slade carried his mug to the kitchen and resisted the urge to chuck it against the wall. He rinsed it and set it in the dishwasher, then turned and found Rocky smirking at him.

"You're such an idiot," Rocky said.

Slade crossed his arms and leaned against the counter. The alternative was taking a swing at his friend. "Thanks for pointing that out. Sounds like you two are having fun."

Rocky nodded. "We are. She's amazing. Funny and sexy and…"

"I don't want to fucking hear it," Slade growled, pushing off the counter to stalk out of the room.

Rocky put a hand on his chest to stop his progress. Slade looked down at it, debating breaking a few of Rocky's fingers.

"She's totally hot for you," Rocky said.

Slade snorted. "Since you two are such good friends, I'm sure you know she turned me down three times. And not just that, but she thinks I'll have her fired if things don't work out. So, no, you're wrong. She sounds like she's having a great time with you."

Rocky nodded, a smug grin on his face. He was inching closer and closer to earning a few broken fingers. Maybe a nose, too.

"We are having a great time. You know why? Because she doesn't want me, and I don't want her. She's beautiful, but she doesn't see me. I'm okay with that, because I'd rather keep all my fingers straight." Rocky lifted his hand from Slade's chest and flexed them.

Slade's lips curled up on the edges. Sometimes knowing

each other really well was as much of a curse as it was a blessing.

"I'm heading out for the night. Dex and I are the last ones here. Kyra wants to stick around for a while and look for apartments online. I told her it was fine," Rocky said.

"Alone? You're leaving her here alone?" Slade asked, angry his friend would put her in that position.

Rocky shook his head and backed out of the room. "Nope. You're still here. I'm leaving her here with you."

Slade opened his mouth to say something, but Rocky gave him a mock salute and walked away. He waved to Kyra on his way by. Dex was already at the door waiting for Rocky.

And then there were two.

Slade wasn't sure if Kyra knew he was in the building or not, but he didn't want to freak her out. He went back to his office and sat down in his chair. He didn't try to be quiet, but he didn't stomp around either.

She was crazy about him? Rocky's words rang in his head. There was no damn way. She spent every moment they were alone trying to get away from him. She wasn't crazy about him. Rocky was wrong.

Slade shook his head and unlocked his computer. While he was there, he figured he might as well get some more work done.

Slade dug into the kidnapping case they were working on. They had a few leads, but nothing had panned out. He didn't have anywhere near the computer skills of English or Dex, but he had a few tricks of his own when it came to finding people.

He buckled down and focused, putting all thoughts of being alone in the building with Kyra out of his mind. He heard her move once in a while, but she stayed in her office and he stayed in his.

His eyes were strained and tired from staring at the screen for so long, but he wasn't willing to stop. He was likely to have a mess to clean up when he got home since Howler hadn't been out in hours, but he'd deal with that, too. Slade refused to leave Kyra in the office alone.

Slade shook his head and debated getting more coffee when he heard her sigh in the room next door. Her chair squeaked, then her footsteps tapped lightly on the floor.

"Oh. I didn't know you were still here," she said, stopping in front of his door.

Slade nodded. "Rocky told me they were leaving. I didn't want you alone in the building."

A smile turned her lips up. "Thank you. I really appreciate that. I wasn't thinking about leaving alone when I decided to stay." She took a step into his office. "You look exhausted."

Slade shrugged. "I'm fine."

Kyra wrinkled her nose. "Don't you know fine usually means anything but fine?"

Slade huffed a laugh. "I don't want you here alone."

She took another step closer. "Can I ask you a question?"

Slade leaned back in his chair and nodded. He stretched his arms and linked his fingers behind his head. Kyra's gaze caressed his muscles before jerking away to stare at... not him.

"Why did you ask Rocky to help me out?"

Slade shook his head and dropped his arms. He leaned forward again, resting his forearms on his desk. "You said you didn't want me, Kyra. I'm trying to do the right thing here. I'm keeping my distance and giving you space or whatever."

"I never said I didn't want you."

"You made it pretty damn clear what you think of me," Slade said quietly. He wasn't the kind of man who would force himself on a woman, and he damn sure wasn't going to push to be involved with one who had such a low opinion of him.

"I had this job when I first moved here," she said, taking another step closer. "I got the job over the phone. My boss never saw me before I arrived, but on day one, it was clear he wouldn't have hired me if he saw me."

"Why?"

Kyra gestured to herself. "I'm not perky and cute. I dress in dark clothes to try to make myself look smaller. I wear loose clothes. I blend in. I also don't smile much. That was a big one for him. He told me I have such a pretty face and that I should smile more."

"What the fuck?" Slade growled.

Kyra shrugged like it was no big deal. "Women who look like me get that all the time. 'You have such a pretty face' is code for if you weren't so fat, guys would want you. All women are told they should smile more. Research shows that skinnier people are more successful at work. It's all society's way of making curvy women feel like we're not good enough."

"That's not true," Slade argued.

"It is."

"No," Slade said, shaking his head. "I'm not saying it doesn't happen. I'm saying it's a load of fucking shit."

Kyra smiled. "Anyway, so my old boss... he told me I should smile more. I was working in an office and was the first person a customer would see. I listened to him and started smiling when I would greet customers. It seemed to put them at ease, so I relaxed just a little bit and smiled more around the office. A few months later, right before performance reviews, my boss asked me out. He said I was pretty when I smiled and he wanted to go out with me."

"What did you say?"

Kyra shrugged. "I said no. If he didn't like me for who I was, he wasn't the man for me. I knew he tried to get me fired right after I started working there, but the owners told him no. He didn't like me until he thought I was an easy mark."

"What happened?" Slade asked, even though he was sure he already knew the answer.

"He gave me a bad review. Said he was told by multiple customers that I was rude and unhelpful. He claimed we lost business because of me. I was still on probation, so the owners let me go."

"I'm gonna fucking murder him."

Kyra chuckled. "Rocky asked me for his address so you could line it with explosives."

"You told Rocky?" Slade asked, changing the person he wanted to kill.

"He asked me why I wanted someone else to train me. He said you made it sound like I asked for someone else."

"You—"

"I know," she said, holding up her hand to stop him from talking. "I took what happened at my old job and assumed the same would happen here. I tried to stop it before it did."

"I'm not him, Kyra. That's not me. It's not any of us. Besides, if it was a choice between me and you, I'm pretty sure they'd all choose you," Slade said.

Kyra laughed. "This is your family. These people love you. All of you are a team, and I'm the newbie who's going to come in and blow it all up."

"Why do you think that?"

Kyra shrugged. "I've seen it happen too many times. And I wouldn't want them to choose me. You're the one they've known forever. But after just a few days working here and one night with all of them, I want to be a part of this group."

"You are," Slade said.

Kyra shook her head. "I'm an employee. I'm not really a part of the group."

"Everyone loves you. Rocky busted my balls about you today. He wouldn't do that if he didn't like you."

"What do you mean?"

"He set us up."

"How?"

"He left when he knew I was still here and made sure I was going to stick around so you weren't alone."

"Why would he do that?" Kyra asked.

Slade looked up at her and grew hard at the look in her eyes. She wasn't even trying to tempt him, but her barely restrained desire pulsed through the air between them. She was trying to keep it in check, but Slade liked blowing things up.

"He said you're totally hot for me."

11

———

Kyra's cheeks burned hot with his words. She felt like such an idiot. "How much did he tell you?"

Slade shrugged.

Kyra shook her head. "Fine, yes, we were talking about you the other morning when you walked in. I like to draw. And you have a really nice face. I didn't mean for Rocky to see it."

"You did a drawing of me?" Slade asked, his brows going up. The edge of his mouth quirked into a grin, and those damn arms of his went back on his head.

He was a fucking god. Kyra had enough trouble getting a guy who looked like he was an accountant or sold insurance to pay attention to her, but a man like Slade... she still couldn't believe he wanted her.

"I... it was just one, and I..." She sighed and met his gaze. No sense hiding it. "Yes."

"Can I see it?" he asked, surprising her.

"I... um, it's personal."

Those damn brows went up again. "You showed Rocky."

She shook her head. "No. He just saw it. And then used it to tease me all week about having a crush on you."

Slade stood and moved around his desk. He was stealthy, and fast, and was in front of her before she could take a breath.

"Show me, Kyra."

The command in his voice had all her parts standing up and taking notice. Kyra thought of herself as a feminist, and a champion of women, but she was still a woman who liked a man to take care of things once in a while. Taking out the trash, fixing the car, and ensuring she had orgasm after orgasm in the bedroom.

At least, in her fantasies, that was the kind of man she always wanted.

Kyra turned and walked out of the room without a word. She intended to grab her notebook and bring it back, but Slade followed her into her office. She flipped back from the page she made notes on about available apartments to the drawing she did and handed it over.

His eyes went wide, then sank to half-mast. His mouth parted just enough to let his tongue out to run over his lower lip. He exhaled softly and set the notebook down.

His gaze collided with Kyra's and she lost her breath. She was glad her desk was between them because the way he looked at her made her feel exposed.

"This is how you see me?" he asked, his voice low and rough in the quiet office.

She shrugged, unable to push a word past the lump in her throat.

"Kyra, you're fucking killing me."

"Wh... Why?" she stammered.

He moved to the edge of her desk, then kept going around it. She was trapped between him and the wall. Her pulse throbbed, setting a beat between her thighs as he drew closer to her.

"That isn't a normal drawing, sweetheart. That's a snapshot of what I look like when I want to fuck you. And if that's how you think of me, I get why Rocky said what he said. You are hot for me." Slade flashed her a cocky grin.

Kyra pushed at his shoulder, but he barely moved. The only thing it did was put her in contact with him. Her hand stayed there, holding on to him. She didn't want to let go.

"Kyra, you will never be fired or reprimanded or used as an example or anything for being involved with me. I will sign anything you want me to sign saying you can sue the fuck out of me and the whole company if I ever make you feel pressured or uncomfortable. I don't care about any-damn-thing except you. That face... that's how I feel. I want you."

"Why?" she blurted.

"Because you're smart and funny and creative. Because you help people even when you should be letting them help you. Because you don't give up and you fight for what you need, although you could fight a little harder for what you want. Because you've been torturing me all fucking week, sitting in this office laughing. Not with me. Because you're gorgeous and I want to strip off all this black you're wearing and see the beautiful colors of your skin." He trailed a delicate finger down her neck. "Like this right here, where you're flushed pink. I want to see how far down it goes. I want to watch your whole body. I want you, Kyra. I've never made that a secret. But I will walk out that door, go straight to the bathroom, and fuck my own hand right now if you tell me no."

"What?" she gasped.

"You can say no, Kyra. Any time you want. It might kill

me to have to jerk off so much when I'd rather be inside you, but this is your show here, sweetheart. I'm just a very willing participant."

Kyra swallowed roughly. Her hand was still on his shoulder, and his was still teasing her throat. Every brush of their fingers on the other sent her temperature a little higher. She was sure she would burst into flames if she didn't have him.

But it wasn't just about sex. He was a good man. He was a man she could fall in love with. She didn't want to, so she shut down her heart and let her body take over.

She curled her fingers around his shoulder and pulled him closer. His hand slid up and wrapped around the back of her neck, immediately taking control. He tilted her head less than a second before his lips crashed into hers.

They met with parted lips and eager tongues, neither of them waiting to get a taste. Kyra sucked in a breath, bringing her chest into contact with his, and he growled.

Slade turned them and broke the kiss. Kyra whimpered at the loss until he reached behind her and swept everything off her desktop except her computer. She gasped, then clutched at him when he lifted her up and replaced all her stuff with her ass.

"I'm going to break it," she said, embarrassed and scared.

"No, you're not. Every other couple in this office has had sex on these desks. I promise, your beautiful body is not going to break it. I could climb up here with you and it would be fine. I won't let anything happen to you, Kyra."

Her heart ached at the care in his voice. She tried to shove it back in the box, but it wanted to stay out and enjoy the show. Slade... it was like he knew what she needed to hear. Kyra had never known anyone who saw her the way he did. Not that she showed him all of her, but he saw through the mask she wore to catch glimpses of the person underneath.

"Relax, beautiful," Slade murmured against her ear. "I can stop if you want me to."

She shook her head and grabbed him. "Don't stop."

He chuckled. "Thank God."

His hands went to her thighs and eased them apart. He stepped in between. He was much taller than her, and with her ass on the desk, she felt even smaller next to him. He leaned over her, teasing her as she tipped her head back. When he ducked down to meet her lips, he didn't slow down.

Kyra gasped against his lips and held onto him as he laid her back on the desk. He followed her with his body, pressing his thick cock against her stomach. She moaned softly, wanting desperately to touch him.

His hands went to both sides of her face and pressed her hair back. He pulled away and looked at her from an inch away. "You're so damn beautiful, Kyra. I feel like an asshole right now, but I don't know if I can wait to get you to a bed before I have you."

"I don't want to wait. Please."

Slade groaned and sealed his lips over hers again, sliding his hands down her body until he caught her thighs. He lifted them up and positioned himself between her legs, thrusting against her.

"Oh, God," she whimpered. "That feels so damn good."

He chuckled. "Imagine how good it'll feel when we don't have clothes on."

"Please tell me you have condoms here," she said.

He nodded. "Lots."

She sighed and dragged his lips back to hers. Her heart whispered not to get attached, but the rest of her body was back in charge, and it was *not* saying no to the beautiful man with the impressive cock that was making her want to come before he even took one stitch of clothing off her.

Oh, no, Kyra was going to get some. And nothing was going to stop her.

SLADE THRUST his tongue deep into her mouth and fought the urge to tear her clothes off and bury himself in her. He wanted her, no question about it, but he wanted to savor her. To enjoy every sound and taste and touch. He didn't want to miss one second of his first time with her.

And yeah, he knew it wouldn't be the last. Not by a long shot.

Her warm heat beckoned him deeper, but he was focused on kissing the hell out of her first. She let him lead, but she wasn't afraid to tell him what she liked. She sucked hard on his tongue, making his cock ache for the same attention. Then she tilted her head the opposite way and led them in a taste test of the other side of their mouths.

Slade eased his hands up until he could cup her jaw. She had the most beautiful neck. He couldn't wait to taste it, but having his hands there and knowing he was in control of her every move made him even harder.

He pulled back and looked into her heavy-lidded eyes. She struggled to meet his gaze, trying to drag him back for a kiss. "Look at me, Kyra," he snapped.

Her eyes opened lazily. She grinned like she was drunk. "Why are you all the way over there?"

He smirked. "I just wanted to look at you for a minute. Your eyes are sexy as hell. I like watching them, seeing what you're feeling."

She closed her eyes and pulled back. If he hadn't been paying attention, he wouldn't have noticed it. She didn't like being so open and vulnerable. She wanted her secrets.

He wasn't having that. He wanted to know everything. "Open your eyes or I stop."

She opened again, and there was fire there. She didn't like that option, especially because she wanted him as much as he wanted her.

"Good. I want to watch you when I make you come. I want to see you when I fuck you. I want to look at you when I explode deep inside your pussy. Don't fucking hide from me, Kyra."

She drew in a shaky breath and leaned toward him. "Please, Slade."

"With pleasure," he growled. He brought her lips back to his, but he refused to let her control anything. She fought him when he held her head where he wanted it, but she gave up when he sucked hard on her tongue. That made her whimper.

When she wasn't fighting, he released her head and slid his hands down to her pants. They were thin and light, but they were still pants, which meant no fucking access. He found the zipper and slid it down while he kept kissing her. He pushed her pants off her hips, the desk restricting him from getting them all the way off.

"Lift," he growled, pulling back from her just enough to issue the command.

She did as he asked, and Slade tugged her pants and panties down her thighs. They caught on her low heels, but he didn't care. He could get to where he needed.

Kyra kicked her shoes and bottoms off while Slade lowered to his knees in front of her. "Let me see you, Kyra."

She watched him as she spread her thighs wide enough

for his shoulders. He loved that she wasn't shy and didn't try to hide from him.

"Come closer to me."

She eased closer, her bare ass squeaking on the solid desktop.

Slade slid his hands beneath her cheeks and tugged her forward until she was barely on the edge. She leaned back, propping herself up on her hands.

"You're fucking perfect," Slade groaned. He pulled his hands out from under her and traced her seam with one finger.

She jumped at the soft touch but spread her thighs ever so slightly wider. Her breath hitched.

He eased her flesh apart and slipped a finger into her. She was tight, drawing his finger in as he learned her body. His gaze flickered between where his finger disappeared into her and her face.

She watched him, doing as he asked and letting him see her.

Slade shifted forward, drawing her scent inside him. Her channel tightened on his finger when he swiped her flesh with his tongue.

"Oh, God," she moaned, her hips shifting up.

Slade wanted to taste every inch of her. He slid his tongue between her lips and licked from one end to the other. He pumped his finger inside, giving himself a taste of her on the way out. He replaced his finger with his tongue, and she moaned again.

He pressed her thighs wider and swiped his tongue through her folds. He pushed two fingers inside her, and she gasped.

"Yes."

Slade wasn't sure how long he could hold out, but he

was enjoying himself. A thrust in, and a swipe. Another plunge, and a suck. One more slam, and a flick. With each movement, she grew more incoherent. Her body trembled above him, readying for her release.

Slade wanted to prolong it, but he also wanted to watch her. His desire to watch won out, and he curled his fingers and sucked hard on her clit.

She came with a shout that would have scared everyone if they weren't alone, but they were blissfully alone on a soundproof floor that no one could get into without authorization. Kyra's body pulled at Slade's fingers, wanting more from him. All he wanted was to watch her do that again and again.

But he needed to make one change first.

"Take off your shirt," he demanded.

"Wha... what?" she gasped, her brain foggy from the orgasm.

"I want to see how far that flush goes. I want to watch your breasts turn red when you come. Either you take your shirt off or I remove my hand and I do it myself."

Kyra almost fell onto the desk in her hurry to pull at her shirt. Her stomach shook with the effort it took to hold herself upright, especially when Slade pumped his fingers deep into her again.

"Oh, God," she cried out, her shirt forgotten.

"Shirt, Kyra," Slade commanded her.

She fumbled again and almost got it around her neck when he drew her clit into his mouth and sucked hard.

She came with a shout and dropped back onto the desk.

Slade released her and said, "Shirt."

She struggled to sit up and yanked her shirt off. Her bra followed quickly, leaving her entire body naked for him.

"Fucking hell, you're gorgeous," he groaned. "I might not be able to wait."

"Don't wait," she begged.

He shook his head. "I might come in my pants just from looking at you."

"No," she whined. "Please, Slade."

"One more," Slade said.

"I need you," Kyra said.

"Trust me, sweetheart, the feeling is mutual."

He withdrew, making her whimper, then added a third finger and thrust into her, hard and deep. She froze, then relaxed, her entire body liquid on the desk. Her thighs were wide, and all of her was primed and ready to come hard.

He flicked her clit with his tongue as he fucked her hard with his fingers. She twitched and jerked, but she didn't move far as the pleasure built up inside her. Then she cried out, and he knew she was there.

He sucked down hard on her clit and she lost it. She came instantly, flooding his hand and overflowing onto his tongue. Slade watched her curves shake, the ripple of her orgasm making her breasts bounce and her entire body tremble. She was fucking gorgeous.

She screamed his name and flailed with the strength of her orgasm, unable to stop the train.

"Oh, God. Holy fuck. Yes, Slade. Oh, yes!"

He licked her clean while she came back down and slowly withdrew his hand. She quivered at the movement and tried to meet his gaze.

"I've never come like that," she said softly, sounding drunk.

"Good," he said.

"I thought I was going to die."

"That's the best kind of orgasm."

Kyra chuckled. "You're magical."

Slade rocked back on his heels. "You're going to give me a big head."

She gave him a sultry smile and said, "I was kind of hoping I already did."

"Trust me, you did."

"Good," she said with a smirk.

Slade stood and stripped off his shirt. Kyra propped herself up and devoured him with her eyes. Watching Kyra's eyes light with desire made him feel like a fucking god.

He went to his jeans next and didn't waste any time dropping them and his boxer briefs to the ground. He grabbed the condom he set on the desk and tore it open, watching Kyra chew on her lip. He rolled the condom on and positioned himself between her thighs.

She lifted her feet and set her heels on the edge of the desk next to her ass. Slade groaned at how open she was to him.

"I want to taste you again," he admitted.

"I need to feel you," she argued.

"Later," he negotiated.

"We'll see," she said.

He nodded. "Definitely later."

She opened her mouth to argue, but he plunged into her in one move, and whatever she intended to say turned into a long, low moan.

"Oh, fuck, yes," Slade said in agreement.

"That's what I was going to say," Kyra said.

Slade chuckled and brushed her hair back from her face. She turned her head and kissed his palm. He leaned over her and claimed her lips with his. She kissed him leisurely, like he kissed her, neither of them in a hurry to end their night.

Slade withdrew slowly while they kissed, easing his body in and out of hers. She lifted her hips to meet his, but it was slow, easy. Like they had all the time in the world and couldn't care less if it took just that long to let go of each other.

Kyra slid one of her feet around his waist and rested it on his lower back. Slade slid his hand over her leg, loving one more connection with her.

Lazily, they moved together. Tongues sliding alongside each other while bodies did the same. The unhurried pace allowed Slade's orgasm to sneak up on him, and when it did, it demanded he take her hard.

He slammed into her, unable to stop his body. She tightened around him in an instant and threw her head back.

"Oh, God," she moaned.

Ripples gripped him, drawing him in and telling him she was right there with him. He pulled back and thrust into her again, and she let go.

Her orgasm tripped his need into overdrive. He lost all thought of everything except Kyra and needing more of her. He cupped her hips and pounded into her again and again until his balls drew up tight and burst, pouring himself inside her.

His legs shook with the power of his orgasm, but he forced himself to stay upright. Stay inside Kyra. Because he wasn't done with her yet. Far from it.

12

———

Kyra laid on the desk and wondered if she'd ever had sex even close to what she just had with Slade. It was better than just sex. It was like an experience, a life-changing, soul-crushing, world-breaking experience.

Because she knew she'd never have sex like that again.

Her high school boyfriend wanted to have sex. They were both virgins, and she thought they were in love. It didn't take long for Kyra to realize she was wrong. The sex was rushed and frantic, like most teenagers, but afterward, she didn't have a feeling of bliss or joy like in the movies. She was just different.

Being with Slade, in a way, was like that all over again. When it was over, Kyra knew she would never be the same again. As a teenager, she'd lost her virginity, and not to a guy who loved her, but to a guy who convinced her having sex would mean they'd be together forever.

He was wrong, and Kyra decided sex wasn't really that great. Parts of it were good, but it marked a moment in her life that she forever looked back on and said things changed because of it. She changed because of it.

Over the years, other experiences altered the way she viewed sex. It got better, and she enjoyed it more often than not.

But sex with Slade was like starting all over again. It was going to change her forever because there was no way she could go back to the kind of sex she was having before and enjoy it. It was like having Dom Pérignon and then trying to drink sparkling wine. There was no damn comparison. But she couldn't afford Dom every time she wanted a drink, so she was going to live her life disappointed because she knew how good amazing really was, and it was out of her reach.

Slade reached for her and tugged her up and into his arms. He was sweaty, and his heart was pounding. For half a second, Kyra wondered if he was feeling the same thing she was, but she dismissed it.

She'd never had Dom Pérignon sex. Not even close. It wasn't her that made it so amazing, it was all him. Which meant he'd had Dom Pérignon sex before.

Kyra almost let it depress her, but she wasn't going to do that. She had the best sex of her life, and that was something to celebrate. When it was over and he was done with her and he moved on to have Dom Pérignon sex with someone else, then she could be sad. But until that happened, she was going to enjoy every fucking minute.

Literally.

"You're definitely going to kill me," Slade whispered against her neck. He slid his tongue over her sticky skin, then suckled on her jaw.

Kyra resisted the urge to moan and fall right back in. She wasn't sure her body could handle more orgasms after the powerful ones he handed her. He was truly a master.

"If you do, I'll definitely die a happy man," Slade continued. "That was... I don't think there are words to describe how good that was."

Kyra nodded, knowing she couldn't say anything that would help. She was just as lost as he was.

He eased his hold on her and kissed his way to her lips, teasing them apart. He swept his tongue through her mouth and pulled back enough to whisper, "Come home with me."

"Why?" Kyra blurted.

"Because I want you in my bed. I want you again. I want you all night."

"We have to work tomorrow."

"We can call in sick."

"I just started here Monday. I don't think I get sick days yet."

"I'll grant you a sick day. Better yet, a sex day."

Kyra chuckled and shook her head. "I can't. I need this job. It's a very tempting offer, but I need the money to be able to afford my own apartment."

Slade kissed her jaw, then pulled back, lifting her with him. "How did the search go?"

She shrugged. "There's a decent amount out there, but a lot of it is out of my price range. Unless it's in a shitty area."

"We'll give you a raise," Slade said.

Kyra chuckled. "Again, it's only my first week. I'm not going to ask for a raise."

"You're not asking."

Kyra narrowed her eyes. "You do realize this is still kind of the same thing as I worried about, right?"

"What?" he asked, genuinely confused.

She shook her head and smiled. He was adorably clueless, which was the only reason she didn't rush out of there. "We just had sex, and now you're trying to bribe me into more sex with days off and more money."

Slade pulled back, his face twisted in pain. "I didn't mean to make it sound like that."

"I know," Kyra said, reaching for him before he got too far. "I know."

"Are you sure? I just want to spend time with you. And I don't want you in an unsafe apartment."

She nodded. "I know. And thank you. I've been on my own for a long time. I've been basically taking care of myself since I was a teenager. I appreciate it, but I'll make it work."

"We all take care of each other here. We're a team, but we're friends. Family, really. You're a part of that now."

Kyra nodded, her heart going all gooey again. She hadn't had a real family... ever. Her own family would have gladly forgotten she existed, and she never let anyone else close enough to think of them as family.

But Slade and the rest of the team were close. It didn't matter that she'd only known them for a few days, they were inside her.

"Thank you," Kyra said softly.

Slade kissed her temple and pulled her off the desk and to her feet. "If you won't come home with me, we at least need to head out. I need to let Howler out."

"I'm sorry. I shouldn't have stayed so late."

Slade cupped her jaw and forced her to meet his gaze. "You didn't do anything wrong. This was perfect."

She grinned. "Yeah, it was."

He leaned over and kissed her again. Heat pooled inside her, readying her for Slade again. He pressed her back to the desk, but she shoved him off.

"Howler," she said with a laugh.

"Who's that?"

Kyra chuckled and shook her head.

"You're far more tempting. Are you sure I can't talk you into coming home with me tonight?"

Kyra shook her head and reached for her clothes. "Not tonight."

"But sometime, right?"

Kyra looked at him over her shoulder and nodded. "Definitely."

How could she resist?

BOBBY PACED the basement and looked at the plans they already had. He'd been working on this for years. He knew what he was destined for, and greatness was headed his way.

His old man always told him he wasn't going to be anything, but he would show him. The stupid motherfucker never even realized what his son was planning, right under his damn nose, for years.

But Bobby was smart. He spent the last five years waiting for the time to be right. And it was. Step one was already in the bag. Step two was going to be just as easy. And step three... that was the one Bobby was really looking forward to.

He looked at the schematic for the next bank they were going to hit. The cash they took from the first one was enough to set them up for a while, but he didn't want to be set up for a while. Bobby planned to be set up for life. He was going to take out his old man and as he took his dying breath, Bobby would make sure he knew who came out on top in the end.

Footsteps behind him told him Stevie was headed down the stairs. When he made it to the concrete floor, Bobby turned to look at him.

"Figure this one out yet?" Stevie asked.

Bobby nodded slowly, facing the wall again. The projector they bought from a yard sale the summer before was the best little investment they'd made. They could print out the bank plans at the library, then enlarge them with the help of the projector. They drew right on the wall of the basement, then covered it back up with insulation when they were done. The cops could walk into the basement and never know the whole plan was right in front of them.

"I think we need to put Mario in charge this time."

"You really think he's ready for that?" Stevie asked.

Bobby shook his head. "No, but I don't think we have a choice."

"Why not?"

"Because my face is all over the fucking news," Bobby growled. He still couldn't believe anyone got a good enough look at him to detail so much to a sketch artist. Bobby did what he could to hide his real appearance while not being obvious, but whoever described him saw right through the prosthetic adjustments he made to his face.

"How the hell did someone do that?" Stevie asked.

Bobby glared at him. "I have one guess."

"Really?" Stevie asked, picking up what Bobby implied.

"It's hard to believe there's another option. Like Mario said, we weren't invisible to everyone in the bank," Bobby growled.

"I don't know. I have a hard time thinking either of them would rat you out."

Bobby shrugged. "The list he gave us didn't tell me much. It's the only answer. But if Mario is the face next time, he's the one going down if everything is perfect. Let's see them describe him to a sketch artist."

Stevie chuckled with Bobby. Insurance policies were

cheap when someone had something to hide. Put them out in the open and the whole game changed. Bobby was ready to change the game. And he was going to let Mario go down if he had to.

IT WAS hard to believe it was only her first full week of work. Kyra walked into the office Friday morning wearing her standard uniform of black pants and a dark blazer with a lighter colored shirt underneath. Pink today, because she wanted to feel a little feminine and pretty.

She kicked herself for not going home with Slade after they slept together, but she knew it was better that way. It gave him a night to think about if he really wanted her and gave her a night to distance herself.

They weren't in a relationship, and he didn't owe her anything. She didn't want to be one of those women who became someone else because of a man. So, she was going to stick to who she was and what she wanted. A new apartment where she could dance in her underwear and take baths and draw while she sat on the couch watching TV instead of feeling like she couldn't leave her bedroom.

Kyra got a cup of coffee and settled at her desk. She hoped Slade would train her again, but she didn't want to ask him. Instead, she just got her hopes up with she sipped her coffee and went through her emails. She was about to go find out what she needed to do for the day when Dex walked into her office.

"Hey, Kyra. I'm going to work with you today, if that's okay."

Kyra nodded, trying not to be disappointed. She straightened the inbox on her desktop surface, thankful it didn't break when Slade shoved it off her desk. She tried not to think about what he did after that, but her mind was stuck there, wondering if it was the last time.

"I know Rocky showed you some of our programs and a few things you can use to monitor what we're all doing. He said he got you started on some of the admin tasks. Dunn asked me to show you the accounting software we use. We're all pretty horrible with paperwork, but in order to get paid, we have to do it. Have you used billing software before?"

Kyra nodded. "Yep, lots of times. I'm pretty comfortable with most of the common ones."

"Good, you can probably show me a few things," Dex said with a chuckle. He pulled a chair over next to her and sat down. "You ready to get started?"

Kyra nodded.

They'd been working for a little over an hour, Kyra clicking through their accounts and double checking all the invoices that had been sent. She found a few that weren't sent out and Dex approved her to send them since they were due. She also found a few things they needed to pay and processed those. None of it was complicated for her, and Dex seemed impressed.

"I don't even want to think about what else we missed before you got here," Dex groaned.

Kyra laughed. "I guess I'm paying for my salary."

"More than," Dex said with a grin.

"We need to talk," Dunn said, sticking his head into Kyra's office and interrupting them. "Now. Conference room. Everyone."

Dex nodded and followed Dunn with Kyra right behind them. She took a seat next to Dex and wasn't sure whether to be thankful or not when Slade was the last one in the room and had to sit next to her.

She hadn't seen him and found herself hungry for a sign from him. His gaze slid over her as he took the chair next to her and pulled it back to the wall so he was next to her but not close. Kyra pasted a smile on her face and reminded herself she didn't want special treatment at work. It didn't matter that they had sex on her desk twelve hours before, she needed her job and she was there to do it, not to worry about Slade.

"There's been another bank robbery," Dunn said with no preamble, attracting all of Kyra's attention. "Same MO, same neurotoxin. Same everything. Patrick asked if the two of you will go to the scene and try to help out. He knows it's a big ask, but—"

"I'll go," Slade said before Dunn could finish. "Anything to catch those bastards."

"Good. Kyra?" Dunn asked.

All eyes swung to her. She felt the weight of their question. She could say no, but if she did, these guys could get away again. If she said yes, she might help. She nodded. "I'll go."

"Are you sure?"

Kyra nodded again. "Yeah. I took this job because I want to be able to help. I'm not out there doing the work, but if I make things easier for all of you, you can catch the bad guys. I can't say no to something like this because I'm scared."

"Okay. They need you there ASAP. Do what you need to do and head out," Dunn said. "Everyone else, we have an update on our missing person."

Kyra and Slade left the room. Her hands were shaking, but she knew it was the right thing to do. Kyra made it to her office and woodenly packed her bag. She took her notepad and a few pencils in case she talked to any witnesses who could give her a description of the men who were there.

Slade walked back to her door and asked if she was ready.

Kyra forced her head to nod and followed Slade out of the office and down to the garage. He unlocked a black SUV. She got in the passenger side and waited for him to get in the driver's seat.

He pulled out like it was just another day at the office. For him, it was. She was happy for his solid, steadiness beside her. It made her feel like maybe she would be okay.

They didn't speak on the drive to the bank. Kyra wanted to ask him if he was upset with her or something, but it wasn't the time, and she wasn't that person.

He parked outside the bank amid the police cars and turned off the SUV. When Kyra didn't make a move to get out, Slade turned to her.

"You okay?" he asked. His voice was gruff, like he'd been chewing nails all day.

She shook her head. Every inch of her body was vibrating with fear. She wasn't sure she could do it.

"I know," Slade said, as though she spoke aloud. "But this isn't the bank we were in. This is a different bank and we're safe."

"Are we? Is anyone?" Kyra asked, her voice panicked. "They're still out there. They're hurting more people. How are we safe?"

"We're here right now to help catch them. To end this. There's no reason to worry right now."

"Isn't there?" Kyra asked, looking up at Slade. He was watching her closely. "How are you just totally fine right now?"

He breathed a laugh and shook his head. "Trust me, I'm not. I want to grab your hand and never let go. I want to drive away from here and hide in my bed all day like I told you last night. I don't want to be here. I want to be buried deep inside you and forget there is a world outside the two of us. I fucking hate this. All of this." He gestured to the bank in front of them. He sighed. "I don't know how I'm supposed to act around you now, so I'm kept my distance this morning. And here? Walking into another bank?" He shook his head. "I'm not okay, Kyra."

"I don't want you to keep your distance," she said softly.

His gaze snapped to hers. "Good."

"I—"

Whatever she was about to say was cut off by the hard press of his lips to hers. He pried her mouth open and forced his tongue inside. She moaned and clutched at him, letting herself sink into him.

She fought with him, chasing his tongue through her mouth. He was a masterful kisser. He groaned and slid his hand to her throat. The touch was gentle and controlling at once. Without a doubt, she would do whatever he wanted.

Then he pushed back, separating them. He panted, their mixed breath steaming up the windows of the SUV. Their eyes locked together, both of them staring and on edge. Kyra would happily dive back in, but—

"We need to get inside," Slade said. "But this isn't over, Kyra. I'm nowhere near done with you."

Her body shook for an entirely different reason as his heated words sank into her. She bit her lip, and he cupped her jaw, tugging her lip free with his thumb. She licked his thumb, and he growled.

"You're going to fucking kill me, Kyra."

"But you'll die a happy man," Kyra repeated his words from the night before.

Slade nodded once, his eyes blazing with need. "Fuck, yeah, I will."

Slade got out of the SUV without another word. He stood at the front, waiting for Kyra. When she felt like her legs would support her, she fell out and met him. Slade reached for her hand and they walked into the bank together.

13

————

SLADE NEVER WOULD HAVE ADMITTED HOW TERRIFIED HE WAS to anyone else, but he felt like Kyra needed to hear he was scared, too. It was the honest truth, but walking in with her next to him made him feel like he could do it.

Patrick was just inside the door talking to another officer when Slade and Kyra walked up. The officer outside stopped them, but Slade called out to the Captain. He nodded and the officer let them by.

"Thanks for coming," Patrick said, glancing at their joined hands.

Kyra tried to pull away from Slade, but he held tightly to her hand. He needed to feel her touch, even if it was just her hand in his, if he was going to get through this.

Slade nodded and looked around the bank. It was a slightly different setup than the one they'd been in, but similar. The guard at the door was dead, but this time there were three other bodies on the ground. The officers were bagging the deposit slips on the table to the right by the door. The tellers were toward the back on the left with a snaking line in front of them. The biggest difference between this bank and the one they had been in was the position of the offices. Instead of being beyond the table with the deposit slips, the offices were farther back. The bank was narrower but deeper.

"What do you need us to do?" Kyra asked.

"Look around first," Patrick said. "If anything pops out to you, notify one of the officers. We might ask you to talk to some of the people. We were starting to think there was an inside person at the other bank, but it's hard to believe they have an inside person at both."

"Do you know for sure these are the same attackers?" Slade asked.

Patrick shook his head. "No. We're going off the assumption they are since it's so similar, but we're keeping our eyes open for everything. We wanted you two here in case you see something we don't see that tells you it's the same men or not." He leaned in closer. "I'll be honest, we're fucking lost with this one, and we need help. All our leads have been dead ends, and I fucking hate that. The picture you drew has been on the news for what, almost two weeks? But nothing's turned up. People are ignoring it now. We need to find these assholes."

"Agreed," Slade said. He looked down at Kyra and said, "Let's take a walk."

She nodded and let him pull her away from Captain Patrick. He could feel her body trembling as she followed him deeper into the bank. Slade released her hand and slid his arm around her waist, pulling her body closer to his. They walked side-by-side, taking steps together and swinging their eyes around as they moved through the bank.

"Are we allowed to talk?" Kyra asked.

Slade nodded. "Of course. What do you want to talk about?"

Kyra rolled her eyes at him. "About this. And... ours."

"Okay, talk. What's on your mind?"

Kyra stopped where they stood and spun in a circle. Slade let his hand fall from her waist and watched her as she scanned the bank. "Okay, this layout is very similar to ours. The front is nearly identical. The biggest difference is the position of the offices, but both are away from the view of most people. I've been in banks where the offices are a part of the open area near the tellers, either desks spaced apart or glass cubbies. This is an older style."

Slade nodded. "I noticed that, too. You're right, though. It is an older style. I wonder if that means their security system is also older."

"I'm not worried about that right now. Look at the people. We have no way of knowing who works here and who doesn't, but look at the people."

"What about them?" Slade asked, staring at the group Kyra was studying.

"It's about the same number. We had three tellers and seven customers. There were also two managers in the back, and the security guard. Thirteen people. There are thirteen people here, too. If you include the four bodies."

"How is that significant?" Slade asked. He wasn't saying she was wrong, but he couldn't imagine how it would matter, either.

"I was a criminal justice major in college. I wanted to be a cop. I loved it, but..." she gestured to her body "...I don't have the physique for it. I remember from one of my classes that criminals who pull off things like this sometimes have a magic number. They know how many people they think they can subdue, or at least how many they can handle. More and they won't attempt the job. Less and they'll go ahead with it. It makes me wonder if these guys were in the bank, this one and the other one, before they did this."

Slade nodded. "It's almost guaranteed they've been here. The problem is until we know what they look like, there's no way to go through all that footage to try to find them."

"But we know what they look like," Kyra said. "You and I saw them. The one. I didn't get a good look at the others before they put their masks on, but we saw the one."

"We don't know if it's the same people."

"So, we ask around. We show them the sketch."

Slade shook his head, putting his hand on hers. "We can't."

"Why not?" Kyra barked. The excited smile fell off her face at his refusal.

"It's leading them. It's giving them a suspect before they give us one. It's not a good idea because it could lead to the police chasing the wrong person and the true criminal getting away."

"Shit," Kyra said. "I should have remembered that."

"You haven't been doing this work. It's okay. For what it's worth, your physique is fucking perfect."

Kyra looked up at him, her eyes going from annoyed to heated in an instant. Her lips curled up into a smile. She shook her head and closed her eyes, then drew in a deep breath. "Thank you. Now what?"

"Well, we could go back to my place like I wanted to do last night," Slade said with a waggle of his eyebrows.

Kyra chuckled and shook her head. "I meant with the bank."

Slade shrugged and pulled her close. "You didn't say no.

I'll take it. As for here, let's look at the other similarities and differences and talk to some people... Wow, that man looks just like the bank manager."

"Who?" Kyra asked.

Slade nodded to the man in the middle of the crowd. He had more hair, and he was taller, but he looked just like the other bank manager. The one with the keys who disappeared with the pregnant teller.

Kyra turned and found the man Slade was talking about and jerked back. "They have to be brothers or something. That's a really weird coincidence, isn't it?"

Slade nodded slowly and grabbed the shirt of a cop walking by. "I need a list of all the people who were in this bank during the robbery. Now."

The cop looked at him and nodded. "Yes, sir." He rushed away to do what Slade asked, and Kyra chuckled.

Slade raised an eyebrow at her.

"You about made him pee his pants."

Slade shrugged. "He needs to learn how to handle himself if he's going to be a good cop. Part of that is not letting his guard down or losing it with a witness or another officer."

Kyra giggled. "I don't think it was either of those things. I think it was the fact that you're twice his size and could squash him without even trying and there would be nothing he could do about it."

"Then maybe I just inspired him to bulk up."

Kyra grinned and slid her gaze down his arms and across his chest. Slade just stood still and let her look. His strength didn't save them from the bank robbery, but it might come in handy for something else.

Like getting her naked again. He was okay with that deal.

Kyra watched Slade as he observed the room. He took in everything around him. She wondered what he was thinking, but she wasn't brave enough to ask.

The officer came back with the list Slade asked for and handed it over before rushing away again. Slade scanned it quickly and pointed to a name. "It's the same last name. That can't be a coincidence."

Kyra shook her head. "It would be a pretty big one if it is. Do you think they're the ones that are helping pull this off?"

"Only one way to know." Slade nodded to Captain Patrick, and he walked over.

"Do you have something?"

"A few things," Slade began. "This layout is very similar. Not exact, but close. Tellers up front, offices closed off from the rest of the area. It's easy to separate the two and not see what people in the other area are doing. But the biggest thing we've noticed is a connection to the staff. Our bank manager appears to be related to a staff member here."

"What?" Patrick barked.

"We recognized him," Kyra said. "He looks just like his brother or cousin or whatever. I thought he was going to be killed when they took him to the back of the bank with the teller. But he walked back out again after the police arrived. This guy looks very similar, and they have the same last name."

Patrick waved over one of the other cops and told him to pull the man to the side for additional questioning. It was nearly impossible to imagine they weren't involved.

"Thanks," Patrick told them. "We couldn't have done this without you."

"We can stick around if you want," Slade offered.

Patrick shook his head. "I didn't mean to drag you two into this all day. I just wanted fresh, trained eyes on it. I'll tell you, these guys are smart. They definitely know what they're doing. And we can usually figure out something about why they're doing it, but with them, we're just chasing our tails. Hopefully, you guys gave us a lead we can use to find them."

"Keep us posted," Slade said, extending his hand.

"We will," Patrick answered, shaking it. He turned to Kyra. "Thank you for coming along. How's the new job?"

Kyra smiled and shook his offered hand. "Good. Although, it's only my first week. I still have a lot to learn."

"Keep away from this guy and you should be fine," Patrick teased Slade.

Slade rolled his eyes and shook his head. "You're just jealous because I can bench more than you."

Patrick chuckled and clapped Slade on the back. "I'll catch up one day."

Slade laughed with him and jerked his head in a good-bye. Then he put his hand on the small of Kyra's back and led her to the door.

She liked that part.

Slade opened the door for her at the SUV and waited until she was settled in the seat before closing it. He jogged around the front and slid in next to her. "Want to get a drink?"

"It's not even lunchtime," Kyra said with a laugh.

"I need a drink. Being here... do you want me to drop you off at the office or do you want to go with me?"

Kyra met his gaze and nodded. "I want to go with you."

Slade started the SUV and backed away from the bank. He turned the SUV around and headed toward the office, then turned and pulled into a parking space on the side of the road.

Before they got out, he thumbed a text and said, "Just letting Dunn know we're getting a drink. In case he needs us for something."

Kyra nodded and waited for him to finish. When he opened his door, she opened hers and met him on the sidewalk.

"Right here," Slade said, nodding to a hole in the wall bar that had a small neon open sign glowing.

The inside wasn't much more impressive than the outside. Slade pointed to a table for Kyra to sit while he went to the bar and ordered for them. Kyra looked around the tiny space. It was dark, so it took a minute for her eyes to adjust, but when they did, she was able to see the short, wooden bar surrounded by stools and the scattered tables. There were no dartboards or pool tables or anything else. Next to the bar was a hallway that she assumed led to the bathrooms and storage area, but that was it.

Music played softly in the background, but there was nothing to do in the bar except drink. At the moment, Kyra was okay with that.

Slade set two glasses on the table and took the seat across from her. There were two other chairs, but with the size of Slade, Kyra wondered how two other people could possibly sit at the same table.

"What is it?" Kyra asked, lifting the glass of amber liquid.

"Scotch. We need something good and strong right now." He picked up his glass and clinked it against hers, then took a sip. "Damn, that's good."

Kyra brought the glass to her lips. She'd never had scotch. She wasn't sure it was something she liked, but the first taste didn't make her want to spit it back out. It was strong but smooth with a burn that followed the liquor down her throat to her stomach.

"You're not a scotch drinker, are you?" Slade asked.

Kyra shook her head. "I'm not much of a drinker at all."

"Is there a reason?"

Kyra shook her head again. "Not really. I drink wine, but usually only when I'm by myself. I don't have a group of friends like you do to spend time with."

"Why did you move here?"

Kyra looked at him and debated telling him the same thing she told almost everyone else. She mentally shook her head and decided to tell him the truth. "My parents have always favored my older brother."

"I'm sure that's not true," he said quickly.

She smiled. "It is. He's perfect. He's the kid every parent wants. He says the right things and does the right things and looks the right way. I'm not any of those things, so my parents favored him."

"That's not what parenting is," Slade growled.

Kyra shrugged. "Maybe, but it's what my parents did. When I was in college, they decided to move to be near my brother. They sold the house I grew up in and left. I decided there was no reason for me to stay close to them when they really didn't care if I was around."

Slade reached across the table and set his hand over Kyra's. "I'm sorry."

She avoided his gaze and nodded. "It's fine. It's been almost ten years since I've lived near them. I don't really know why I moved here specifically, but it seemed like a good place to land. I've lived in a few different places and was looking for a change from the West Coast. A college friend was from the area. She had a friend casually looking for a roommate, which is how I ended up with Autumn."

"And now you're getting your own place?" Slade asked, still holding her hand.

Kyra nodded. "I hope to. I need to start actually going to look at places instead of just browsing online."

"Another apartment or a house?"

"An apartment. I can't afford a house yet."

"And you aren't sure if you want to stay," Slade said, reading her mind.

"I've been here for years. I'm not going anywhere."

"Good," Slade said, finishing his drink. He rubbed small circles on her wrist with his thumb. "What are we doing after this?"

"Um, going back to work," Kyra said, stumbling over the words. His thumb was more than a little distracting.

"Are you sure about that?"

Kyra nodded. "Probably for the best. If I'm going to afford a new apartment."

Slade grinned. "Probably smart."

Kyra watched Slade's thumb silently, knowing he was staring at her. She'd never known a man like him, one who was blunt about what he wanted from her but also respected that she was her own person and didn't push for more than she was willing to give. It was as intoxicating as the scotch.

"Come over tonight," Slade said softly.

"Why?" Kyra blurted.

"Because I want to be with you again. In a bed."

Kyra grinned. "I figured you were done with me after last night."

Slade shook his head. "Hell, no."

"You didn't come in to train me today," she said, hating herself for sounding like a needy girlfriend instead of a one-night stand.

"Dex was already lined up to work with you today. There were things he needed to show you. It made sense."

"But you didn't... never mind."

"I didn't what?" he asked with a grin. His thumb continued to rub circles on her wrist.

Kyra sighed. "You didn't want to sit next to me in the conference room and you didn't say hi when you came in this morning."

His grin widened. "Keeping tabs on me?"

"No," Kyra said immediately.

"You were the one who said you weren't sure about us. You turned me down three times. I haven't hidden the fact that I want you, but I am not the kind of man who is going to force himself on a woman. You say no, I back off. Which is what happened when I asked you to come home with me last night. But if you say yes again, trust me, sweetheart, I'm all in."

Kyra couldn't stop her grin or the desire racing through her. She wasn't sure it was a good idea, but the thought of being alone again was not appealing. Especially on the heels of another robbery.

Her smile faded with her desire as she thought of the people who wouldn't get to go home that day.

"Why did they kill more people this time?" she asked softly.

Slade drew in a breath. "I was wondering that, too."

She shuddered. "That could have been us."

Slade nodded.

"I wish we could have helped more."

"We gave them something. Hopefully, it leads to whoever is doing this."

"I hope so," Kyra said, draining her glass. "Should we go back to work?"

Slade nodded and carried their glasses back to the bartender. He met her at the door and guided her outside and to the SUV again. When he climbed in his side, Kyra leaned over and turned his face to hers.

"I'm not saying no," she said softly.

Slade grinned. "Good." He leaned forward and pecked her lips quickly, then turned on the SUV and drove them back to work.

14

———

Slade stuck close to Kyra the rest of the day. He told himself it was to make sure she was doing okay, but being around her helped calm him down.

Dex smirked every time Slade walked in the door with a cup of coffee or a snack, but Kyra didn't seem to mind. It was only when Rocky pulled Slade aside that he realized he wasn't being as subtle as he thought.

"You doing okay?" Rocky asked, following Slade into his office.

"Yeah, why?"

"Uh, because you went to the scene of another bank robbery this morning. You can play it off all you want, but I know it messed with your head."

"I'm good," Slade said, not meeting his friend's gaze.

"Okay, then how's Kyra?"

Slade shook his head. "Better than I expected. She's shaken up, but she wants to catch these guys."

"It's the same group?"

"We don't know. It's a similar layout to the bank, and there was one guy at this one that we think is related to the manager at the other one, so it's easy to make a connection."

"That seems really easy," Rocky said.

Slade nodded. "I've been thinking that, too, but Patrick and his guys will figure that out."

Rocky nodded. "You up for some company tonight?"

"Yeah, Kyra's coming over."

"She is?"

Slade nodded, trying not to grin.

"So, leaving you two here together last night was a good thing?"

Slade chuckled. "Very. I think I owe you for it."

Rocky shook his head. "No thanks necessary. But fair warning... Lily's rounding up the troops. She's not going to let you be alone tonight."

"I wasn't going to be," Slade groaned. He wanted to get Kyra naked as quickly as possible.

"Keep your clothes on until after we all leave. You know it's impossible to talk Lily, Kelsea, Pilar, and Ashleigh out of taking care of someone. Dunn said Ash is nesting, and she was always the one who might help call them off. Just be prepared to be invaded."

Slade nodded, thankful for the warning. Even though it would delay his plans to get Kyra into his bed, he was grateful that they all wanted to be there for him. And for Kyra, too. He was sure she would have been invited.

Slade called Patrick to see if they got anything out of the guy he and Kyra pointed out and if there was anything else going on. Unfortunately, he didn't get good news.

"The guy isn't a manager. He's a teller. He was the one they took to the back with the manager. The guy said he felt like they were looking for him, almost like they were trying to establish a connection. It's too easy," Patrick said.

"That's what we were thinking, too. Did you get anything out of the rest of the witnesses?"

"We got a good sketch, we think. It'll go out on the news tonight. Looks nothing like your guy, though."

"Well, if they keep two under masks and one out front, it makes sense they'd change who's seen," Slade said.

"I agree. It still feels like yours. We're missing something, though. I don't know what it is, but we're missing something."

Slade sighed and leaned back in his chair. He looked at the ceiling and tried to figure out what could be going on. "What are they taking?"

"That's the thing... it seems random. Cash, of course, but none from the tellers this time. At the first one, they took cash from tellers, but they also asked for cash that was being pulled out of circulation. This time they were able to get stacks from the vault. And they wanted items from deposit boxes both times, but the managers said it seemed like they picked numbers when they walked into the room. Nothing about it makes sense."

"Is it for sport?"

Patrick breathed heavily through the phone. His voice dropped when he said, "I'll fucking kill them myself if they're doing this for kicks."

"We can't rule it out. They killed both guards. I'm assuming this one tried to stop them."

"Yeah. But it's not like we can tell guards they should let them go. It's their damn job to do something."

"What about alarms? Were silent alarms tripped at either one?" Slade asked.

"Good call, and no. At both places, one of the managers said they hit the alarm button. Managers out of view of the front, so they could easily alert us. Both times, we didn't get calls until the guys left and people could use their phones."

"So, they're stopping the alarms somehow."

"Yeah, and we don't know how they're doing that, either. The alarms seem to be functioning, but they don't."

"Do you think English could take a look at it? Maybe we can go by there Monday?"

"Sure. My guys have looked, but they can't find anything. I'll put you both on the list. Anyone else need to be on the list?"

"See you Monday, Captain."

His laughter rang in the air before Slade hung up.

Slade checked with English that he was free on Monday since it was already late on Friday afternoon and worked a little longer, then decided to call it a day. He retrieved Kyra from her office and ushered her out of the building.

"What was that all about?" she asked when they were in the garage.

"We need to go to your place and get your stuff for the night."

"Okay, but do we need to do it now?"

"Did you get a call from Lily today?"

Kyra nodded slowly.

"She's invited everyone over to my house tonight. Including you."

"What?" Kyra blurted, stopping in the middle of the driveway.

"She takes care of people. It's her thing. And she heard about the bank and decided we needed to get together tonight. She didn't want either of us alone. Everyone gets together at my house, which I encourage, so she told everyone to be there for dinner."

"They all know I'm coming over?" Kyra squeaked.

"Not yet, but they will know when your car isn't there and you don't leave."

"But... I... um..."

"Do you want to drive yourself home and come over like everyone else?" Slade asked. He didn't want to ask the question. He wanted to just demand she get in the fucking truck with him and stay, but it had to be her choice.

She stared up at me. She took a deep breath and shook her head. "Not really. I'm sorry, but all this is a lot for me. I feel like we're jumping in here and I'm not sure if that's what is happening."

Slade cupped her arm and led her out of the driveway in case a vehicle came by. "I have a sister. She's a few years younger than me. She tells me all the time that women need to know what's going on when they're with someone, so, this isn't a fling, Kyra. If I was just trying to get in your pants, we would be done. I like you, and I really like getting naked with you. I'm not saying this is a forever kind of thing because I don't know, but I'm saying I want to see you tonight. I want you in my bed tonight. I want you at my house tonight, and I want to kiss you in front of all our friends and not worry that you're going to get mad at me."

' Kyra smirked and shook her head. "I think I would like your sister."

Slade grinned. "She takes after her big brother."

"Oh, do you have a brother, too?"

Slade scowled at her, and Kyra just laughed. And got in his truck.

KYRA WAS unsure about letting Slade into her bedroom, but she couldn't really leave him in the living room either. She'd never had a man, or anyone, in her room. It was her sanctuary. The place where she was herself and didn't worry about what other people thought about her.

Which was to say it was kind of a mess.

She rushed through her room picking up drawings and grabbed the rainbow bras she had hanging everywhere. She learned to be professional in her outward appearance, which meant dark, neat clothes, but underneath, she wore bright, bold colors that were too loud for most people. She loved them.

Slade lifted a grape bra from her chair and dangled it on one finger. "You should wear this tonight. And only this."

Kyra tried to snatch it from him, but he pulled it out of her reach.

"I'm going to keep this one. You can model it for me later. Got any panties that match?" He folded the bra delicately and put his hands on his hips. He looked ridiculous with the bright purple bra against his black tee and jeans.

Kyra's cheeks burned with the admission that she had panties that matched all her bras. Since it was the only clothing that she actually liked, besides her pajamas, she splurged. She bought coordinating panties in multiple styles so she could wear what she felt like when she wanted.

"Show me," Slade demanded.

The rough edge of his voice sent a shiver down Kyra's spine. She pointed to the dresser where she kept her panties and said, "Top drawer."

Slade crossed to it in three steps and pulled the drawer open. His tongue slid across his lower lip, and he groaned. "I think we need to take them all."

Kyra laughed. "You're insane."

"And you're keeping secrets from me. You had on black panties last night with a black bra."

"Black is a good color. You're wearing black right now."

Slade nodded. "Black is a great color, but it's not you. You're a rainbow person. Why do you hide these under your black clothes?"

Kyra snorted, ignoring his comment about her being rainbow. No one knew she preferred bright to bland. "It's usually frowned upon to wear your underwear on the outside of your clothes."

"Then you need new damn clothes," Slade said. He closed her panty drawer and opened the next one.

Kyra tried to stop him, but he opened her pajama drawer. She didn't wear anything scandalous, but she liked bright, soft, sensual pajamas. Not that she ever shared them with anyone, but she liked the feel of soft stuff on her skin when she slept.

Slade's eyes lifted to hers. Heat poured out of him, flooding the air between them. He dug out his phone.

"What are you doing?"

"I'm calling off the party. You're going to model for me tonight. They all need to stay the fuck home."

"Don't do that," Kyra argued, crossing to him and putting her hand over his phone. "They're your friends."

"And I'm going to be walking around all night with a fucking hard-on because of you."

Kyra grinned. "Maybe I can take care of that for you." She didn't wait for him to respond before she dropped to her knees in front of him. She pulled at his belt and unzipped his jeans, then shoved them and his boxer briefs down.

His cock sprang up at her, and she licked her lips. She half thought he would argue, but he didn't say a thing. When she looked up at him, he was staring at her.

"Am I dreaming?" he whispered.

She shook her head and smiled.

"Thank fuck for that."

She licked the tip of him and tasted the saltiness of his skin. She wanted to take it slow, but she could feel the tension in his body at just being exposed. He was already ready to blow.

She opened her mouth and sucked him inside. He groaned and immediately slid his hands through her hair. He was big, too big to fit all the way in her mouth, but she wanted to use only her mouth.

She withdrew slowly, then sucked him back in. He groaned and thrust into her mouth, pulling her head back the second he did it.

He tilted her chin up to meet her gaze. "Are you okay?"

She nodded and turned her head back to her task. She wrapped her hands around his thighs and let him help her set a pace he enjoyed. He worked opposite her, thrusting in when she sucked him, and retreating when she pulled back.

His pace increased quickly until he was in control of her entire body. Heat pooled in her belly and her panties soaked through. He fucked her mouth, taking what he needed from her. She let him, wanting to make him feel good.

He grunted and thrust harder, nearly tripping her gag reflex, but she relaxed and let him slide in deeper. He swelled between her lips, then plunged in and stilled, holding her head against his body as he jerked and emptied into her mouth.

Kyra wanted to slide her hand between her thighs and relieve the pulsing need he created, but she was focused on Slade. The big, beautiful man who acted like he'd never had an orgasm as good before her.

"Fucking hell, Kyra. I don't know how you blow my damn mind every time, but you do," he breathed. He let her pull back, then lifted her to her feet and kissed her, swiping his tongue through her mouth.

She wrapped her arms around him and held on. His hands skimmed down her body, then back up to cup her heavy breasts.

Flames licked over Kyra's body with his touch, but she knew they had to go. It was going to be bad enough staying after everyone left and having them all know what was going to happen, but showing up to his house late and both of them looking thoroughly fucked was even worse.

"We have to go," she said, trying to pull herself away.

"Fuck them. We can stay here."

"I have a roommate."

"Dammit," Slade breathed. "Fine." He smirked at her. "I plan to make that up to you later."

"I plan to let you."

He bent to scoop up the purple bra he dropped sometime after she dropped to her knees. He turned and grabbed a pair of pajamas that wasn't particularly sexy but was Kyra's favorite pair. It was a soft cotton set, light purple with colorful llamas all over it. "We're taking these." He opened the top drawer again and fingered his way through her panties until he found a pair of boyshorts that matched her bra. "And these."

"I would have figured you for a thong kind of guy," Kyra teased.

He shook his head. "Nah, they tend to ride up my ass."

A surprised laugh burst from her. Slade just winked.

Slade wouldn't let himself tell Kyra to pack for the whole

weekend, but he didn't mind when she added enough clothes to stay with him for at least that long.

He carried her bag to his truck and stole a kiss from her before he ushered her inside. He reached for her hand and wound their fingers together while they made the drive north to his house.

No one was there when he pulled in, which meant he might have a minute to make Kyra crazy before they were invaded. He grabbed her bag and bounded up the steps to his house. He could hear Howler through the door.

"Wow, he's loud," Kyra said.

"He is. But you don't know what a softie he is until you get inside. He sounds like he might eat your face."

Kyra snorted. "True. He's definitely a sweet dog."

Slade unlocked the door and opened it gently to give his lump of a dog a chance to move. He learned shortly after he bought the house that Howler sat right on the other side of the door when Slade was unlocking it. If he opened it too quickly, he would hit Howler.

As soon as they were inside, Kyra sank to the floor to say hello to Howler. The greedy thing flopped onto his back and spread his legs, showing off his junk.

Kyra just laughed.

"I'm glad you didn't laugh at mine," Slade said.

"You didn't lay it all out there for me. I had to work for yours."

"But if I'd done that, you wouldn't have been interested?"

She shrugged. "I like a little mystery. Besides, if you did that at the bank, or the hospital, I think you would have ended up in jail."

Slade chuckled, but just the mention of the bank set him on edge. It wasn't that he couldn't think of it, but he wanted to figure it out. He knew there was a way to find them. There always was. There was a connection. Criminals weren't as smart as they thought, and if they were, they got cocky eventually. They always screwed up. And it was his job to make sure he was there when they did.

Kyra cooed and rubbed Howler's belly. She bent down to kiss his nose, and he let out a fart that scared him. He jerked up and smashed his nose against Kyra's cheekbone.

"Ow, shit," she gasped.

Howler tried to move away, but he couldn't roll over with her leg in the way.

Slade reached down and grabbed him, setting him on his feet, then reached for Kyra.

"Is he okay?" she asked.

Slade nodded, loving that she was worried about the dog before she worried about herself. "He scared himself."

"Did I hurt him? He hit me pretty hard."

"Did he hurt you?"

She shook her head. "I'm fine. Is he?"

Slade looked at his dog, one leg in the air, licking around his cock. "He's trying to rub it in that he doesn't need a woman."

Kyra looked at Howler and gasped, then started laughing.

She was beautiful when she laughed. Slade just stood there and watched her and wondered why he was lucky enough to be in the bank with her that day. He could have gone forever without knowing Kyra. But he met her, and he was pretty sure she was going to be his new favorite toy.

15

Kyra couldn't remember the last time she laughed so much. She was sure everyone was just trying to keep her and Slade distracted, but they were really good at it, and really funny.

"You should have seen the look on his face," Jack said, twisting his lips and drawing back. "He was somewhere between shocked and horrified and didn't know where to land on the spectrum."

Kyra laughed with the rest of the group. Slade drew her closer to him on the couch. He'd barely let go of her all night, which she didn't mind at all.

"I really thought we were all done for," Jack continued. "But Slade pulled it off and got us out of there. I've never known anyone to sweet talk the enemy like he did."

"He's good at sweet talking people," Kyra said with a laugh.

Slade pulled back and looked at her. "Really? That's your answer?"

She just laughed, and he pulled her back in and kissed her neck. "You'll be sorry you said that later."

Kyra was sure he was wrong about that if the tone of his voice was anything to go by. Just having him whisper against her ear made her shiver.

"So, Kyra, what's your story?" Pilar asked. She turned her dark brown eyes to Kyra and smiled. Kyra liked her the last time they met and knew there wasn't anything malicious in the question, just curiosity.

"Well, I'm from California, but I'm not close to my family, so I moved out here a few years after college. I've lived in a few other places up and down the West Coast and wanted to try the East Coast. I have a degree in criminal justice, but I never thought I could pass the physical test, so I never became a cop. And working as an assistant or admin has been good. I don't mind the work and the hours are usually pretty regular."

"What do you do when you're off work?" Lily asked.

"Um, not much," Kyra said with a chuckle. "I've explored the city and the local area a bit, but I don't really have a favorite thing to do or anything."

"What about your drawing?" Slade asked.

"You draw?" Kelsea asked.

Kyra nibbled her lip. She didn't tell a lot of people about her drawing. Most thought it was a waste of time or a silly thing, so she kept it to herself. She wasn't sure if she should be upset that Slade mentioned it, or happy he realized it was an important part of who she was.

"She's very talented," Rocky said with a smirk.

Kyra fought off her grin. "I like to draw, yes."

"The drawing on the news of the guy from our robbery is hers," Slade provided for the group.

"Wow," Ashleigh said. "That's definitely impressive."

"Thanks. It's really just a hobby, but I like it," Kyra said.

"We should go to one of those places where we paint a

picture sometime," Kelsea said. "I've always wanted to do that."

"Let's go after this baby is born," Ashleigh said, rubbing her stomach. "He's making me miserable lately."

"Do you think that means he's coming soon?" Lily asked.

Ashleigh shrugged. "The doctor says she wants him in for a while longer. I'm not due for a three more weeks, and since I'm old, she wants to keep him inside as long as possible."

"I hate that they say you're old," Pilar said. "Women have babies all the time. Teenagers can do it, but for a woman like you, it's negative."

Ashleigh nodded. "Trust me, it's not fun. You should all get pregnant soon so they don't make you feel like you should have a cane or a walker to get through your pregnancy."

Kyra smiled with the rest of them but didn't say anything. The women all knew she couldn't get pregnant, but thankfully, none of them said anything around Slade and the rest of the guys.

"I think it's time for dessert," Lily announced, getting up from her seat. She turned to Archer and reached out her hand. "Come help me."

Archer didn't hesitate to put his hand in hers and follow her to the kitchen.

Kyra always wanted a relationship like theirs. They fit together. She was funny and talkative, and he was quiet and strong. They clearly adored each other, and watching them was like watching a movie. It was rare they weren't touching if they were in the same room, and if they went too long, one of them always went over and kissed the other.

Kyra watched them and the other couples and let herself dream for just a minute. Dunn rubbed Ashleigh's round belly, whispering something no one else could hear. Jaymes kissed the side of Kelsea's head and squeezed her hand. Jack was the life of the party, but when he looked at Pilar, all humor disappeared and was replaced with love.

Being loved was something Kyra never experienced. Not from her family or from another person. She didn't like being jealous of other people, but she was. Love always seemed so easy for people who weren't her. Kyra didn't know how to let people in, how to love them. She tried, but it always failed and she was always left thinking she just wasn't worthy of love.

"What are you thinking about?" Slade whispered in her ear.

She forced a grin and shook her head. "Nothing."

He studied her carefully, clearly not buying it, but he didn't push.

Lily and Archer brought cake over for everyone. Kyra happily accepted a piece because everything was better when cake was involved. She could smell the tart lemon scent before she stabbed her fork through the soft cake. The glaze on top held it together until she got the bite to her mouth. It was sweet but not overpowering. The cake melted instantly on her tongue. The glaze was the perfect compliment, adding touches of sweetness to the lemony flavor.

"Wow, this is good," Ashleigh said. "Is this the same cake you made for my baby shower?"

Lily nodded. "It is. You seemed to really like it, so I wanted to make it again."

"It's delicious," Ashleigh said.

"It is," Pilar agreed. "So good."

Everyone else chimed in with their approval as slices of cake were distributed to the entire group. They all ate silently, only pausing to shower more well-deserved praise onto Lily.

"Where do you find time to bake when you work all day?" Kelsea asked. "I feel like I can barely pick up take out on my way home half the time."

Lily laughed. "It's relaxing for me. I bake before I go to bed and let it cool overnight half the time. Or if I have a rough day, I might bake a cake for dinner."

"Why do we not get together at your house?" Kyra asked.

The rest of the group laughed.

"We're still in an apartment," Lily said. "Jaymes and Kelsea, and Jack and Pilar live in the same building."

"That's pretty cool," Kyra said.

"Kyra's looking for a new apartment," Slade said. "Are there any open in your building?"

Lily shook her head. "Sorry, but no. We just had someone new move in, but I don't know of anyone leaving soon."

"That's okay," Kyra said. "Finding a decent place to live isn't easy."

"No, it's not," Pilar agreed. "I used to live with my brother, and we didn't have the nicest place. We had to stay under the radar, though."

Kyra was about to ask why when Slade squeezed her thigh. She looked up at him, and he shook his head almost imperceptibly. She nodded, understanding not to ask.

She pasted on a smile, but it bothered her. She was on the outside. She wasn't one of them yet. They invited her in, but she wasn't a part of the group. If she and Slade weren't together, she wondered if she would be there at all.

Kyra kept quiet the rest of the night, only speaking when someone asked her a question. She felt awkward and uncomfortable, like she should go, but she didn't have her own vehicle. She was stuck.

What was she thinking?

SLADE NOTICED Kyra was quiet and started making noise to the others about leaving. They were resistant, but it was getting late. Ashleigh was half-asleep on Dunn when he stood and announced they were going to head out.

"Aren't we going to build a fire?" Ashleigh asked.

"Not today. You need some sleep," Dunn said, helping Ashleigh to her feet.

She let him pull her up and leaned into him for support. Dunn had told them all Ashleigh was falling asleep at the drop of the hat and extra crabby when he woke her up to carry her to bed.

"I think we're going to head out, too," Archer said. "You guys ready?" he asked Jaymes, Kelsea, Jack, and Pilar.

Pilar nodded. "Yeah, it's been a long week for me."

The rest of the group filed behind them, grabbing snacks on their way out the door. Rocky, Dex, English, and Mason talked about going out. Normally Slade would be with them, looking for a woman to fall into for a little while, but he didn't need to look far. He already had one.

When the door closed behind the last of them, Slade turned to Kyra, hoping she was ready for bed, and found her chewing on her nail.

"Will you take me home?" she asked without looking at him.

"What? Why?"

"I just think I should go. I'm not here for the right reasons."

"What does that mean?"

She finally looked up at him and glared. "It means I've been fooling myself that I'm a part of this group. It means I came over here tonight thinking I was one of you, but I'm not. I'm an outsider, and I just want to go home where I don't trick myself into believing something that isn't true."

"Where is this coming from?" Slade asked gently.

She shook her head and averted her gaze again.

Slade walked over to her and lifted her chin. Her skin was soft under his rough finger. He wanted to slide his hands over her entire body, but first he needed to understand what happened that turned her cold. "Talk to me."

"I can't have kids," she said suddenly, meeting his gaze with a sad one of her own. "I know you want a family, and you want someone to get pregnant, and you should have all that. But you're not going to get it with me."

She pulled away from him before he could wrap his head around what she said. As she stalked to the other side of the room, Howler followed her. When she stopped, he sat on her feet, either to stop her from leaving or to show his support. The move softened her features and distracted Kyra while Slade processed her words.

Kyra crouched and scratched Howler's head. He sat there, not moving, like he knew it was for her instead of himself.

"I told you I have a sister. Do you remember?"

Kyra nodded.

"What I don't tell people is she's adopted. It's no one's business, and to me, it doesn't matter. I remember when she came home, a tiny pink thing that cried and wiggled and my parents told me I had to protect. And I did. It never mattered to me that she and I didn't share the same DNA. She's my sister, and I love her. My parents love her. She's a part of our family."

"Okay?" Kyra said.

"What I'm saying is getting pregnant isn't the only way to have a child. My mom couldn't get pregnant after me, but my parents still had a second kid. Do I want a family? Yes. But I've never been selfish enough to dictate what that family needs to look like. Families are all different."

"You have a family," Kyra said softly. "The people who were here tonight. They're your family."

He nodded. "They are."

"I'm not a part of that."

Slade chuckled. "You've known us a few days. That's barely long enough to remember everyone's names, let alone know everything about us."

"You wouldn't let me ask," she said quietly.

"What?" he asked, confused.

"When Pilar was talking about her brother, you wouldn't let me ask."

Slade closed his eyes and shook his head. "That's what this is about. That wasn't fair of me. Maybe I should have, but Pilar's brother was killed a little over a year ago. He was a member of a cartel, and they came after him when he handed over information to help take them down. Juan was an informant for us, so we all knew him. And liked him. She doesn't talk about him much."

"Oh, God. And I was going to ask her," Kyra breathed.

Slade nodded. "That's why I told you to stop. Partly for her, but also because I knew you would feel horrible once she told you." Slade took a chance and moved closer. "There's a lot of history between all of us. That doesn't mean we don't want you to be a part of the future, but it's going to take some time before you know all the stories."

"What's your story?" Kyra asked.

Slade smirked and took another step toward her. "I'm just an ordinary guy—"

"Who likes to blow shit up?"

He chuckled. "Yeah, there's that. I grew up in Kentucky. My parents are still happily married. My sister is one of my closest friends. I left my high school girlfriend to join the Navy, and it was the best thing I could have done for either of us. I signed up to be a SEAL and defended my country for sixteen years. When I got out, we all moved here and started F-BOMB."

Kyra narrowed her eyes. "I feel like there are a few missing pieces in that story."

Slade grinned. "There are, but that's part of the story that comes later."

"What parts?"

Slade sobered and put his hands on her waist. "I was a POW for almost two weeks."

"What?" she breathed. She slid her hands up his chest, and he let the softness of her touch ground him.

Saying the words out loud was supposed to help him get past it, but it almost always brought back memories. With Kyra right there, he was able to let thoughts of her push the memories to the side.

"Are you... Did you... I don't know what to say," she admitted.

He shook his head. "You don't have to say anything. It's a part of my story I don't talk about, but one I want you to know exists."

"Oh, God, I'm so sorry."

He smiled and pulled her in close, wrapping his arms around her body until they were touching from shoulders to knees. "Thank you. For telling me about yourself and for listening. Do you still want me to drive you home?"

She shook her head and held on tighter.

"Then can I finally take you to bed?" he asked, a hint of teasing in his tone.

"Yes, please," she said with just as much humor in her voice.

Slade lifted her into her arms, earning a growl from Howler when her feet came out from under him. Kyra shrieked and wrapped herself around him.

"You're going to hurt yourself," she said. "Put me down."

Slade shook his head and patted Howler's head, then cupped Kyra's ass. "I got you."

She looked down at him, the green of her hazel eyes vibrant and flashing. She liked being taken care of. She liked not having to do all the work. And he sure as hell loved being the one in charge.

Slade stalked to the front door and double checked that it was locked, then circled to the back door and checked that one. When he was satisfied that they were locked in, he headed for his bedroom.

"You're going to hurt yourself," Kyra said again.

"I might," Slade said, "but it's not going to be from carrying you. I might throw my back out making you come. I am an old man."

Kyra laughed, her body relaxing against his.

Slade stepped into his room and turned on the light. It was more of a mess than usual since his nights had been filled with wild dreams of Kyra. His blankets were twisted and half-thrown off the bed. A pair of shorts were hanging off the edge of his laundry basket. His pillows were haphazardly on the bed.

But Kyra didn't seem to notice or care. She only had eyes for him. And when he carried her to his bed and laid her down, nothing else in the world mattered.

16

Nothing mattered to Kyra besides the feel of Slade on top of her. She wasn't going to think about the stories she didn't know or about him being held captive. If she did, she'd never be able to enjoy the amazing man making her feel good.

And she felt really damn good.

She'd never been with someone who could lift her, let alone someone who could carry her around like she weighed nothing. But Slade made her feel normal. Like she wasn't curves upon curves.

When he pulled back from their kiss and looked at her on his bed, his gaze sparked with desire. His eyes roamed her body from her head to her hips and back again. His erection grew against her thigh, telling her he was just as ready to get naked as she was.

"Seeing you in my bed... damn, sweetheart. I didn't think anything could compare to watching you on your desk, but having you here is making me feel like a kid who just figured out what to do with a woman."

Kyra smirked. "You were definitely the kind of kid who explored a lot, weren't you?"

Slade shook his head. "I had my fun, but only one woman at a time. That way I can devote all my attention to making you feel good."

Kyra grinned. Slade slid a single finger from her knee up to her hip, barely touching her. The black leggings she wore to work were comfortable enough to hang around in, but they definitely got in the way when a man was touching her and making her feel amazing. She wiggled and tried to shove them down, but Slade was positioned between her thighs and didn't look like he was ready to move.

He lifted her shirt, exposing her stomach, and slid his tongue along the band of her panties. She stopped trying to tug off her leggings and held his head in place. He smiled against her skin and placed kisses up her stomach to her belly button. Then he used his tongue to taste her skin again.

"I'm taking my time with you tonight," Slade said softly. "We hurried at the office, but you're in my bed, and I'm not letting you out until you can't walk or remember anything except my name."

"Oh, really?" she asked with a smirk. "You think that's possible." She was already writhing with need and hoped goading him would make him go faster.

He nipped the flesh covering a rib and lapped at the wound. Then he kissed it and looked up at her. "Yes, it's possible. And no, I'm not going to go faster just because you're not used to waiting for your orgasms."

"Maybe I should just take care of them myself." She lifted an eyebrow in challenge.

"You can go right ahead, but I get to watch."

Heat raced through Kyra's body. Masturbation was a

private thing for her. She'd never shared it with anyone, even the admission she did it. The idea of him watching her both excited and terrified her.

"I'll make it worth the wait," Slade said, sealing his lips over hers hard. He thrust his hips against hers, letting her feel his thick erection.

She moaned around his kiss and clawed at his back, even more desperate to come. She lifted her hips to feel more of him, and he responded in kind, thrusting against her again and again.

Kyra pulled back with a cry as her body tightened with need. "Oh, God."

"Don't stop, Kyra. Let me see you come. Get that pussy ready for me." He thrust against her again and again, holding himself up on his hands and staring at her.

Kyra could feel his eyes on her, but she didn't care. He felt amazing. She pried her lids up and looked at him, and the look of pure pleasure on his face shoved her closer to her orgasm.

His jaw clenched hard, fighting his own need to come. He devoured her with his eyes. Seeing how much he wanted her made her even more free.

Kyra let go of her resistance and wrapped her legs around Slade. The shift had him hitting exactly where she needed him. She moaned long and loud, something she never let herself do before him. It spurred him on, and Slade lost himself in making her come.

Kyra reached for him, needing his strength to let go. He wrapped an arm around her and lifted her body to his, pressing them together. She almost cried with how cared for he made her feel.

Then she did cry, for a very different reason, letting out

all her desire as her orgasm tore through her. She held on to him, her entire body wracked with tremors.

Slade slowed his thrusts and let her down easy. He laid her on the bed and followed her down, resting his weight on her. "You're fucking gorgeous when you come. I need to see that again and again. Tell me you'll stay here for a few days. Stay through the weekend."

"I can't! I need to go home. And I probably don't have enough clothes," Kyra said, while inside she was ready to burst.

Slade growled. "Who said anything about clothes? I plan on keeping you naked all damn weekend. Stay with me, Kyra."

She nodded, admitting only to herself there was nowhere else she'd rather be.

SLADE COULD BARELY CONTAIN himself when she nodded. It was slight, but he saw it, and he wasn't going to let her take it back. She was his. For two full days, she was his. And he meant what he said about keeping her naked. As much as possible, she was going to be out of her clothes.

Speaking of which...

"You're wearing far too many items," he growled, lifting her shirt. He skimmed his fingertips over her impossibly soft flesh and pulsed against her thigh. Her cheeks pinked at his touch, something he loved. She definitely hadn't been with the right men, but Slade wasn't going to wish that was different. If she were with men who were better to her, she might not have stayed single long enough for him to find her.

He kissed her softly while he teased her skin, keeping

his hands away from her breasts. He wanted to touch them, but he wanted her begging for it before he took her. She was going to lose her damn mind if he had anything to say about it, and he had plenty to say.

"You feel so good," she whispered against his lips. Her entire body vibrated against his, like she was trying to make more contact with him but didn't want to be too forward.

Slade was all about a woman who knew what she wanted and wasn't afraid to go get it, as long as she let him be in charge of when she got there. "Gonna feel even better when I get inside you."

"Yes, please," she said with a smile.

"Not yet," Slade said, pulling back to put a small gap between them. "We haven't made it to ten yet."

"Ten?" she asked, confused.

Slade eased his way down, kissing and licking her stomach when he reached her bare skin. "I told you the last time you were here you were going to get at least ten orgasms. I'm not a man who passes on a promise."

"I don't think I can do that," she said quietly, chewing on that lip of hers.

Slade growled and leaped up, capturing her lip between his and sucking hard. She released it with a pop, then moaned loudly.

Slade rolled his hips against hers and sucked her lip into his mouth. She moaned again, wrapping her thighs around him again and taking what she needed from him. He fucking loved it.

"Oh, God, yes," she said as she came, the sound muffled by his hold on her lip.

"There's two," Slade said. "And leave that lip alone or I'll never be able to finish what I started."

She immediately clamped down on it and gave him a teasing smirk.

"You're just asking for me to withhold a few of those orgasms, aren't you?"

She shook her head. "No. But I do like the look of you losing your mind."

"Trust me, Kyra, I'm losing everything when I'm with you."

He meant the words as a teasing response, but as soon as they were out of his mouth, the weight of them hit him. He stared into her eyes as she processed the same words he was trying to figure out. If it were any other woman, he'd be backtracking and explaining, but with Kyra, he knew it was the truth.

She was quickly becoming more than a simple addiction. She mattered to him. He wanted her, but not just for a night or a few.

It had been years since he felt so connected to another person. Since he wanted to let someone in. But she was already in. He wasn't sure exactly when it happened, but she'd snuck under his defenses when he wasn't paying attention and there was no way she was leaving now.

"I feel the same way," she finally whispered.

Slade leaned forward and captured her lips again. All his control fell to the floor, and a sense of urgency overcame him. He had to have her, and he couldn't wait another minute.

Kyra shoved his shirt up, the same hurried need pushing her movements along. Slade pulled away and grabbed his shirt by the collar, yanking it off and throwing it aside. Before he pressed her to his mattress again, he slid down her body, nipping at her stomach. He tugged her leggings down as he moved, catching her panties with them and drawing both off until her lower half was bare to him. He kissed and licked his way back up while she cast her shirt and bra aside.

"That's much better," he whispered against her hip. "God, you're beautiful."

"I want to see you," she hissed as he nipped her thigh.

"Yes, ma'am," he said, standing to remove the rest of his clothes.

She licked her lips and watched him as he lowered his jeans. He kicked them to the side, then hooked his thumbs in his boxer briefs and dropped those, too.

Kyra drew her lip between her teeth again, and Slade pounced on her. "That's my lip," he teased, plucking it from her teeth with his thumb.

"I want to taste you again," she said.

"Later. I need to be inside you first. Now."

She spread her thighs and allowed him to settle between them. Her wet heat beckoned him, and he almost forgot a condom. He dragged himself away, tugging the drawer open and sending everything inside crashing to the front. He pushed it all back and grabbed a packet, tearing it open and rolling it on before he positioned himself at her entrance again.

"Kyra," he said, tilting her chin so she met his gaze.

"Yeah?"

He didn't say anything, just stared into her eyes as he slid home. Her breath hitched, but her eyes stayed locked on his, neither of them ready to break the spell holding them together.

He withdrew until just the tip stayed inside her, then slid back in slowly. The need to have her was still there, but the urgency faded once he was inside her.

She trailed a finger down his chest and circled his

nipple. His body jerked at the intimate contact. She went lower, finding one of his many scars. Slade let her touch him as he slowly made love to her, her hands mimicking the strokes of his body.

Down and in. Up and out. Her hands spanned his chest and abdomen, seeing all of him. He watched her the entire time, learning what she liked as much as he learned what mattered to her.

She didn't like him being hurt, but she loved when he tilted his hips. She didn't like when he withdrew, but she loved when he groaned in pleasure. She didn't like—

She laughed. Mid stroke, she laughed. Slade froze, wondering what in the world she found funny when he was getting closer and closer to losing his entire fucking mind, and maybe something else, to her.

"Howler," she said, tears leaking from her eyes.

Slade turned his head, spotting his rude ass dog sitting just inside the bedroom door. His head was tilted to the side like he was examining their technique. And critiquing it.

"What are you doing?" Slade yelled, unable to stop his smile.

"He's watching us," Kyra said with a laugh. "That's kind of creepy. Does he always do this?"

Slade's gaze snapped back to hers. He thrust in hard and deep, knowing she liked that. She moaned, her eyes fluttering closed. She grabbed onto his biceps and arched her back.

"You're the only woman I've had in my bed since I've had him," Slade admitted.

"That's not possible," Kyra argued.

"I didn't say you're the only woman I've been with, but you're the only one I've ever had here. No one else has ever shared this bed with me," Slade said, pausing deep inside her. His cock twitched, aching to pound into her. She needed to understand she wasn't a run of the mill fling for him. She was special. Different. *His.*

"Oh," she said.

He raised an eyebrow. "That's all you have to say?"

She looked up at him, the magnitude of what he said reflected back in her eyes. "Thank you."

Slade tucked her hair behind her ear and leaned forward. He kissed her softly, letting his hips move again. She pulled back with a moan... and Howler barked.

Kyra laughed again. Slade groaned and glared at his dog.

"He's trying to move in on what's mine."

"Yours?" Kyra whispered, all humor gone.

Slade's gaze snapped back to hers. "Mine."

Her entire body shivered at the possessive tone of his voice. She grew slicker instantly. That frenzied need was back.

Slade withdrew, then slammed into her. She let out a moan that set Howler off again, but neither of them stopped to pay attention. Slade needed her, and he couldn't wait another second.

Kyra dragged his lips to hers and plunged her tongue into his mouth. Slade answered her with a thrust of his tongue and his hips, making her even wetter. She began to tighten around him, her body taking what it needed from his.

Slade opened his eyes, needing to see her when she came apart. She was already watching him through their kiss. He'd never kissed anyone with his eyes open before, and the instant jolt of connection sent his hips into overdrive.

Everything inside him demanded Kyra was his. Not just for now. Not just for the weekend. For a long, long time. He wanted a life with her, a future. All the things his friends had with their women, Slade wanted with Kyra.

He saw it all in her eyes. She was wrestling with the same realization. Whatever was happening between them wasn't casual. It wasn't going to end soon. If it ended, it was going to be big and messy and hearts would be shattered.

But Slade wasn't going to let that happen. Kyra was his, and she was going to stay his.

The bed dipped beside them as Howler jumped up to join in the fun. Slade wasn't in the mood to share, but he couldn't risk hurting his other favorite creature.

"Shit, sorry," he murmured, pulling back from Kyra. "I'll lock him out of the room."

Howler laid down above Kyra's head, watching Slade.

She shook her head and locked her legs around his hips before he could pull out. "Don't... stop. Please. He's fine. I'm not into audiences, but he's not going to tell anyone about all my flabby bits bouncing around."

"Your flabby bits are perfect. Watching your body move is fucking killing me."

Her cheeks turned pink, and she clamped down on her lip again.

Slade growled and leaned over her, sucking on her lip and pounding into her. He was close, and he wasn't going to last long, which meant she needed to come. Fast.

He slid a hand between them and teased her just enough to find her clit. He barely touched it and she let out a long, low growl that startled Howler. The dog watched her, and Slade did the same.

She was beautiful. Her hair was a wild mess on his sheets. Her body was perfect against the gray cotton. That flush he dreamed about traveled all the way from her cheeks to her belly button. He wanted to follow the same path, and then keep going.

He hardened and lengthened inside her as she came. Her channel locked down on his cock, holding him deep inside her. He pulled back just enough to get a good stroke in and shook the bed with the force.

Minds and hearts were tangled up with limbs and words. Slade had never fallen for someone like that. Like he couldn't stop himself. She was it for him. The person he was meant to protect and love and cherish forever.

He held on to her as she moaned and whimpered through her orgasm, then finally let himself feel the pleasure of release. He pumped hard into her, letting her body take all of him. She held him tight, whispering words he couldn't understand while he wondered if it would always be that good with her.

As he collapsed onto her, both of them sticky with sweat and worn out, he couldn't wait to spend the rest of his life finding out just how good the two of them would be the next time.

17

———

Kyra ran her fingers over Slade's short hair and held him to her chest. He'd barely had time to collapse on top of her before he was asleep. She thought he was joking at first, but he was out.

She loved the feel of his weight on top of her. Knowing he trusted her enough to pass out.

Howler whimpered above her head. Kyra reached up and found his head, thanks to his attempt to inhale her hand. She scratched under his chin and rubbed his belly. Howler settled down, and it wasn't long before his breathing evened out and he fell asleep, too.

Kyra laid there, wondering what they did that wore them out so much. She looked down at Slade and itched to draw a picture of him. He looked so peaceful, his head resting on her breast, his hand under his chin. She could picture a little boy that looked just like him, and her heart ached for him.

He would give all that up for her? She wasn't sure she could let him. It was one thing for her not to be able to have biological children, but there was no reason he shouldn't.

She told herself she should leave. Order a car to pick her up and just go. But she couldn't bring herself to do it. He laid there on her, making it harder for her to breathe, and all she could think about was wanting to stay there forever.

She saw in his eyes how much he cared. She was sure he could pull one over on a woman without much thought, but she felt like he wasn't doing that to her.

A silent tear slid down her cheek. She wiped it away. He did what she knew he would do. He burrowed deep inside her and set up residence in her heart. She didn't want to admit it, but she was in love with him. She'd only known him for two weeks, but she was in love with him. From the moment she saw him, when he was trying to help her in the bank, a part of her loved him. And every moment they spent together since then only made her fall harder.

She didn't have enough experience with men in general to know what she should do. She wanted to talk to someone, a girlfriend who could give her some advice, but she didn't have anyone. Lily and the others were great, but they were Slade's friends. If things ended, they would still be Slade's friends, but not hers.

Kyra was alone. With a man and a dog she loved surrounding her, she was alone.

Slade nuzzled against her and kissed the side of her breast, waking up as he slid out of her. She missed the feeling of him deep inside instantly and wondered how quickly he would recover. She'd never been like that, but she couldn't wait to have him as many times as possible before he came to the same realization she did.

"Mine," he whispered against her flesh, licking his way to her nipple.

Kyra's body responded instantly, tightening with need once more. She held his head in place and let out a breathy sigh. She stopped thinking about him moving on or about the babies he would have with someone else and gave in to the pulsing desire filling her body.

"Mine," Slade whispered again, almost like he was saying it in his head and didn't realize the word was leaving his mouth. He was claiming her, making her his.

Didn't he realize she already was?

He kissed his way south and settled between her thighs, only meeting her gaze to whisper, "Mine," before he licked and kissed and drove her out of her damn mind.

SLADE LOST count of the number of times he and Kyra had sex by the end of the weekend. He was sore in the most wonderful way from using all his muscles to please her. And what he wondered was right. It got better each and every time. Although he wasn't sure how that was possible since every time he slid into her he lost his fucking mind.

They were laying on the couch, both of them sweaty and sated from their latest round. She'd given up on clothes sometime around lunch that day and was stretched over him without a thing on. He pulled on his boxer briefs to let Howler out, but he happily spent the rest of his time naked and pressed against her sexy body.

"This is such crap," Kyra said, rolling her eyes at the TV. "People don't fall in love like this. I mean, really? How could someone agree to marry another person without meeting them?"

Slade shrugged. "Some people think love is something that grows over time."

"I'm not one of them," she said firmly. "Love is a force. It's something you can resist, but when it comes for you, it knocks you off your feet. Love doesn't grow. Because if it did, fewer people would get divorced or split up or be miserable."

"Not everyone who's meant to be together is willing to try," Slade said, stroking a fingertip down her spine. He fucking loved that she shivered against him but didn't stop her tirade.

"True, but there are so many people who say they stayed for the kids or they thought they were in love. They wanted to be in love. They wanted it to last forever. They were trying. But it wasn't there. It's sad, but if they were doing everything they could, and love never happened, then it proves love isn't something that you can just wait for and it'll show up one day."

"You seem to know a lot about this," Slade said. He didn't like the jealous feeling coursing through him. He wanted to come out and ask her who she fell for, but he didn't really want to hear about some ex who broke her heart.

Kyra clammed up almost instantly, as if she knew what he wanted to ask. "I just...love hasn't always been easy for me."

"Sorry," Slade said. He wanted her again, something that felt impossible. He wanted to show her that he loved her. That he agreed with what she said. Love was a force. A force that definitely knocked him on his ass. He'd gone from not knowing she existed to wondering how he lived without her in just a few weeks. If he hadn't watched Archer, Jack, and Jaymes fall in love so quickly, and Dunn resume things with Ashleigh just as fast, he never would have thought it could be real. But it was. Kyra was his. He wasn't letting her go.

"I told you about my parents. There were times I wondered if they even loved each other, but when they were with my brother, they were different. It always felt like when I was around, they blamed each other for me not turning out like they hoped, but with my brother, they were vying for credit."

Slade flipped her over and covered her body with his. She squealed but spread her thighs to welcome him in between. "They don't deserve any credit for how amazing you are. And they don't deserve your love. I know they're your parents, but you're definitely better off without them."

She nodded. "I know, but it sucks. They're the people who were supposed to love me." Her voice shook with emotion.

Slade gathered her close and kissed her tears as they fell. He grew hard between her thighs, a hazard of being so close to her. He ignored his throbbing cock and focused only on Kyra and making sure she was okay.

"I wish I could fix this for you. That I could tell them what an amazing woman you are and make them see you for who you are."

She laughed mirthlessly. "They know who I am. That's why they don't want to be around me. They want me quiet and toned down. They want me thin. They want me to be a carbon copy of them. Country club, nose in the air, nothing out of place. I'm not any of those things."

"You're perfect," Slade said with a growl. "If you were that person, we wouldn't be here right now. You'd be on the other side of the country, miserable because you couldn't draw or wear your purple panties or dance in your underwear."

"How did you...?"

He smirked. "Yesterday? When I came in from walking Howler? I about came in my shorts, watching you shake these sexy hips in only your panties. You had your earbuds in and didn't hear us. I wanted to join you, but you looked like you needed a minute to yourself." He brushed the hair off her forehead and smiled. "I told you, I don't know everything about you, but I really like all the things I do know."

"Slade," she said softly.

She shifted beneath him and his cock lined up perfectly with her entrance. He stilled. The desire to slide into her was overpowering, but he didn't have a condom. They used the one they had on the coffee table already, and getting another one meant going to the bedroom. He didn't want to leave her.

"Please," she said, her breath hitching in her chest.

"We don't have a condom out here."

She looked at him and cupped his jaw. "It's been a long time for me. Before you... and I've never..."

She moved again, and he sank into her just a bit. Her heat sucked at him, demanding he give in. "In high school, I went without a few times, but not since then. I'm clean, Kyra. I'm good. But I don't want to risk anything with you."

"I told you I can't get pregnant," she said softly.

He shook his head. "I wasn't talking about that. I just meant I don't want to hurt you, sweetheart. I don't want anything to happen. Or you to regret this. Us. Any of it."

She smiled. "I won't. I... promise."

He let her pull his lips down to hers and when their lips met, he thrust inside her. He stilled, unable to move or he knew he'd come instantly.

She was home. Kyra was his home. She was everything he always hoped he'd find. And she was right there, with him, and he was never walking away.

TEARS BUILT behind Kyra's lids, but she refused to let them fall. Slade was... perfect. She'd never known a man who could make her feel like she wasn't missing out on the love of her parents because he would love her enough to make up for it. But Slade made her think things that couldn't be true.

As he moved inside her, she squeezed around him, nearly losing her mind at the feel of him. She'd never had sex without a condom. Even once she knew she couldn't get pregnant, she refused to take the chance that she would get something.

But everything was different with him. She trusted Slade. She couldn't explain it, but she knew he wouldn't risk hurting her.

"Look at me, Kyra," he grunted.

She struggled to open her eyes, knowing her tears would fall out.

"Sweetheart, let me see you. All of you," he said, his voice strained as he held back. "Kyra."

She finally opened her eyes and met his. His face changed instantly, concern replacing the passionate desire she saw when she opened her eyes.

"What...?" he asked, stilling before he began to ease out.

"No, don't," she said quickly. "You just... it's good."

He seemed to understand what she wasn't willing to say. He grabbed her hands and locked their fingers together, raising their hands over her head. He pumped into her, brushing her entire body with his on every stroke. He rubbed her clit when he thrust in, and she hoped she wouldn't scream the words that were on her tongue.

Slade held her gaze as they moved together, operating as one to chase the common goal. The thick head of his cock dragged across her channel, lighting up every cell inside her. She was close, so close, but she wanted to come with him.

"Slade," she whimpered.

"Just let go, sweetheart. I'm right there with you. Always."

He slammed into her, setting off a series of fireworks inside her. Warmth and bliss filled her as her mouth opened in a silent cry with her orgasm. Slade thrust deep into her once more, then spilled himself into her. The feeling of him pulsing inside nearly set her off again. She never thought she'd find someone who made her feel loved, but she had.

Which only meant it would be that much worse when things ended. Because for her, they always did.

"What are the tears for?" he whispered against the shell of her ear. He kissed her neck, sending shivers through her body.

"I... um..."

"You don't have to tell me," he said softly. "As long as you're okay."

She nodded. "I'm better than okay."

Slade pulled back just enough to meet her gaze. "Me, too." His stomach growled loudly, and they both laughed. "Okay, well, maybe I'm hungry. But other than that, I'm better than okay, too."

Kyra smiled and wondered how in the world they found each other, and how she got so lucky that for a little while, she got to love a man like him.

AFTER DINNER, Kyra said she needed to go home. Slade was not okay with that option.

"I thought you were going to stay the weekend. The weekend isn't over."

"I need to get clothes for work and see if my last paycheck came yet. They were supposed to mail it out this week. I have a few apartments to look at, and if I find one I like, I'll need that money for a security deposit."

"I'll take you home, but only if you come back here tonight. I'm not done with you yet."

She gave him a sad smile that made him wonder what he said that put the look on her face, but it was gone the next second. "I think I can handle that."

They got dressed, Kyra in her matching purple bra and panties covered in something dark and drab and not her at all, and Slade drove them to her apartment complex. He didn't love it, but he thought it was better than a lot of the places he'd seen. The doors were secure, and she had a roommate, which meant someone was there to make sure Kyra was safe.

Of course, Slade wanted her to just move in with him instead of finding a new place, but he couldn't ask her that yet.

He followed her to her floor and into the apartment. The TV was on, and a blonde woman sat on the couch in front of it. She turned her head when Kyra and Slade walked in.

"Good, you're here. Oh, um, hi. I'm Autumn," the woman said, pasting on a smile and walking over to Slade. She extended her hand and let her eyes scan his body.

She was attractive enough, but she was not Slade's type at all. She could use a little more weight on her, and the come hither look in her eyes did nothing for his cock.

Slade shook her hand and said, "Nice to meet you. I'm Justin." He wasn't a big fan of his given name after being called Slade for almost half his life. Justin felt like another person.

"Justin," Autumn said, rolling the name around in her mouth. "Kyra doesn't bring her friends over very often. I'm sorry we haven't met before."

Kyra tried to move toward her room, but Slade grabbed her around the waist and pulled her to his side. "Well, we're not friends. I've been buried deep inside her all weekend, and definitely not in a friendly kind of way. More like a this-is-my-woman-and-I'm-going-to-fuck-her-senseless kind of way."

He intended his words to shock Autumn into walking away, but instead they seemed to turn her on. "I like that kind of way."

"Me, too," Slade said. "With Kyra. I'm not on the market. If you'll excuse us, we're just getting some of her things."

Slade steered Kyra toward her room before Autumn could get any closer. He seriously feared for his cock with a woman like her around. She was the type who'd cut it off and hang it on the wall like a trophy if she could.

"You could have talked to her," Kyra said as soon as the door was closed behind them. "She's probably more your type."

Slade tightened his grip on her hip and turned her to face him. "She's not my type. I only have one type and her name is Kyra."

"But what you said sounded like you were trying to tempt her."

Slade chuckled and shook his head. "I was trying to make sure she knew I wanted you, not her. She clearly didn't get the message." He narrowed his eyes. "And neither did you."

Kyra shook her head. "I'm not the woman who ends up with a guy like you."

Slade slid his hand over her cheek and smiled. "You should be. I'm not going anywhere, Kyra. Not without you by my side. Or under me. Or on top. That was fun, too."

She smiled.

"Do I need to prove to you that I'm hard right now because I have you in my arms or are you going to trust me that every time I told you how beautiful you are and every time I buried myself in you and every time I kissed and touched and licked and sucked on you it was because I want you, Kyra. You're the one I'm here for. You're the one I'm taking back to my bed tonight. You're the one I can't get enough of."

She didn't say anything for a minute, and Slade lost his patience. He scooped her up and spun them, pressing her back to the door. Kyra tried to push him away, but Slade wasn't having that.

"You're mine, Kyra. I don't know how to get that through your head, but you're mine. Every inch of you. You're mine, sweetheart."

She stopped resisting him and melted in his arms. They kissed hurriedly, and stripped each other just as quickly. And when he sank into her, with her back against her bedroom door and nothing between them, he almost told her he loved her.

Almost.

18

THE OFFICE WAS QUIET ON MONDAY. KYRA WASN'T ENTIRELY sure what to make of it. She didn't expect it after the previous week when everyone was there almost every day.

Slade told her a bunch of the others were on an assignment. Something to do with the missing woman case that came in the week. Kyra wasn't sure if she could ask questions, but Slade answered them anyway.

"They think they found her. There's a commune not too far from here that brings in women for the men who live there. Some are there by choice, or at least that's what they've said. The ones who don't appear to be... it's not an easy place to go. Without someone willing to press charges or testify, they go free."

"I didn't even know places like that existed."

Slade nodded. "The world is pretty ugly. It's sad."

English joined them in the break room and asked what time they were going to the bank.

"The bank?" Kyra asked.

Slade nodded. "The guys who've hit the two banks are somehow turning off the security measures in place.

Managers have said they hit the silent alarm, but in both cases, nothing has been sent out. Captain Patrick said English could have a look. See if he can figure out what's going on."

"I wondered about that," Kyra said. "It seemed strange to me they were able to do whatever they wanted. I figured they had a bank employee involved, but it makes sense they messed with the alarm, too. I remember waiting for sirens and wondering if I should be relieved or not when I didn't hear them."

"Why would you not be relieved?" English asked.

Kyra shrugged. "I think I watch too many movies. Whenever the police arrive, a hostage always dies in the movies."

"Someone died anyway," Slade said quietly.

Kyra nodded. "Yeah, and that doesn't make sense to me, either. They could have just pushed him out of the way. Why shoot him?"

Slade and English shook their heads.

"Getting inside the mind of a criminal isn't easy," English said. "And it isn't fun."

"Very true," Slade agreed.

"So, what time? Ten?" English asked again.

Slade nodded. "Yeah, sounds good."

English sipped his coffee as he left the break room. Kyra popped a bite of her bagel into her mouth and chewed. "Is the bank open?"

Slade nodded. "The one we were at is. The second one doesn't open until the end of the week. They had the scene all weekend and turn it back over tonight or tomorrow."

"It seems fast," Kyra said.

Slade shrugged. "It's a business. They have to get back to work and show people their money is safe. When there is a shooting at a bank, they move on quickly, like nothing happened."

"I can't fathom it. Although, I do need to go to the bank," Kyra said.

"See? Business as usual."

SLADE DECIDED to go with English to the bank. He wanted to see for himself what was going on. It was a case that bothered him. He didn't like having unsolved cases, but when he was one of the victims, he liked it even less.

English was silent as they rode over, which wasn't any big shock. He'd always been the strong and silent type, the kind of person who would listen and give advice when needed, but didn't spend a lot of time on words just for the sake of saying them.

When they got out of the SUV, English looked up at the building. "I've never been here before."

Slade shook his head. "I hadn't been, either. Patrick suggested we start with this one since it's still closed. The other one will be a little trickier because we need to work with a bank employee, but we can get in without any trouble."

"Kyra seems nice," English said on their way to the door.

"Yep," Slade said, his back stiffening.

"I think she's good for you."

English didn't wait for a response before he walked off, leaving Slade to wonder if there was more to the comment.

By the time Slade caught up to him, English was at the door. He flashed the order he had from Patrick, giving them unlimited access to the scene, and the officers let them by without question.

"What did you mean by that?" Slade asked English.

"By what?"

"That Kyra is good for me."

"You don't think she is?"

Slade shook his head. "That's not what I said."

English sighed and met Slade's gaze. "You've been beating yourself up for years. Since before we met. You thought you ruined Jessie's life by walking away from her to sign up. You regretted leaving Megan behind when she needed her brother. You've blamed yourself for a lot of things because you chose a career of service that meant not being there for the people you loved. We all did, but for you, it was always different. Like it was deeper. It only got worse after... But Kyra almost seems like she's healed a part of that. You're happy with her. So, I think she's good for you."

Slade thought about what English said and knew it was true. He'd never let a woman in the way he did with Kyra. Even Jessie didn't get as deep, and they were together for years before he left and joined the Navy.

There was a part of him that wanted to turn and run from Kyra because she got too close, but a bigger part of him wanted to grab a hold of her and never let go.

His lips curled up as he thought about the way she did that the night before. After they got back to his place, it was like she finally accepted what he kept telling her. He wasn't interested in her roommate, or anyone else. He was crazy about her.

Crazy in love.

When Slade finally looked up to say something to English, he was gone. Slade just shook his head and moved toward the offices where he was sure to find him.

English was behind a desk, buried deep in computer stuff that Slade didn't understand. He could hold his own with a computer, but he didn't have anywhere near the skills that English had.

It wasn't long before the resident computer expert was leaning back. "They're good," he said, staring at the screen. "I'm better, but they're good."

"You figured it out?"

"The system is completely fine. There is absolutely no reason it shouldn't have worked."

"What does that mean?"

"It means one of two things. Either they rerouted who the alert went to, or they had something that made it seem like the alarm worked but it never did."

"And I repeat, what does that mean?"

"It means I have to keep digging. This is hardwired into the system, so for it to not work, the connection needs to be cut somewhere. It's possible, but it's unlikely there is a physical limitation that Patrick's guys didn't find. It would be obvious. Do you know if this was tested?"

Slade shook his head and said, "I assume so since Patrick couldn't figure out what was wrong. If it was still not working, something would have tipped him off, right?"

English nodded. "Yes, but I still want to double check."

"How do you find out who the alert went to?" Slade asked.

"That's a trickier question. We have to trace the signal, but if they changed it, we might never know."

"Seriously?"

English nodded. "Unfortunately, yes. It looks like these guys are smart. They knew what they were doing."

Slade shook his head. "And they're going to get away with it."

English clapped him on the back. "People always make

mistakes. They get too greedy or cocky or slip up. There's always a way to find the bad guy. We always did."

Slade nodded, letting English's words sink in. He hoped he was right, but Slade didn't have the same level of confidence. The guy who stared him down was definitely cocky, but that was day one. The longer he went without getting caught, the worse he would be. But that didn't mean he would make a mistake. He was one of those people who was in control of everything except his anger. That was what would do him in.

Slade just wondered how many other people the piece of shit would take down with him when it happened.

"They're on their way," Stevie said, tossing the phone onto the table as he took his seat on the couch.

Bobby nodded. "Both of them?"

"Yeah. Mario said she was there. Tried to get out of bringing her, but I said it was better for her if she wasn't alone."

"Good."

Bobby sat in silence, running through the lines in his head. He was furious, but he knew his anger wasn't what would get through to them. He'd tried anger in the past, but the only thing that spoke to them was fear.

Bobby knew exactly how to make them scared. So scared they would piss themselves to do everything he asked.

Stevie laughed at the show on the TV. Bobby nearly flinched. He was so inside his own head he'd forgotten about the TV and Stevie sitting next to him.

Stevie was a simple man. He liked to be entertained. Sometimes that meant a woman, sometimes that meant a stupid show, and sometimes that meant more money than he could spend in a lifetime. It wasn't much to ask for, not in Bobby's mind, but he wasn't as simple as his friend.

Bobby liked things orderly. He liked to know what was going to happen. Surprises were never good for him. Surprises meant the difference between life and death. Between a quiet night and a beating. Between terror and relaxation.

The surprise he got the night before was not a good one. And he had to make sure the lies he told were seen as the truth or the next surprise was going to be new bracelets for him to wear on his way to jail.

Jail wasn't an option, which meant Bobby needed to keep Mario in line. Mario was the complicated one. He always had been. Sometimes Bobby wondered if Mario had a conscience that was too big for the rest of them, but Mario was smart. He was the one who helped them with the surveillance at the bank. And he could talk his way out of things. He was smooth and looked like a good person.

It was the only reason Bobby could think of that landed Mario his girl.

She was the wildcard in all of this. She was an unknowing and disagreeable accomplice. She didn't plan to be a part of everything, but she didn't stop them when she saw them walk in either. Bobby was almost sure he'd find Mario on the doorstep the night after the first robbery, bags in his hand after she kicked his sorry ass out. It was a risk Bobby was willing to take.

But she didn't, which made Bobby wonder who the woman really was underneath. So, he did a little digging.

Bobby wasn't the only one who knew how to get shit done. Seemed Mario's girl was a scrapper. She'd lived in her fair share of shitty places, and being with Mario was a big step up for her compared to some of them. She was smart enough to know what she had, and Bobby hoped she was smart enough to know what could be taken away from her.

A knock dragged Bobby out of his thoughts. He didn't move, letting Stevie pull himself from the show when they knocked a second time.

"Hey," Mario said, letting Stevie pull him in for a hug when they shook. He held onto his girl with his other hand, his gaze searching the dark room for Bobby.

"Hey, Bobby," Mario said, stepping past Stevie and dragging her with him.

Bobby watched them, not giving anything away with his gaze. He sat in the armchair, his back to the wall so no one could sneak up on him.

"What's going on?" Mario asked, taking a seat on the couch and pulling her down next to him.

She was nervous. It was obvious in the way her eyes darted around the room. She'd only been there once or twice. She wasn't usually invited since she wasn't a part of their plans, but tonight, she was.

"Good to see you both," Bobby said after a minute. He kept his eyes locked on hers.

She noticed the threat in his gaze and stiffened her chin. She wasn't afraid of him. She'd faced worse. Bobby was looking forward to making that change. He was the worst thing she'd ever sat in front of.

"Is everything okay, Bobby?" Mario asked. His voice held a slight tremor. He was already scared. Smart man. His hair was slicked back from his face in something that was supposed to be stylish. He looked like he recently got it cut. He was out there living a life like a normal person. The drawing of him on the news wasn't as accurate. Mario could still live his life.

"Are you two headed out?" Bobby finally asked.

Mario nodded. "Yeah, we were going to dinner. Do you want to join us?"

She grabbed his hand, squeezing it tighter. Her other hand slid up his arm, holding him back. She knew Mario would choose her if he had a choice. If...

"Thanks, but I'll pass. Tonight."

"Oh, okay. So, um, what's going on? Stevie said you needed to talk to me." Again with the shaky voice. Bobby was starting to wonder why he let Mario get involved with them. He wasn't the ruthless one they needed. She was.

"Actually, I was hoping for a word with Sara," Bobby said, sliding a glare to Mario before focusing on Sara again.

Her hand slid over her round belly, holding the baby Mario put there. A family. A son, Mario proudly told him when they found out.

Bobby hated them both for it, but he couldn't let it show. If he let it out, it would mean he still cared what his own old man thought. He didn't. The fucker could rot for all Bobby cared. After Bobby had the chance to return all the favors he bestowed on his son growing up. Bobby would make sure he felt all the pain, but he was a better man. He would make sure his father didn't live long enough to suffer. He would put a bullet in him the same way he did those other bank guards. His buddies. Neither of them recognized Bobby, Jr. He was as invisible to them as an adult as he'd been as a kid when they saw his father backhand him or throw things at him and did nothing. They got what they deserved. And he will, too.

"What do you need with Sara?" Mario asked, his voice full on shaking. "She didn't do anything."

"No, but she might one day. Maybe that kid comes out, and she decides she wants it to go to one of those fancy preschools. Or it needs braces. Or maybe college. And Sara is sitting on a golden ticket. That bitch who saw my face told the cops. She drew that picture. And I need her to shut the fuck up."

"What does that have to do with Sara?" Mario asked.

Bobby was losing his patience with Mario. He was a sniveling little bitch. Sara sat there, silent, holding her belly like that would do something. If Bobby wanted to hurt her child, she wouldn't be able to stop it. They both knew it.

"She's going to get the woman's address for me."

"You know I can't do that," Sara said.

Bobby grinned. If she was speaking to him, she was in. The shell had cracked and fear was spilling out. Her fingers gripped her belly tighter, holding on more securely.

"You got me the list of everyone who was in the bank. You can get me her address, and you will."

"Why would I?"

Bobby leaned forward and showed off his teeth. "Because if you don't, I'll use my own golden ticket."

"What are you talking about?" Mario asked. For a guy who was so smart with computers, he was dumb as a box of rocks.

"He's saying he'll turn us in," Sara provided. "Do you really think I'm afraid of jail? I'm pregnant. I can easily find a lawyer who will take one look at me and know I didn't mastermind anything."

Bobby chuckled and steepled his fingers together in front of his face. "You're smart. Already figured it all out, I see? Well, maybe I won't go to the police. Maybe I don't need to. Maybe I should just cut that baby out of you right now and watch both of you bleed to death right here on my floor."

By the time he finished speaking, all humor was gone

from Bobby's voice. He held Sara's gaze, a single tear dripping from her bottom lashes to race down her cheek.

"What the fuck, dude?" Mario asked. "You're scaring her. You can't threaten her like that!"

"It's not a threat," Sara said quietly. "He's evil. He's not afraid of doing whatever needs to be done."

"She's a smart one," Bobby said to Mario. "You should really try to keep her around."

"You're supposed to be my friend, Bobby," Mario said, the hurt in his voice making Bobby sick.

"And you're supposed to be something more than a waste of fucking space," Bobby shouted back. "Do you really think this is all about you? That we did this job because of you? No. Stevie and I have been planning this for years. We just needed a third. You fit the bill. But you're running around scared and acting like you're going to get caught. And if you do, I want you to know exactly what will be waiting for you when you get out. A dead girlfriend and baby. Because if you snitch on us, there won't be enough stitches in the world to put them back together."

Mario's eyes went wide with fear before he put a hand over Sara's belly. "Stay away from them."

"Bring me her name and address," Bobby said. "She dies or you die. It doesn't really matter which one to me."

19

SLADE WATCHED KYRA SLEEP AS THE SUN FILTERED THROUGH the curtains of his room. Howler was curled up on the other side of him, snoring. Slade wanted to sleep, but he couldn't. He knew he was missing something about the robbery and couldn't figure out what it was.

Kyra stirred in her sleep and rolled over. When her hand brushed his chest, she sighed softly and snuggled closer to him. Slade shifted to his back and pulled her against his side. She didn't wake up.

He turned everything over in his head. The computer rerouting the call so the police weren't notified about the bank, the signal jammer to make sure no one in the bank could call or text, and the glasses that hid their faces from the moment they walked in. Someone inside the bank had to be working with them. Someone had to have planted the deposit slips and the candy.

Slade wondered about the teller. Kyra ate the candy in front of her. Did she provide it? She clearly didn't eat it or she would have been knocked out. The police questioned her, though. They dismissed her. Said they didn't believe she was involved. When he got to work, Slade needed to read over her interview again and see if they asked about the candy.

"Hey," Kyra said softly, her voice thick with sleep.

"Good morning," Slade said, turning off his mind to focus on the beautiful, naked woman in his bed.

"Everything okay?"

Slade nodded and shifted on top of her. She parted her thighs and smiled when he fit perfectly between them. "I'm always good when you're around."

She breathed a laugh. "You're good for my ego."

He leaned forward and kissed her gently. "You're good for me."

She blinked slowly at him, still waking up as she let his words sink in. "You're good for me, too."

He smiled and kissed her again, this time taking it slow. She was like all the best things in the world at once. He already couldn't imagine his life without her, and he didn't want to. She was it for him, and he planned to tell her. Soon.

He was half an inch from sliding into her when Howler whined. Slade pulled back with a groan and glared at his dog. "Really, dude? Now?"

Howler whimpered again and stood on the bed. He barked once, then jumped down. Kyra giggled.

"Don't move. I'm coming back." He climbed out of bed and took the covers with him, exposing her naked body. "Damn, I hate walking away from you."

She chuckled. "It's for like five minutes."

"Too long," Slade said.

Howler barked again, letting Slade know he better hurry or he was going to have a mess to clean up.

Kyra climbed off the bed and went to him. "I'm going to

start my shower while you let him out. I'll be wet and warm and waiting for you when you're done."

Whatever blood Slade had left in his head raced south. He groaned and nearly dropped to his knees right then. She was perfect. And she was all his.

But Howler let out a yelp that said he was about two seconds from having an accident.

"Go," Kyra said with a husky laugh. She turned and walked into the bathroom completely naked.

Slade debated for a second, then took off for the living room. He didn't bother covering up, knowing putting clothes on over his throbbing cock would only make it worse.

Howler spun in a circle when he saw Slade and howled for him.

"I know, I know. Sorry, dude. If you still had balls, you'd understand." Slade opened the back door and poor Howler barely made it off the patio before he lifted a leg to pee. He didn't even finish peeing before he was moving to squat. It would have been a very bad morning if Slade chose Kyra over Howler.

When Howler finished his business, he trotted back to the door, tongue flopped to the side. He followed Slade inside and went straight to the kitchen for his breakfast. Slade rinsed and refilled the water bowl and scooped food out for Howler. He watched for a minute as Howler dropped to the floor and happily lapped up his water before switching to the food.

Slade made sure the door was closed so Howler didn't run out and went back to his bedroom to find Kyra. She was still in the shower, her body covered with soapy bubbles that ran in rivulets down her curves. Her eyes were closed as she rinsed her hair, and Slade just stood there watching her.

He almost lost her before he even found her. Getting her to agree to see him was a challenge. He loved her, but he needed to go slow telling her. He wanted to tell her in that moment, but he was sure it would scare her off, so he kept his mouth shut and grinned when she opened her eyes and saw him watching her.

"You're not joining me?" she asked, turning her back to him.

"Just enjoying the show."

She grinned, her cheeks pinking before she ducked her head to hide them. She enjoyed his words, but it was obvious no one had ever told her how beautiful she was. Slade was happy to have that honor all to himself but hated that she didn't have more confidence. She was a strong, smart, stunning woman, and she needed to know it.

Slade stepped into the shower and pressed himself against her back. She leaned into him, tilting her head back to rest on his shoulder. He loved the way every part of her responded to his touch, like her body knew it was made for his pleasure.

He slid his fingers down between her legs and lazily played with her clit. She moaned softly, spreading her thighs wider for him.

Slade could spend all day making her come, but she would lose focus and worry about work if he didn't hurry. He reached lower and slid the tip of his finger inside her, then dragged it back to her clit and made quick work of her first orgasm, sending her up and over in just a few minutes.

She panted in his arms, clutching tightly to him. "Shit, that was fast."

"I didn't want you worrying about work like you were yesterday," Slade whispered against her ear.

"What's work?" she asked with a grin.

He spun her in his arms and pressed her against the wall. He devoured her mouth, needing to get a taste of her. If they had time, he'd lay her on the bed and have her for breakfast, but they wouldn't make it to work if he did that.

While he kissed her, he lifted her and wrapped her legs around his waist. It was harder in the shower than against her bedroom door, but he knew she liked being held. And Slade fucking loved anything that made her feel good.

He slid into her easily, her orgasm and the shower making their bodies wet. He groaned at the feel of her body sucking him in deeper and nearly came when he was fully inside her.

"Kyra," he groaned. "Oh, God, Kyra. You feel so damn good, sweetheart."

"You, too," she said. "It's never been like this before. Not for me."

"Me either. This is all us."

She looked at him for a long moment as though she didn't quite believe him. He just held her gaze, letting her see everything inside him. He wanted her to know his whole truth.

When he started to move, she rested her elbows on his shoulders and wrapped her hands around his head. They kept their eyes locked together and moved as one. When he came, she did, too, and he swore he saw love in her eyes.

KYRA KNEW STAYING at his house was a bad idea. She couldn't keep her distance and find a way to not involve her heart when she was with him all the time.

Instead, she slept in his bed, ate his food, enjoyed his shower, and gave him her heart. She was completely gone for him. She'd never known love could feel the way she did. It was like a low grade flu where she felt sick all the time, but with moments of the greatest joy she'd ever known.

Nothing was ever going to be the same again.

After their shower, Kyra and Slade dressed and had breakfast. Their drive in to work was quick and quiet, but a comfortable quiet that said they were content and at ease. When they got out of the truck and headed for the elevator, Slade reached for her hand and she held his without considering another option.

The office was quiet again, something that Kyra wasn't sure she'd ever get used to. After working in offices where clients came and went on the half hour, working somewhere that could go days without seeing a client was strange.

After they had coffee, Kyra and Slade went to their own offices. She went through the emails she'd gotten overnight, including two from Dunn about the case half the team was away working on. The father of the missing girl was coming in at one, and the team was expected back just before lunch. Dunn had a few things he needed Kyra to do, including scheduling an appointment with a potential new client for the following day and picking up lunch for the team.

Kyra went through the motions of her morning, vaguely aware of Slade next door. She wondered why he was so quiet on the ride to work and what he was thinking before she woke up. Maybe he was getting sick of her being around all the time. Maybe she should give him a little space. After all, it was almost lunch, and she hadn't seen him since they got to the office. Usually, he would be in her office every thirty minutes.

Kyra decided to stop by the bank to deposit her last paycheck from her previous job on her way to pick up lunch for everyone. She had her eye on a couple of apartments and wanted to set up appointments to view them toward the end of the week. If she liked one of them, she wanted to know the money was in her account if she needed to write a check. And going to the bank would give her a few minutes alone without wondering what Slade was thinking or doing.

Voices filtered down the hall, letting her know the rest of the team was arriving. She wondered if they had any luck finding the missing woman and assumed they didn't if they were back and simply scheduled a meeting with the father. She hoped they would find the woman soon.

Kyra grabbed her purse and headed toward the door. Rocky was in the hallway and said hi.

"Hey. I'm going out to get lunch now, but I need to run by the bank first, if that's okay."

Rocky nodded. "Yeah, that's fine. Thanks for getting lunch. It was a long night."

"Any good news?"

Rocky shrugged. "We didn't find a dead body. Some-times that's the only good news."

The magnitude of what they did hit Kyra, and she nodded. Rocky continued to his office as Kyra walked to the elevator. She hoped she was never in a situation where they needed to rescue her.

When Kyra parked outside the bank, she sat in her car for a minute. She wasn't sure she wanted to go inside, but being a smaller local bank, there weren't a ton of branches.

"I can do this," she said softly to herself.

She brought her own deposit slip and had everything ready so she didn't have to touch anything inside the bank. Her knees shook as she walked to the door, and pulling it open and walking inside felt like she was stepping back in time.

It had only been a few weeks since she was there, face

down in front of the teller, but it felt like a lot longer. Everything about her life had dramatically changed since that day.

"Can I help you?" someone said.

Kyra turned and saw a security guard standing near her. He was alert, watchful. He had to know what happened to the man he replaced.

Kyra shook her head. "Sorry. It's my first time back."

His brows went up before he nodded once. He understood. It didn't mean he was going to blindly trust her, but he got it.

Kyra pulled her gaze from him and looked at the tellers. When she saw the pregnant woman she'd spoken to that day, she was shocked. Kyra was sure the woman would never have come back. She was tough.

Kyra got in line and waited until the teller called her.

"Can I help you?" she asked, looking up to greet Kyra. "Oh, it's you."

"Hi," Kyra said, rushing to the woman's window. Sara. That was her name. Kyra had forgotten it. "How are you?"

"Um, I'm good. Really good. I was, um, I was thinking about you today. How are you?"

Kyra grinned. "Good. It's a little weird being back here."

Sara tilted her head. "You haven't been back since…"

Kyra shook her head. "I'm surprised you are. If I were you, I would have run screaming in the other direction."

Sara smiled sadly. "I didn't think it would really matter where I went."

Kyra nodded. "Yeah, I get that. The fear follows you everywhere. Can I ask…?" Kyra glanced at Sara's round belly.

Sara cupped it tighter, her grip on her unborn child firm. "Good. No concerns."

"That's good news. I'm so sorry."

"Why? You didn't have anything to do with it."

Kyra nodded. "True, but going through all of that was horrible for me. It had to be that much worse for you."

Sara shook her head, her jaw a little stiffer. "It's fine. Is there anything I can do for you today?"

"Oh, yeah," Kyra said, handing over her deposit. "It's crazy, but all this kind of changed things for me. I got a new job and met a great guy. I'm looking for a new apartment so I can finally be out of the one I'm in. I never would have expected so many good things to come out of something so bad."

Sara nodded politely. "That's good." She typed in the computer. "Where are you looking for an apartment?"

"Somewhere close," Kyra answered. "I work not far from here, and I like being in the middle of everything."

"I have a... friend with an apartment to rent. Great location, affordable, and really nice lighting. I could reach out and see if he can show it to you sometime," Sara said, half-watching Kyra and half-paying attention to what she was doing.

"Really? That's so sweet of you. That would be great."

Sara smiled. "Do you have time today?" She grabbed her phone and sent a text.

Kyra nodded. "I can meet this afternoon. I have to get back to work shortly, but my schedule is pretty flexible."

Sara checked her phone, then wrote something down on a sheet of paper. "Send a text to this number when you can head over. He'll text you the address."

Kyra happily took the sheet from Sara and thanked her. "I'm so thrilled I saw you today. Thank you. I'll reach out to him soon."

"He'll be waiting to hear from you. Good luck."

"Thanks, Sara. Have a great day."

Sara smiled at Kyra, then turned to the next customer in line.

Kyra clutched the paper to her chest and walked out of the bank. It was going to be a good day.

KYRA PICKED up the lunch order and drove back to the office. She couldn't stop smiling at her good luck. She made sure she had Robert's number in her pocket and grabbed the bags of food and headed for the elevator.

She swiped her badge and heard voices in the conference room. She wasn't sure if they were in a meeting, so she quietly moved everything through the door so she didn't disturb them.

Then she heard her name.

"Slade would have quit if we didn't hire Kyra," one of the guys said. Dex maybe?

"Yeah," another joined with a laugh, "he was pissed we were considering anyone else." Was that Jack?

"We had to. Even before we knew the circumstances, it wouldn't have been smart to only talk to one person. We had to find the best person for the position."

"Slade found someone for his favorite position."

The first guy laughed.

"He thinks with his dick more often than not."

"True, but they weren't sleeping together when we hired her."

"No, but he wanted her. That's why he pushed for us to hire her. He kissed her at the hospital."

"No shit?"

"Yep. When it ends, and you know it will, it's gonna be ugly around here."

"Hey, Kyra," Dunn said from the end of the hall. "Lunch. Thank you."

Kyra was still frozen, her heart split in half and her pride shattered. The only thing that made her move was when Jack and Dex stuck their heads out of the conference room. They saw where she was standing, and their eyes got wide with the knowledge that she heard what they said.

Kyra pasted on a smile and handed a bag to Dunn, then carried the rest to the break room. She set everything on the table and asked Dunn if she could have the afternoon off to go look at an apartment.

"Yeah, sure. Did you eat yet?"

She nodded, lying her ass off so he didn't press her to stay any longer.

"Okay. Oh, did you get that appointment set up for tomorrow?"

She shook her head. "Sorry. I tried to call but there was no answer."

"Could you try them again? If they still don't answer, I'll call later, but I want to make sure we get them on the books."

Kyra smiled at him and nodded. "I'll take care of it."

Dex and Jack stood sheepishly by the door. When she walked toward them, head held high, Dex said her name.

"I need to make a call. Excuse me."

Dex and Jack let her pass without another word. She was vaguely aware of Slade's office being empty, but she had to use her energy to schedule the appointment for Dunn and see the apartment Sara told her about.

The potential client answered the phone, and Kyra was able to put them on the schedule. While the guys were eating lunch and distracted, Kyra decided to set up the meeting to see the apartment.

Robert said he was available to meet whenever she could be there. He sent her the address, and Kyra asked if she could meet him in fifteen minutes. He said he'd be waiting for her.

Kyra took a deep breath and blew it out slowly. She grabbed her purse again and left the building. It wasn't until she got in her car that she let herself be upset by what Dex and Jack said.

They didn't want to hire her. Slade talked them into it. All because he wanted to get in her pants. She wouldn't have believed it if it were anyone else, but Dex was in her interview. He knew exactly who she was before they offered her the job.

Yet again, Kyra wasn't quite right.

Well, she'd show them. She was good at her job, and they could all kiss her ass. Including Slade. He got what he wanted. Kyra was ready to get what she wanted.

She drove to the address Robert gave her and parked in the lot. It was a big building, and beautiful. Kyra wasn't sure how the apartment was so affordable, but Robert confirmed the price when they set up the appointment. Kyra marveled at the lobby and the elevators when she punched in the floor number from the text.

The doors opened, and Kyra turned right, heading toward the apartment number. She scanned the doors until she found the one she was looking for. She took a deep breath and knocked, pasting on a smile as the door swung open.

"Hello, Kyra. It's nice to see you again," said the man with the ice-blue eyes from the bank. Then he yanked her inside and slammed the door behind her.

20

"Where's Kyra?" Slade asked when he walked into the break room. He went to view the recordings from the bank and thought he had a lead. But he wanted to talk to Kyra. "Her car isn't here."

"She went to see an apartment," Dunn said around his food.

Jack and Dex avoided his gaze. Everyone else ignored him.

"When is she going to be back?"

"Tomorrow, I guess," Dunn said.

"You just gave her the rest of the day off?"

Dunn shrugged. "She seemed like she really wanted to get out of here. She did everything I needed her to do for today. We would have found things for this afternoon, but aside from the meeting in thirty, it's a quiet day. I didn't see an issue with it."

"Do you know where the apartment is?" Slade asked.

Dunn shook his head. "I didn't ask. Why? What's going on?"

"I think the teller was involved with the robbery."

"What are you talking about?" Dunn asked.

"The pregnant teller. I was going over the video again. When the guy who did all the talking walked in, she seemed to recognize him. It was subtle, like she wasn't expecting him to be there, but I think she knows who he is."

"Did you tell Patrick?" Dunn asked, his voice changing from disinterested to concerned.

Slade nodded. "Yeah, and she left work. She was there for the morning, but before lunch, she told her boss she wasn't feeling well and needed to leave."

"You said she's pregnant," Dunn said with a shrug. "It happens. Ash feels like crap almost all the time."

"This woman's phone is off, and her apartment is empty. Like grabbed her go-bag and left empty," Slade said. He paced the small break room, feeling like a caged animal. "Kyra was going to go to the bank today."

"That doesn't mean anything. She might not have gone yet," Dunn said. His voice held concern. He'd been there, worrying about the woman he loved. He knew what Slade was feeling. But that didn't make Slade feel any better.

"What if she did? What if this woman followed her or —" He cut off when his phone rang. "Yeah?"

Patrick confirmed what Slade feared. "We pulled surveillance from today. Kyra was there. She talked to Ms. Martin. They exchanged something, a slip of paper, but we don't know what was on it. Kyra left on her own, and it appears she was fine."

"What time?" Slade demanded.

"She left the bank at eleven-oh-seven."

"Thanks," Slade said, hanging up as he took a breath. Maybe it was all a coincidence. "She left the bank before lunch. You said she brought this here?"

Dunn nodded. "Yeah, she dropped it off. I didn't talk to

her for long, though." He turned to Dex and Jack. "Did you two talk to her?"

Slade shifted his gaze to them. Both averted their eyes and shook their heads, not saying a word. Jack was never that quiet.

"What happened?" Slade demanded. He leaned on the table in front of them and glared hard at his friends. He never understood a man who would choose a woman over his best friends and brothers, but in that moment, Slade was ready to tear them apart if they did anything to hurt Kyra.

"She overheard us talking, we think," Jack said.

"About what?" Slade asked.

"About you pushing us to hire her because you wanted to sleep with her," Jack said, barely meeting Slade's gaze.

"You said what?" Dunn asked, joining Slade to tower over Dex and Jack.

"She's awesome and was the best one for the job, but it was pretty damn obvious that if we didn't pick her, Slade would have lost his shit," Jack said, trying to defend himself.

Dunn focused on Dex. "You were in those interviews with me. You know she was good. And we agreed we wanted to hire her no matter what everyone voted."

"Yeah, but I mean, come on. Slade would have lost it if that wasn't the case," Dex said.

"Are you saying you only agreed to hire her because you're afraid of Slade?" Dunn asked.

Dex glared at him. "No, I'm not. Kyra was the best. She also has him all twisted up and could blow up everything we've created here."

"You guys said the same thing about Ashleigh," Dunn said menacingly.

"And Pilar," Slade provided with a glare toward Jack.

"And it didn't happen," Dunn said.

"Do you want me to walk?" Slade asked calmly.

"This is what I'm talking about," Dex said with a sigh.

Slade shook his head. "I'm not willing to walk because I'm pissed. I'm willing to walk because if you don't trust my judgement, then I shouldn't be a part of this team."

"What does judgement have to do with anything?" Dex asked.

"He's saying he's in love with her," Archer provided from his seat at another table. "He's saying he trusts her and he wants to be with her and if we're not okay with that, then he'll leave. He'd rather leave this team than have to walk away from her."

"Kyra was the best candidate, but can you honestly tell us that you wanted us to hire her because she was good? Because you didn't know shit about her resume when you pushed us to give her an interview. She was some woman in the bank, and you wanted to bring her in so you could sleep with her," Dex said.

Slade took a breath and stood to his full height. He looked at the men who'd been there for him through the worst days of his life. The days when he wanted to put a bullet in his head so the memories would stop haunting him. The days when he was so broken and hurt that he thought he would die.

He didn't talk about it with them. Not much. Even though they all knew what he'd been through, none of them knew how hard his road to recovery was. Not just physically, but mentally.

"I couldn't help her. In the bank, I couldn't help her. I felt the effects just before she went down. I went to her, but I couldn't do anything. I was trapped, again. I could see some of what was going around, but most of it, I watched in her eyes. She was there. She was the only person who was there with me. And I couldn't help her. Just like none of you could help me," he said quietly.

He met the gazes of the men surrounding him. Men who'd told him they would have given their lives for his many times over. He knew they all meant it, too. They would have, without a second thought. But they couldn't help him anymore than he could help Kyra in that moment.

"Did I think she was beautiful?" Slade continued. "Yes, I did. But that wasn't why I wanted you to give her a shot. No, I didn't know her resume. But I didn't ask Dunn to hire her. I asked him to call her for an interview. I figured we could get her resume and take a look and if she was decent, then we could talk. It was a chance for her. Something I didn't have the power to do in the bank."

"Slade, I'm sorry," Dex said.

Slade turned and glared at him. "Do you really think that little of me? That you believed I would hire someone to work here just so I could have a convenient fuck?"

"I—"

"Don't talk to me right now. I need to find Kyra."

Dex didn't say anything else before Slade walked away. He went into Kyra's office first and found a phone number written in handwriting he didn't recognize with the name Robert above it. He wondered if that was what the teller gave her. But who was Robert? Slade pocketed the number and kept looking for anything that could help him.

He pulled out his phone and opened the Find My Friends app. In their line of work, being able to locate someone was sometimes a matter of life and death. They required everyone to be on the same network, just in case. Which meant Slade should be able to see where Kyra was.

Except he couldn't find her.

Something didn't feel right. He went back to the break

room. "If Kyra's phone isn't coming up, what does that mean?" he asked English.

"It could mean her location is disabled or that her phone is off," he said.

"Do we have a way of knowing which?"

English shook his head. "Why would she turn it off?"

"I don't know. Is there a way to look at where she went today?"

English shook his head again. "Not a great way. If she used her phone, it might have hit different towers and we can get a rough idea of where she's been, but it's not always accurate."

"We need to check. Now."

"What's going on?" Dunn asked.

Slade shook his head. "I don't know, but this isn't like Kyra."

"I don't want to start something here, but how well do you know her? Do you know this isn't like her? Maybe she heard everything these idiots said and decided she needs a break from you and the rest of us," Dunn said.

Slade shook his head. "I know her. She wouldn't turn her phone off. She'd ignore me so I know she's pissed, but she wouldn't turn off her phone." He dug the paper out of his pocket and handed it to English. "Trace this, too. I don't know who this is, but Patrick said the teller gave Kyra something. If the teller knew the guy, she could have sent Kyra right to him."

English took the paper and led the way to his office. Slade followed him, standing over his desk while English worked. After a few long minutes, English turned one of his screens toward Slade. "This is her path today. Roughly. It looks like she left here a little before eleven and this tower is the one by the bank. She hit this one, which is probably her picking up lunch, then she's back at the office. She was here for a little while, then she hit this tower and her phone went off."

"What's near there?" Slade asked.

English shrugged. "Everything. It's in the center of downtown. There are bars and restaurants, hotels and apartments, the Falls, everything."

"So, nothing to help us figure out where she actually is?"

English shook his head, looking as defeated as Slade felt. "I'm tracing the number you gave me. If I can get a hit on where that is, it might help us."

Slade nodded. "Good. In the meantime, I'm going to see if I can learn more about this teller. She has to have a father for that baby."

English nodded, staring at his screen as Slade left his office. Slade hated the idea of Kyra being in trouble. He didn't know it for sure, but he'd rather be overbearing than be called in to identify her body.

He was not going to lose her.

Kyra glared at the man named Robert. She knew her opinion of him didn't matter to him, but she was not going to sit there and let him think she was happy to see him again.

"You created quite the problem for me," Robert said. "I heard you were the one who did the drawing of me. You must have done that of the man you saw before the drugs worked their way into your system."

"What difference does it make?" Kyra asked.

"Because I can't go anywhere now. You ruined everything."

"You didn't hide your face. Everyone in there saw you."

"No, they saw the man I wanted them to see. You had to go and smile at me. You paid attention. You were the problem. That's why you're here."

"Was Sara working with you?"

His eyebrows went up. "Are you two friends now? She said she didn't know you."

Kyra hated that it upset her to learn Sara was involved. She always thought she was a decent judge of character, but she'd been proven wrong more than once today. First with Slade, then with Sara. Slade only wanted her there for sex, which explained why he was distant all day, and Sara only wanted her gone so she didn't get caught, too.

Kyra wanted to just cry, but she knew she couldn't give up. It was just her and Robert in the apartment. If she caught him off guard, maybe she could overpower him and knock him off his feet. Or just knock him out. Her hands were zip tied behind her back, and he'd taken her purse and smashed her phone so no one could trace her location, but she would find a way.

"You're not friends," Robert provided. "No, she doesn't make friends. Sara... Sara's a snake. She delivered you to me. You thought she was nice, but she's evil, too."

Kyra didn't answer him, just glared again.

Robert smirked at her.

A knock on the door drew Kyra's attention. Hope filled her. Could someone have found her? "Help!" she called out. "Help me!"

Robert rolled his eyes and slapped her, his knuckles connecting with her cheekbone. Pain exploded at the impact and she fell silent, knowing that pain wouldn't be the worst she felt if he had anything to say about it.

"They're not here to save you," Robert said as he walked

to the door. He opened it wide. Sara and two other men walked in. One of the men looked scared. The other looked like he was as evil as Robert. "It's about fucking time."

"She was trying to run," the evil man said. "She fucking kicked me."

"And you saved the pleasure of killing her for me? How generous of you," Robert said with a grin.

"Why would you kill her, Bobby?" the scared man asked.

Robert, or Bobby, got up close to him. He pressed his forehead to the other man's and clapped a large hand around his neck. "Because your girlfriend is a cruel bitch who will turn me in to save her own sorry ass. She's not who you think she is, Mario." Bobby pulled back and looked at Sara. "Are you?"

Sara just glared at him.

"What are you talking about? What is he talking about?" Mario asked.

Bobby released him and moved to stand in front of Sara. "She's not a good person, Mario. Sara... well, Sara had a pretty rough childhood, and she spent a lot of years doing whatever she had to do to survive. For some of those years, she was a prostitute. For others, she was a thief. She's been in and out of jail, but I don't think that will bother you as much as learning that she's not even Sara Martin."

"Please, don't," Sara said quietly.

Bobby just grinned. "Her real name is Amber Grey."

"So?" Mario said.

Bobby smirked. Sara dropped her head. "Don't worry, you can look her up later. What matters right now is that whoever she is, she's going to pay for what she did."

"What did she do?" Mario whined. "You told us it was either Sara dies or this woman dies. She got you what you wanted."

Kyra's breath hitched. She knew it was possible she was going to die, but hearing it so plainly, like it was no big deal to any of them, hit her. She really was going to die. She was going to die with no one who loved her, in love with a man who didn't care as much about her as she did about him. She had no family and no friends. She was alone.

Tears slid down her cheeks, but she couldn't wipe them off. They soaked into her collar. Kyra almost laughed at herself when a tear snaked between her breasts and into her bra. She wore the shirt for Slade. It was one of her brighter tops, one that made her feel more like herself. And instead of having it drive him crazy all day with the low neckline and the fabric that clung to her breasts, she was going to die in it.

"He never intended to let me live," Sara said silently. "He just wanted to kill both of us."

"No," Mario said, stepping forward. "You're not going to kill anyone, Bobby. Too many people have already died."

Bobby didn't hesitate before he punched Mario square in the face. Mario stumbled back, grabbing his nose and howling as blood poured from it.

Sara moved toward him, but Bobby pulled out a gun and pointed it at her. "Sit down," he demanded.

Sara took a breath and moved toward the couch. She sat next to Kyra, close enough that Kyra felt the other woman's leg against hers. She flinched, but there was nowhere to move to on the small loveseat.

"Don't fucking move," Bobby said. He turned to the third man. "Did you take their phones?"

The guy nodded. "Yeah. They're in the river."

"Good. Then it looks like we're all alone."

21

———————

Kyra looked around the room and wondered how in the hell she was going to get out of there. The building was nice, but that only meant the walls were well insulated and no one could hear what was happening next door. It wouldn't be until her body started to smell that she'd be found.

Despair threatened to overtake the terror she felt. So many things she'd never get to see or do. She thought about the drive to work that morning. And spending the night with Slade. Even her parents and her brother. She'd never see any of them again.

Kyra sucked in a breath and sat up straighter. She wasn't going to die like that. She refused. She had to fight. Even if fighting got her killed faster, she had to fight.

She opened her mouth to interrupt the men arguing, but Sara nudged her. Kyra looked over at the woman who betrayed her. Sara nodded behind them, moving her head just enough that Kyra wondered if it was a twitch. She did it again and shifted her eyes.

Kyra looked. Sara had an old flip phone. She raised her eyebrows, and Kyra nodded.

Sara leaned back and slid the phone into Kyra's hand. Kyra opened it and paused. The smart thing would be to call 9-1-1, but she knew police procedures took time. Plus, it relied on the operator to route her call to the right people and for the officers to get there in time.

She knew Slade's office number. She'd called it enough over the last week. She could call him, and if he answered, he could save her.

The hurt part of her didn't want to put her trust in him again, but the part of her that wanted to live knew he was her best chance at survival.

"What the hell are you doing?" Bobby asked, glaring at Sara and Kyra.

"My stomach hurts," Sara told him. "Being cuffed like this is going to hurt the baby."

"So is killing you," Bobby said with zero sympathy. He turned back to Mario and the other man. "We have one more place to hit, then we're free. Without these two making noise, we can get through it and move on."

"Are you really going to kill her?" Mario asked quietly.

Bobby turned to him. His entire face changed. With the men distracted, Kyra opened the phone and felt for the position of the buttons. Then she dialed.

"I don't want to," Bobby said. "I never wanted to. But she made everything worse. If you never brought her around, none of this would have happened."

"Hello?" Kyra heard softly from the phone. "Hello?"

She pressed a button, hoping Slade would realize she couldn't talk but was there.

"What the—?" she heard. Then silence. Kyra had no way of knowing if the call was still open or not. She had no way of knowing if her lifeline was connected or not. She had no way of knowing if she'd walk out of that apartment or not.

But she refused to give up.

"WHAT THE FUCK ARE YOU DOING?" Slade barked as English reached for his phone.

English pressed the *Mute* button and slapped Slade's hand. "Whoever just called you is there, but if they can't talk, it means it could be bad if whoever is there hears us talking."

"Kyra," Slade breathed.

English shrugged and shoved Slade out of his chair. "Go get everyone else. I'm going to see if I can trace this number."

Slade rushed out of his office to the conference room. The rest of the team was in a meeting with the father of the missing woman. Slade knew they didn't have good news for him, but it also wasn't bad news, so he didn't feel too bad for interrupting them.

"We need to go," Slade said, walking into the room and staring down Dunn.

Dunn understood immediately and stood. "I'm sorry, sir, but something has come up in another case. I assure you, we have not given up on finding your daughter. And we won't until we bring her home to you."

The man stood and shook Dunn's hand, then allowed Rocky to lead him out of the office.

Dunn turned to Slade. "Kyra?"

Slade nodded. "English thinks she just called my office. He's tracing the number she called from."

"Gear up, everyone. We know what that means."

Dunn followed Slade while the rest of them went to

their respective offices to collect guns and knives and bullet-proof vests.

"Anything?" Slade asked.

English looked up and shook his head. "It's an old phone, one that can't be traced. I'm trying to listen to what they're saying. Hopefully, they say something that can help us figure out where they are. So far, all I hear are muffled voices."

"Turn it up," Dunn said.

The three of them hovered around the phone, listening intently to the voices as the static on the line deafened them.

"Whose apartment is this?" a woman's voice asked.

Dunn and English looked at Slade. He shook his head. Not Kyra's voice.

"Why?" a man answered. Slade couldn't place the voice, but it was vaguely familiar.

"I didn't know you knew anyone who lived in Waterfalls Place," the woman said.

English immediately started typing. He nodded.

"We're heading there now," Dunn said. "I'll call from the SUV and you can tell us anything else."

"I'm going with you," Slade said.

Dunn shook his head. "You need to stay here and listen."

"Fuck that. I need to go find my woman," Slade argued. He got up in Dunn's face, and Dunn glared right back at him.

"When Ashleigh was lost—"

"You didn't fucking listen to me," Slade finished. "You told me you were going no matter what."

Dunn sighed heavily knowing he wasn't going to win that argument. He nodded.

"What's the deal?" Dex asked from the door.

"We know where Kyra is, but I want someone to stick

with English. Listen to this call and relay whatever info comes up to us," Dunn said.

"I'll stay," Mason offered. He stepped into the office, armed to the teeth, and slapped Slade on the shoulder. "Go get your woman. We'll send the PD your way."

Slade nodded and followed Dunn and the others to the SUVs. He only hoped they got to Kyra quickly enough.

"IT'S MY FATHER'S PLACE," Bobby said. He cast his glance around the room for signs of the man he hated. His mom ran out when Bobby was in high school, leaving him behind with his abusive asshole of a father.

"I thought your father was a security guard at a bank, Bobby," Sara said, tilting her head.

"Yeah, so?"

"I'm learning so much about you. Is he the reason you shot the guard at my bank? Harry was a good man. He was kind and generous. He has three grown kids. He didn't need to die," Sara said, her voice full of emotion. Fake emotion. The bitch couldn't care less about another human being if her life depended on it. Hell, her life depended on a lot at the moment, and she still couldn't get it right.

"Was he a friend of yours?" Bobby asked with a sneer.

Sara sighed. "No, but he was always nice to me. He was nice to everyone."

Bobby rolled his eyes. "No one is nice to everyone. People put on a show. They show you the person they want you to see. My father was nice to everyone. He had friends who were always laughing at his jokes and making sure he knew how funny he was. Harry was one of them."

The shock on Sara's face was worth the price of admission for Bobby. She had no idea what he was doing. No clue. She thought he killed those guards for sport. No, his reasons were much better than that. He knew those men. He knew everything about them. He'd grown up with them in his house. And he was happy to repay their kindness with his own.

"You knew Harry?" Sara asked. A single tear slid down her cheek.

"And the guard at the second bank. The bank we're going to hit next... I know that guard best of all."

"You're going to kill your own father? Doesn't he work at Falls Community Bank?"

"Yeah, so?"

"That's a bigger bank. More cameras," Sara said.

Bobby shrugged. "We have it all figured out. And you won't have to worry about it at all anyway because you'll be dead by the time we go. And dear old Dad will take the fall for your deaths while the three of us go find a beach to settle on."

Sara's eyes grew wider. Bobby fucking loved seeing the bitch cower with fear. She was cocky and confident most of the time, with her claws in Mario. She was the one who made him second guess everything. With her out of the picture, Mario would be willing to help again. No more talk about going straight after this score. Everything would be the way it was supposed to be with Sara gone.

"What are we waiting for?" Stevie asked. "Why aren't we just getting rid of them and leaving?"

Bobby turned his gun on his friend. He didn't like his authority or his decisions being questioned. He made the rules. Everyone else had to live by them. If they didn't like it, they didn't have to live.

"It's too early. The bank doesn't close for two hours. If we do this now, and someone hears anything, we're done. We need to wait."

"Seriously? We just have to stand here? I didn't eat lunch."

Bobby rolled his eyes. "Go find something, but don't touch anything. They'll dust this whole place when they find these two."

"Hey, Bobby?" Mario asked. He sat near the door, quiet. "Yeah?"

"Are you sure you have to kill Sara and the baby?"

Bobby went to him and smiled at his friend. Gone was the man who fearlessly stood up to everyone when Bobby was getting picked on in high school. Mario had become a whimpering fool, hung up on one pussy. He needed to learn the world was full of possibilities, and Sara wasn't worth losing himself.

"It's for the best," Bobby said softly. "I know you care about her, but she's not good enough for you. She lied about who she is and she manipulated you. She never really loved you. She just used you to improve her situation."

Mario looked beyond Bobby to Sara. "I love her."

Bobby breathed a laugh. "I know you think you do, but you'll love someone else one day. You'll forget all about her."

Mario gave him a forced smile and nodded, pulling his gaze from Sara.

"You're a monster," Sara growled.

Bobby turned to her with a wide grin. "What is it they say? Takes one to know one?"

"Fuck you, Bobby. I'm not that person anymore. I did what I needed to do when I was living on the streets. But that's not who I am. And I never used Mario. He's a good man. A kind man. And I love him and this baby more than you'll ever love another person. All you do is hate. I've been telling Mario we need to get away from you for months, but you keep pulling him back in. You're the evil one here, not me," Sara spat.

Bobby walked over to Sara and stood before her. She was small, a lot smaller than he was. Size always matters. His father taught him that. When he was a kid, his father was quick to slap him around. Once Bobby got older, his attacks were less frequent but more violent. It wasn't until Bobby was bigger than his father that it stopped. And that was when Bobby left. When he knew he could turn things around on his old man.

And he did. Years of planning, and he was the one with the upper hand.

He swung hard, his palm connecting with the side of Sara's face before she realized what he was doing. She fell to the side, landing on Kyra. Kyra tried to nudge Sara up, but with their hands tied behind their backs, it was more comical than helpful. Bobby laughed.

A growl from behind him had him turning just before Mario hit him. Bobby sidestepped, but Mario still connected with his shoulder. It hurt, but Bobby had been through much worse.

"You're going to regret that," Bobby said, reaching for his gun.

"So are you," Mario said. Instead of doing the smart thing and pulling his own weapon, Mario crouched in front of Sara and Kyra. He righted Sara on the loveseat and cupped her jaw. "Are you okay?"

Sara shook her head, the red skin of her cheek already starting to bruise. A trickle of blood ran down from the corner of her lip. It was just the beginning.

Rage filled Bobby. He pointed his gun at them, ready to pull the trigger.

"No!" Sara said.

Mario turned at her words and found the gun pointed at him. "What the fuck, Bobby?"

"Her or me, Mario?" Bobby demanded.

Mario stood and faced him, positioning himself between Bobby and Sara.

Bobby raised an eyebrow. "Her or me? Are you really going to stand there and protect that bitch, or are you going to make the smart choice and get to live?"

Mario reached behind him, but a knock on the door stopped his movements.

"Who is it?" Bobby called out.

SLADE WAS ready to charge the door, but Dunn refused to go in without knowing what they were facing. The only reason Slade listened was because Dunn said it could kill Kyra.

But he wasn't going to wait long for the door to open up.

"Delivery," Jack said.

The rest of them were plastered to the wall, invisible through the peephole in the door. Jack was dressed as a driver for a package delivery company, down to the hat. If they checked, they would see a regular employee instead of a man armed with stun grenades and tear gas, among other things.

"We didn't order anything," the man inside yelled through the door.

"Someone in there did, buddy," Jack said, adding a laugh like he thought the whole thing was funny.

"Leave it at the door," the guy yelled.

"Sorry, man, but it needs a signature," Jack said. He kept

his gaze focused on the door in front of him in case they looked out.

Dunn signaled to the rest of them to pay attention. If the door opened, Jack would subdue the first guy. The team knew there were three men inside and another woman besides Kyra. They believed the other woman was the teller and the one whose phone Kyra was using to call, which meant she was helping even though she was also believed to be dangerous.

English and Mason reported the argument between the two men. As they waited for the door to open, English said the men were talking quietly, but he couldn't understand them. They were plotting something.

"Everyone be ready," Dunn said softly.

"Listen, man, I got a bunch of deliveries to do after this. Are you gonna sign for it so I can leave whatever this is?" Jack whined at the door. He shifted the package from one hand to the other and rolled his neck. He played the part of the stressed out delivery guy well.

"Give me a minute," the guy inside shouted.

Slade's heart pounded with adrenaline. He was not a patient man, and knowing Kyra was on the other side of the wall and possibly hurt did not make him more patient.

Finally, there was a noise at the door. Jack moved the box back to his other hand so he could grab a weapon quickly.

One lock slid open. The chain on the door was removed. Then the door eased open.

"Finally," Jack said, sounding truly exhausted. "Just sign here." He handed the guy a device that captured signatures. It was enough for the dark-haired man to be distracted.

Jack tossed both a stun grenade and tear gas into the apartment and pinned the guy to the front door. He struggled for about two seconds, then stopped fighting and said, "Bobby took them to the bedroom. Don't let him kill her."

Slade rushed through the smoke, ignoring all the protocols, in the direction the guy at the door indicated. The tear gas was quickly filling the apartment, but Slade could see where he was going. He turned down the hallway and stopped at the closed door to the bedroom. If they had time, they would have had the floor plan for the unit before they went inside, but since they didn't, Slade had no idea if the door he stopped in front of was the bedroom or if Kyra was in there. He just had his instincts.

Slade stopped at the door. His mask allowed him to breathe clean air, but the people inside the room were getting hit with the gas. He did his best to be silent as he lifted his infrared lens to see through the walls. Two figures were on the bed, and two more stood in front of them, guns pointed.

22

———————

Kyra's eyes and lungs burned from the gas, but it was better than a bullet. Or she assumed. She'd never been shot and was really hoping the same would be true at the end of the day.

She couldn't see well, but she could see enough to know the room was almost full with smoke that filtered under the door.

Hope filled her the minute the smoke started seeping into the room. Bobby and Stevie didn't notice it at first as they kept guns trained on Sara and Kyra, but it wasn't long before they started choking and knew what happened.

"Kill them," Bobby said, pointing his gun at Sara. The grin on his face was one of pure evil. Kyra had never seen such menace in her life.

"Who gives a shit about them? We need to get the fuck out of here!" Stevie insisted.

Bobby weighed his options for a second, then moved to the window. Stevie was frantic, trying to smash the window, but it wasn't budging.

Bobby went back to the edge of the bed, coughing and

wiping his eyes as the gas infiltrated his senses. "How did they find us?" he demanded from Sara.

"I'm smarter than you are, asshole," she said hoarsely.

"Bobby, we need to go. Now!" Stevie said. He moved across the room with his shirt over his face and grabbed at Bobby's arm. "Come on!"

Bobby shrugged him off. Stevie finally gave up and went back to the window. The sound of a gunshot and breaking glass echoed through the room the same moment the door splintered in front of them.

Men in masks and head-to-toe black gear rushed into the room, one gun pointing at Stevie, another at Bobby.

"Guns down," the muffled voice of the man behind the mask ordered.

Stevie tossed his immediately, his hands in the air. The broken window helped to dissipate the gas, but Kyra's eyes and throat still burned.

Bobby wasn't as smart. "Who the fuck are you? You're not cops. Cops have to announce when they enter."

"We're not cops," the man said, his gun still pointed at Bobby. "But the cops like us a lot."

Bobby moved to lift his gun, and the other guy growled, "You're not gonna want to do that."

Bobby's head snapped toward him a second before the massive guy cold cocked him. Bobby's limp form dropped to the ground.

Sara coughed again, choking on the air around them. Kyra turned to her, struggling to see her through her own tears. "Sara," she said loudly.

Sara looked at her. "I'm sorry, Kyra." Then she stood. "I was involved with them. I was the one who brought Kyra here. She's innocent and needs to be saved. I don't deserve it."

"No, she saved me. She gave me the phone to call for help," Kyra said, struggling to stand herself.

"What the hell? You called someone?" Stevie choked out. He was on the ground with his arms behind his back.

"I'm so happy you called me," the guy in front of Kyra said.

He flipped off his mask. Slade. She was so happy to see him, but the hurt she felt earlier rushed back in when he leaned forward to kiss her. Kyra turned her head so his lips grazed her cheek instead.

"Kyra?"

"Thank you for coming to save me." She looked up at Dunn when he took off his mask. "I'm sorry, but this job is not going to work out for me. I will stick around if you want me to help train someone, but I will be leaving soon."

"Kyra," Slade said again.

Dunn put his hand on Slade's arm and pulled him away from Kyra. "I understand."

"What the fucking hell?" Slade demanded. "No. I don't understand. What the hell?"

Dunn shoved Slade out of the room and Rocky walked in with Archer right behind him. Dex was lifting Stevie to his feet and leading him toward the door.

"You okay?" Rocky asked, shining a flashlight in her eyes.

Kyra nodded and squeezed her eyes shut, fighting back tears.

"The gas burns. I'm sorry about that. It was the only way."

"I'm fine," Kyra choked out. "Check on Sara. She's pregnant."

"We're going to take care of both of you," Rocky said.

Kyra nodded and wished she'd never walked into the bank that day.

"WHY IN THE fuck are you dragging me out of there?" Slade demanded, shrugging Dunn off.

He was furious. Kyra was quitting, and Dunn was just going to let her. She didn't let him kiss her. She was running from him. No. Hell fucking no. He wasn't having that.

He tried to push his way past Dunn again, but Dunn slammed him into the wall.

"Leave her be for a minute," he said. "She was held at gunpoint. She was tricked by a woman she trusted. And she thinks you're an asshole who only hired her for a fuck."

"And I need to tell her that's not true," Slade argued.

"No, you need to give her a minute. This is not about you, Slade. This is about her. Kyra is the one who matters right now."

"She's the only one I'm thinking about," Slade growled.

"You're thinking about yourself. You don't want to lose her. That's about you, not her. If she's done, you need to let her go."

"She's not done. She can't be," Slade said, the loss of her choking him like it had already happened. "She can't be."

Dunn patted him on the shoulder as Slade sank to the ground. Dunn stood guard at the door, no one in or out, until the police arrived.

Patrick shook their hands and took over the scene a few minutes later. He asked for statements from all of them, and they dispersed with officers to tell their sides of what they walked into.

"Talk to me," Patrick said to Slade. "How the hell did you find these guys?"

"They found Kyra," Slade said simply.

"Well, fuck."

Slade nodded. "The teller was involved, just like we thought. She's in there. They had her at gunpoint, so I guess she wasn't being cooperative or something, but she gave Kyra the ringleader's phone number. This is his dad's apartment. He's a guard at Falls Community Bank. They were going to kill Kyra and the teller and pin the whole thing on the father. English has it all on recording for you."

"Jesus," Patrick breathed. "Talk about a grudge. Any bodies in there?"

Slade shook his head. "All alive. The three men and the teller."

"Damn. All right, tell me what you saw and did in there."

Slade went through the whole thing mechanically. He started with the phone call from the unknown number to showing up at the complex and subduing Bobby. He couldn't let his emotions out because if they did, he wasn't sure he'd be able to stuff them back inside. The woman he loved was held at gunpoint with a killer threatening her. She called him, but when he showed up, she refused to speak to him.

Slade understood how scared she was. He knew the rollercoaster she went on. He'd been there. And when he was saved, he didn't want anyone close to him, either. He wanted space. He wanted to process. He wanted to thank God he hadn't died at the hands of people who had no intention of letting him live.

He'd give Kyra time. If what she went through had her pushing him away, he hoped she could let him back in, eventually. If it was his teammates, he'd fucking kill them.

His anger was still rioting through him when Patrick spoke.

"How's Kyra?" Patrick asked.

Slade shook his head. "She won't talk to me."

Patrick rose his brows. "What happened?"

Slade shook his head again, knowing the truth in his gut. "My fucking teammates happened."

KYRA FELT BADLY for Sara as the police officers swarmed the room and led her out. She was crying when she left and apologized to Kyra, but she still knowingly led Kyra to her death.

Kyra wanted to be understanding that Bobby threatened to kill her if she didn't give him Kyra's contact information, but if Sara had gone to the police, or even told Kyra what was happening, it all would have happened very differently.

As it was, Kyra was not feeling a whole lot of kindness toward the other woman, even if she did help to save Kyra in the end. Even that was likely a hope that Sara herself would also be saved.

"Are you feeling any better?" Rocky asked, walking back into the room.

Kyra sat on the bed, letting the fresh air wrap around her. The gas had filtered out of the apartment and only stung when Kyra took a deep breath.

"I'm fine," she said automatically. She was pretty much done being around anyone from her soon-to-be former place of employment. She felt like a fool for believing Slade cared about her and thinking that she got the job because she earned it. She was sure she was a joke to all of them the entire time she worked there.

"I still think you should go to the hospital and get checked out," Rocky said.

Kyra shook her head. "I just want to go home."

Rocky nodded. He hovered near the door like he was trying to decide if he should stay or go, but after a minute, he moved closer to her. "Kyra, listen—"

"If you're about to tell me I should reconsider quitting or give Slade another chance or not to listen to what Dex and Jack said, I don't want to hear it," Kyra said firmly, glaring at him.

Rocky stopped in his tracks and backed up. He nodded once, then stepped out of the room, standing guard at the door but not speaking to her.

When the police officers finally cleared the scene and asked about taking her to the hospital, Rocky spoke up. "She'd like to go home. I've checked her out and would recommend she follow up with her family doctor if she doesn't want to take another trip to the ER."

"Do you think she's okay to go?" the EMT asked Rocky.

Rocky held Kyra's gaze and nodded. "It wouldn't be bad for her to go to the hospital, but I think she's okay if she promises to get checked out soon."

"I will," Kyra said.

"Well, our recommendation is everyone goes to the hospital, but since you're not in any obvious distress, I can sign off. Do you have anyone at home who can help you if you do have a problem later?" the EMT asked.

Kyra nodded. "I have a roommmate."

"Okay," the EMT said. She signed the paperwork and handed Kyra a copy. "You're good to go."

Kyra thanked her and finally felt better. She went to stand and lost her balance, falling back to the bed again.

"Whoa," the EMT said. "Are you sure she can go?"

"I'm fine," Kyra insisted. She refused to go to the hospital. She couldn't be anywhere in public. She needed to go home and have a good cry and forget all about Slade O'Keefe and her broken heart.

Dammit. She still had things at his house. She shook her head internally. She'd buy new stuff.

She realized she wouldn't be able to move out anymore. She gave up the job she had that allowed her to live on her own. She never should have gone to the bank that day.

Kyra stood again and was able to balance. Her head spun a little, but her hands were zip tied behind her back for hours. And she breathed in tear gas. And she was heartbroken.

Kyra started for the door when she realized she was going to have to walk right past Slade and all the others. Everyone would see her leaving. Tears burned her eyes again, but she refused to let them see her cry. She was the butt of their jokes long enough. They could all kiss her extra large ass.

She took a deep breath and walked out. The living room was quiet, but voices lingered through the apartment. She saw movement in the kitchen but kept walking.

"Don't," someone said firmly.

Kyra didn't stop to look at who was talking. She just continued right out the door and into the hallway.

Police officers were scattered down the hall, but none of them stopped her. She hurried to the elevator and sighed with relief when was there and empty.

Kyra's hands shook as she pressed the button. The doors slid closed in front of her, cutting her off from the people on the floor. She finally looked up and just barely saw Slade rushing out of the apartment.

She couldn't face him. She didn't want to. He would see

all over her face that she'd fallen for him, and he'd laugh at her, too. Dex and Jack were bad enough thinking she was just a plaything for him, but Slade...

Kyra willed the elevator to move quickly. When the doors finally opened on the ground floor, Kyra checked around then rushed for the door. She didn't hesitate before getting to her car and turning the key. She backed out of the spot and drove away, relieved to have made it away from him.

Instead of breaking down while she drove, Kyra made a mental list of all the things she needed to do, starting with finding a new job. She needed a new phone, too. Maybe she could find a job quickly and would be able to find an apartment by the end of the month like she planned.

The thought of searching for an apartment again had fear coursing through her. She wasn't sure she wanted to live alone anymore. She didn't really like Autumn, but she was fairly sure Autumn would call the police if someone tried to kill Kyra.

Hopefully.

Kyra made it home and carried herself up to her apartment. Autumn wasn't there yet, so Kyra went straight to her room, stripped out of her clothes and ran herself a hot bath. She found her iPad under the sketchbook on her desk and turned on some music. It wasn't as convenient to listen to music on her iPad as her phone, but it was the only option.

She set the iPad on her vanity and sank into the hot bath water while music filled her head. She let the heat carry everything away and cried out all her tears.

When the water turned cold, Kyra reluctantly dragged herself out of the tub. She dressed in her second favorite pajamas since her favorite ones were still at Slade's and sat on her bed with her sketchbook and pencils.

Kyra let herself get lost in her drawing, not paying attention to what she was drawing or if it was any good. She just needed to let all her emotions out. One after another, she drew Slade's face. Happy, turned on, excited, thoughtful, caring, frustrated. If she could get them all out of her head, maybe she could get him out of her head, too.

Her heart would be harder to do, but she knew it was going to happen eventually.

Kyra started to wonder if she should leave Niagara Falls. Nothing really held her there, and if there was ever a reason to leave, almost being killed twice and having your heart destroyed felt like damn good reasons to find a new city.

There was a loud knock on her door, one that startled her and brought her back to the room around her. Crumpled papers littered the bed and the floor. The sun was setting outside, a dark orange glow pouring through the curtains. Autumn was clearly home, and pounding again.

"Yeah?" Kyra said.

"What are you doing?"

"Um, nothing. Why?"

"Someone is here to see you."

"Who is it?"

"Uh, just come out here," Autumn said, sounding both concerned and disinterested.

Kyra sighed and pushed off her bed. For about a second, she thought it might be Slade, but Autumn wouldn't have given in so easily if that were the case. Kyra didn't know anyone else, and no one else knew where she lived. She grabbed a sweatshirt instead of putting on a bra and opened the door.

Lily, Ashleigh, Kelsea, and Pilar stood on the other side of her bedroom door with snacks and wine and smiles.

"What are you guys doing here?" Kyra asked.

Lily pushed forward and waved Kyra back into her room. "Archer told me what happened. We came to be here for you."

"And to tell you how sorry I am that Jack is such a moron," Pilar added.

"And because we care about you," Kelsea said.

"What they all said. But I really need to pee," Ashleigh said. "Do you have a bathroom in there? Because your roommate is kind of a bitch."

Kyra pointed to her bathroom, and Ashleigh rushed in. Lily pulled Kyra in for a hug and said, "I'm so sorry about everything you went through today. We brought wine and cupcakes and junk food."

"Why are you all here?" Kyra asked.

"Because we're your friends. And we are here for our friends," Kelsea said.

So much for thinking Kyra cried all her tears. She burst into tears all over again, but this time, she wasn't alone.

23

Slade paced his living room with his keys in his hand. Howler followed behind him, whimpering. They both felt the same way. It wasn't the same without Kyra there. She belonged with them. In his house. In his bed. In his life.

"I'm going to get her," he said to Howler. Howler barked in agreement.

Slade was almost to the door when the bell rang. Howler let loose with a howl that drowned out anything Slade might have said. They both rushed to the door, yanking it open. Slade was sure it was going to be Kyra, back where she belonged. But it wasn't.

"I'm on my way out," Slade told Archer and Jack. Right behind them was the rest of the team.

"No, you're not," Archer said, using his bulk to block Slade and push his way inside.

"I need to go see Kyra," Slade argued.

Archer shook his head. "Nope, you don't. She needs a night off from you."

"How the fuck do you know what she needs?" Slade demanded, ready to put his fist through his friend's face.

"Because Lily and the others are with her right now. Lily already texted me. Kyra is upset and thinks you were only with her for a quick fuck," Archer said.

His words took all the fight out of Slade. He sank against the wall and shook his head. Then he caught sight of Jack and Dex, and the fight was on again.

"You two did this. You two made her think I didn't love her. You made it sound like she was no one," Slade shouted at them as Archer and Dunn held him back.

"Pilar will tell her what an idiot I am," Jack said. "If anyone knows, it's Pilar."

"Yeah, well, you get to go home to Pilar tonight. Kyra is gone. She should be here with me, where I can help her. Where I can tell her she's safe. Instead, she's alone."

"She's not alone," Dunn said. "She'll come around. She knows you care about her."

Slade shook his head. "No, she doesn't. I never told her."

"Why not?" Dunn asked.

Slade chuckled and shook his head. He ran a hand over his short hair and looked at the men around him. These men had been everything to him for years. They were the people he went to, but they were still men. They still kept their emotions in check and refused to show any weakness. Especially to each other.

"When did you tell Ashleigh you loved her? Was it the moment you realized it, or later?" Slade asked.

Dunn nodded, knowing the answer.

"What about Lily? Or Kelsea? Or Pilar? Which of you blurted out how you felt when the emotions hit?"

They all mumbled their agreement.

"I love her. I've wanted this my whole life. I thought I'd have it by now. A wife, a partner, a home in someone else. I was scared it would be taken from me if I admitted to her how I felt. And she was. Because of you stupid fucks," Slade growled, glaring at Jack and Dex.

Dex stepped forward. He still had on his black tee and jeans from work, complete with the ketchup stain barely visible on his right pec. "Don't blame Jack. We all know Jack talks out of his ass and uses the brain in his dick more often and expects the rest of us to do the same. And he wasn't in the interviews. I was. I knew how good Kyra was. I knew it didn't matter what you said, I wanted to hire her. I'm an ass."

"At least you finally admit it," Slade said, his anger still threatening to drown him. "But it doesn't help me."

"I'll talk to Kyra. Let her know none of it was true."

"I think we all need to talk to her," Dunn said. "She needs to know we all wanted her for the job."

"I promised her that getting involved with me wouldn't affect her job. I told her I would never threaten it. The only way she's going to stay is if I leave," Slade said.

"We'll figure out a way for both of you—" Dunn said.

Slade shook his head. "No. If she doesn't want to be around me, if she is done, I can't be there. I can't look at them every day and know what they took from me. I can't trust them. And if I can't trust them, I can't be a part of the team."

The entire room dropped into silence. Dex and Jack looked at each other, then at the rest of the room. Slade hung his head. He felt defeated. He lost too much. The woman he loved, the friends who were brothers, the job that defined him and gave him purpose. All of it was gone.

Archer stepped forward to say something but stopped when a phone went off.

Dunn was frantic when he heard it and dug his phone

out of his pocket. "Shit. Ashleigh. She's in labor. Right now. I gotta go."

"We're all going," Archer said.

"No," Dunn said. "I'll be fine."

Archer shook his head and pointed to the door. "We're all going. Ashleigh is with Lily, Kyra, Kelsea, and Pilar. Lily will get them to the hospital, and we'll all be there for you guys. Let's go."

Slade wanted to let them all walk out the door and lock it behind them, but Archer made him file out, too. They piled into SUVs, Slade with Dunn and Archer, and took off for the hospital.

Archer dropped Dunn off in front and told Slade to go in with him. Dunn looked like he was losing his mind as they ran inside and asked for directions to labor and delivery. They followed directions to the elevator and waited for it to bring them up to the labor and delivery floor. Another nurse's station gave Dunn Ashleigh's room number. Slade followed.

Outside the door, Dunn stopped and put his hand on Slade's chest. "I got this. Thank you. And don't kill those two morons. We will make everything right with Kyra."

Slade nodded, wishing he felt half as confident as Dunn.

He asked someone walking by if there was a waiting room on the floor and followed their directions. He walked in and stopped.

Kyra was sitting against the wall, the late day sun streaming through the windows. It glowed around her, making her shine.

Every inch of him demanded he walk across the room and sweep her up and tell her exactly how much he loved her. But she was surrounded. Lily and Kelsea on one side, and Pilar on the other. And the looks on their faces said they weren't letting him near Kyra unless she said so.

And she definitely wasn't saying so.

He was fucked.

KYRA WANTED to run to Slade when he walked in. Every cell inside her said she belonged in his arms. She ached from holding herself back. It broke her heart, but that was the whole reason she didn't want to go to the hospital in the first place.

When Ashleigh said she was in labor, Kyra thought she was joking. When Ashleigh admitted she'd been having contractions all afternoon and dismissed them as Braxton-Hicks, Kyra started to get concerned. Then Ashleigh's water broke, and she called out as a big contraction hit her, and Kyra about lost her mind.

Thankfully, Kelsea and Pilar seemed to know what to do. Lily called Dunn and made sure he was going to meet them at the hospital while Kelsea and Pilar helped Ashleigh get to her SUV. Kyra was about to wave and say goodbye when they all demanded she go with them.

She really didn't want to, but Ashleigh asked Kyra to sit in the backseat with her on the ride to the hospital. Kyra was sure it was just an excuse for her to go along, but Ashleigh held her hand and admitted how scared she was.

The hospital rushed Ashleigh to a room while the rest of them settled in the waiting room for Dunn to arrive. When the rest of the guys showed up with him, Kyra wasn't sure she could breathe.

"Do you want to take a walk?" Kelsea asked.

Kyra shook her head.

"Need a coffee?" Pilar asked.

Kyra shook her head again.

"Want us to leave so you can talk to him?" Lily asked.

"No," Kyra said firmly.

Lily sighed. "You need to talk to him. Even if it's just to clear the air. He's a good guy."

Kyra laughed mirthlessly. "The night I met all of you, you guys told me he doesn't get attached. That I would be good for him, but he hasn't been in a relationship since you've known him. I should have just listened and kept my distance. Then I wouldn't be sitting here with a broken heart."

"He doesn't look much better," Pilar said. "And I'm pretty sure Jack and Dex are going to have something broken by the end of the night, too."

Kyra looked at the men. Jack and Dex were to the side, watching Slade. He had his head resting on his hands, elbows on his knees, glaring at everyone. Archer, Jaymes, Mason, and English sat together, watching the whole scenario. Rocky leaned against the wall, alternating between staring at the door to the patient rooms and Slade.

"Maybe I should just go," Kyra said softly. "I don't belong here. I'm not a part of this group anymore."

"What do you mean?" Lily asked.

"I quit this afternoon. I told Dunn I would stay until he found someone else, but I can't be here. I never should have taken this job."

Pilar shook her head, her dark hair falling forward to cover her face. Her hands gripped the armrests of her chair. She took a deep breath and stood, smoothing her hands down her cotton shorts before she stomped across the waiting room to Jack.

"What the hell is wrong with you two? How could you make her feel like she doesn't belong here? You owe her an apology! She has done nothing to either of you, and instead of being welcoming and kind, you make her feel like she's a cheap slut. No woman deserves that. I expected better from you, especially you, Jack. I love you, but if you really think that a woman should be spoken about instead of to, and if you think you were in the right, then maybe you aren't the man I thought you were," Pilar said.

Jack stood and reached for her, but Pilar moved away from him.

"Oh, no. You don't get to smooth this over with a kiss and a sweet word or two. Are you the man I fell in love with or are you a Neanderthal who thinks women are only good for the purposes men define them for?" she demanded, arms crossed. Her head tilted to the side in defiance, waiting for his answer.

"You know I don't believe that," Jack said quietly.

"Then why in the world would you say those things about Kyra?" Jack looked behind himself at Dex, and Pilar continued, "Oh, no. You are not going to blame someone else for your actions, Jack Farrell. You are a grown-ass man, and if you can't make your own decisions, then you don't deserve to have a woman like me sharing your bed."

"I..." Jack sighed. "I'm an ass. I didn't think through what I was saying. It was stupid guy talk because I was jealous that Slade and Kyra got to spend their days together. I wish I saw you more, but instead, I go to work and you go to work and we barely have a few hours together every day. I was being a selfish dick," he moved past Pilar to stand in front of Kyra, "and I'm sorry. I shouldn't have said any of those things. Slade asked if you could get an interview. Dunn and Dex described each candidate without telling us who you were, and we all chose the best. You got the most votes, without knowing it was you. And you were the best for the job. You still are. I just wish I'd been smart enough to get Pilar to work there."

Kyra smiled and nodded, but she didn't have any words to say. She understood what he was saying, but she was still hurt. She still felt like an idiot.

"He's right," Dex said, joining Jack. "Dunn and I agreed we wanted to hire you, regardless of what everyone else said. You were the best candidate, even before the bank. We wanted you. And I have no excuse for the things I said. I don't know if you'll be able to trust us again, but if you will, we'd still like you to work with us."

Kyra's gaze slid to Slade. He wasn't looking at them. He was silent. His friends said they shouldn't have said those things, but they didn't say they were wrong. Lily and the others tried to tell her Slade was in love with her, but Kyra knew he'd never look at her the same way. What they had was over, which meant she had to leave.

"Thank you," she said softly. "I appreciate it. I think it's still for the best if I go."

"I'm leaving," Slade said from across the room. His words were quiet and pained, but loud enough that she heard them. "I put in my notice. You can go back to work because I won't be there to make you uncomfortable. I promised you nothing that happened between us would affect your job, and I meant it. So, if you can't be there with me, I'm leaving."

"You love your job," Kyra breathed. He told her it gave him meaning when he left the SEALs. He felt untethered when he retired, and joining F-BOMB with the others made him feel like he had a place. He couldn't quit.

"I love *you*," Slade said, finally meeting her gaze. "The

job is just a job. If I can't have you in my life, nothing matters."

"You don't love me," Kyra said, even as tears filled her eyes. She blinked them away, but they kept coming back.

Slade nodded. "I do. I have for a while. I wanted to tell you before, but I thought you'd run. I know this is hard. I know you don't trust me. You sure as hell don't trust those fuckers. But I love you. I don't want you to look for another apartment because I want you to move in with me and Howler. You're everything to me."

"But I..." she started to argue. Then she stopped. Slade knew everything about her. He knew she couldn't have kids. He knew she liked fancy underwear and pretty clothes. He knew she liked to dance in her underwear and draw. He knew who she was. For the first time in her life, someone knew her and didn't want her to change.

Slade sat patiently, waiting for her to say something.

"I can't let you quit your job," Kyra finally said. "You love it too much."

He shook his head, but she didn't let him say anything.

"When you love someone, you don't let them give up the things that make them happy."

His eyes narrowed as her words sank in. Then a smile curled the edges of his lips up. "Are you saying what I think you're saying?"

She nodded slowly.

"Say it, Kyra. I need to hear the words," he said. His fingers dug into the armrest, turning his knuckles white. His entire body was coiled tight, ready to leap at her.

She smiled, dragging out the moment for both of them. Anticipation was killing her, but she saw it in his eyes. He wasn't going to make her wait to be in his arms again once she said those three words.

"I... love... you," she said softly, staring at him as she said it.

He was out of his chair and across the room in a heartbeat. He swept her up into his arms and pressed his lips tight to hers. His tongue filled her mouth and promised forever, a kiss to seal her fate.

"Well, damn," Dunn said from behind them. "That's some more good news."

Kyra and Slade broke apart, but Slade kept his arms around her. He nuzzled against her neck and asked Dunn, "How's Ash?"

"She's good. Thanks to these ladies getting her here. We have a son. Seven pounds, fourteen ounces. Great lungs. The doc said you guys can come back but only two at a time for right now. Ash is pretty worn out, but she asked for you, Kyra."

"Me?"

Dunn nodded. "She said you were the one who held her hand and told her it was all going to be okay. That you gave her the strength on the ride here that she didn't have inside."

Kyra shook her head. "I didn't do anything. She did the hard work."

"She said she knows what she asked of you wasn't easy, and she's grateful. And she just squeezed out my kid, so I'm going to do whatever I need to do to bring you back to see her. Slade?" Dunn said with a nod.

Kyra barely had time to turn her head before Slade hoisted her over his shoulder and followed Dunn to the door.

"Put me down," Kyra said, slapping his back.

"Only if you go see Ashleigh. And only if you promise you won't run from me again."

He eased her off his shoulder and held her, feet off the ground, until she nodded. "Yes. To both."

"Finally," Slade said. He set her on the ground and kissed her quickly, then grabbed her hand and followed Dunn down the hall.

24

———————

Kyra had tears in her eyes when she took the tiny package from Ashleigh's arms. Slade rocked back. "Fuck me, he's tiny."

"Yeah," Dunn said. The two of them stayed at the door, letting the women talk quietly. "So, you two are good now?"

Slade nodded, unable to tear his gaze from Kyra. She cradled the baby with such love that Slade's cock throbbed with need. He wanted to give her that. He knew she couldn't have kids, but that didn't mean she didn't want to be a mother. Looking at her, it was clear that was a dream she never thought she'd be able to see come true.

Fuck that. It was Slade's job to make all her dreams come true.

"What about Jack and Dex?" Dunn asked.

Slade sighed and shook his head. "I don't know."

Dunn was quiet for a moment, watching Kyra hand the baby back to Ashleigh. "When that last bomb went off, and I knew she was inside, I thought I lost her. I felt like my life was over. And you were standing between me and her."

Slade opened his mouth to argue, but Dunn cut him off.

"It didn't matter that you were right, and I was hurt. You wanted to prevent me from saving the woman I loved. I hated you at that moment. More than I hated Williams. He was the one who tried to send her back to her monster of a husband, but you were stopping me from saving her. If I could have, I would have cold-cocked you and left you on the ground."

Slade chuckled softly.

"Jack and Dex were wrong. They were assholes who have a lot of apologizing to do. But we don't work without all of us together. I don't want to lose you, but I can't choose between you and them, either."

Slade nodded thoughtfully. He leaned against the doorframe and watched Kyra smile. Her eyes kept going to the baby. She put her hand over Ashleigh's. Kyra belonged in their group. She was a part of more than just him. She was a part of all of them.

"I'll forgive them, eventually. Just like I forgave all of you for not getting me out of that shit-hole sooner in the desert."

Dunn rocked back and gave Slade a funny look.

Slade shrugged. "Yeah, I blamed you. I blamed Williams. I blamed myself. I had a lot of fucking blame. I spread it around. I was pissed off. Therapy helped."

"I didn't know. I'm not surprised. I would have felt the same. It killed me not to go after you," Dunn confessed. "They had to hold me back."

"Who?"

Dunn laughed softly. "Williams and Hockley."

"Fucking Hockley," Slade said. "That guy was such an asshole."

Dunn nodded.

"You should have cold-cocked them," Slade said with a wry smile.

Dunn barked a laugh and shook his head. "The things I would do over if I could." His gaze went to Ashleigh.

"You two found a way," Slade said.

Dunn nodded. "We sure did."

Ashleigh tried to get Slade to hold the baby, Daniel Jr., but Slade refused. The baby was far too small for him. He worried he'd break him.

Kyra let him wrap his arm around her before they walked out of Ashleigh's room, but she stopped him and turned back.

"Hey, Dunn?" she said.

Dunn lifted his head and met her gaze. "Yeah?"

"Um, I was wondering if I could take back my resignation?"

He grinned. "What resignation?"

Kyra chuckled and nodded. "Thank you."

"Does that mean you're not leaving?" Ashleigh asked.

Kyra nodded and looked up at Slade. "I'm not going anywhere."

"Good," Ashleigh said with a wink for Slade.

Slade wrapped his arm around Kyra's shoulders and led her back to the waiting room.

The rest of the group took turns going in to see Ashleigh and Dunn. While everyone talked quietly, Slade asked Kyra the question he wanted to know the answer to.

"Do you want kids?" he asked softly.

Her head snapped to look at him, shock and pain in her gaze. "I told you I can't have kids."

Slade cupped her jaw and ran his fingertips along the soft skin there. She was hurt by his question, and after all the hurt she'd been through that day, it was the last thing he wanted.

"I know, and that's not what I asked. I asked if you want

kids. If you want to be a mom. If you would have a family if it were an option."

She looked away from him before she nodded. She pulled at the hem of her shirt and ducked her chin.

"Hey," he said softly. "Look at me."

She lifted her chin and finally met his gaze again.

"I love you. I meant those words. And to me, those are words that say I'm not going anywhere. I want you with me forever. I want you in my bed and in my house. I want to be raising kids with you or dogs, maybe cats if you really want one, or just you, me, and Howler, if that's what you want. We're a family, with or without kids, but I love you."

"Do you want kids?" she asked quietly.

Slade nodded. "I do. I always have. And seeing you with Junior made me ache to get in some practice."

She snorted and shook her head. "You're not going to get me pregnant."

Slade smirked. "That has nothing to do with it. When we have a kid running around and Howler running around, we're going to need to sneak around. I think maybe we should start practicing now. I saw a supply closet down the hall."

Slade nuzzled her neck, and Kyra slapped him. "We are not having sex in a hospital supply closet."

"Then we need to get home because I'm not sure how long I can wait to have you."

"Home? But I don't live with you."

"You should. Or we can buy a new house if you don't like the one I have. I don't care as long as I get to wake up every morning with you in my arms," Slade said, kissing her neck.

"I—"

"Get a room," Lily said from way too close.

Slade looked up at her with a glare. "Got one we can borrow?"

Lily snorted and grinned. "We're ordering pizzas and coming over. I think after everything that happened today, we all need to be together."

"You're inviting yourself to my house?" Slade asked with a grin.

Lily shrugged. "Not the first time. At least I'm bringing food."

Slade nodded. "Good point."

"I think we've all seen Junior. You guys ready to go?" Lily asked.

"Only if you're not giving us the keys to your office," Slade answered, standing and dragging Kyra against his body. She squealed, then melted into him.

Lily shook her head. "Nope. You have a house. You can have all kinds of sex after we leave."

Slade pressed his nose into Kyra's hair and dug out his wallet. He handed Lily some cash and said, "Take your time getting to our house."

Lily laughed as Slade dragged Kyra out the door.

KYRA WRAPPED her hair up in a towel and smiled in the mirror. Slade was behind her, a towel around his waist, just watching her.

"What?"

He shook his head. "You're beautiful. I just like watching you."

"You're weird," she said, feeling awkward.

He moved closer and wrapped his arms around her waist. "Don't get all uncomfortable on me now. You just rode my face like a cowgirl and screamed my name so loud Howler hid under the bed."

Kyra snorted her laughter and looked to where Howler was still cowering, afraid for his life. "I'm sorry, buddy," she said, crouching low so he would come to her.

Howler barked once, then wiggled out from under the bed and scooted across the floor to her. She wrapped her arm around his neck and kissed the top of his head. He barked.

"I'll try not to scare you again," Kyra said.

He howled.

"Oh, no. Until there are little kids running around here who would be traumatized by your screams, we're not going to let him stop us. He'll be okay. Maybe he'll howl with you again."

Kyra laughed. "That was almost worse."

Slade grinned and helped her back to a stand. He slid his arms around her back and pulled her body flush to his. He was already hard again.

"We have people coming over," she said, trying to get away from him.

"They can wait outside," Slade said with a growl, pulling her closer.

The doorbell rang, followed immediately by a knock.

"Go let them in," Kyra said, slipping out of his grasp.

Slade groaned and yanked off his towel. "They have keys."

"What?" she shrieked. "We have to get dressed!"

Slade grabbed a pair of boxer briefs and shorts, then tugged a tee over his head. "I'll save you some pizza. Put on something that'll be easy for me to take off when they all leave."

Kyra smiled at his wink before he disappeared, calling Howler to go with him.

Kyra didn't have a lot of clothes left, so she went with the basics. She put her bra on from the day before, but only had one pair of panties for work the next day, so she decided to go without. Her pajamas were comfortable but also short, and might show off what she wasn't wearing underneath, so she pilfered through Slade's drawer and found a pair of his shorts. She pulled on a tee of his with his shorts and ran a brush through her hair before joining the rest of the group.

"Hey," Kelsea said, seeing Kyra first. "Did we give you enough time?"

Kyra shook her head. "I don't think I'll ever have enough time with him."

Kelsea grinned, her gaze following Jaymes. "I know the feeling."

Kyra laughed. She never thought she'd find a group of people who understood her thoughts. Who were like her, even though they were all a little different.

"Junior is so cute, isn't he?" Kelsea said, her eyes still on Jaymes.

Kyra nodded. "Adorable. Are you guys thinking about kids?"

Kelsea chuckled. "We've talked but not yet. Hopefully, one day soon."

"What are you two talking about over here?" Lily asked, handing over a plate of pizza for Kyra.

"Thank you," Kyra said as Kelsea said, "Babies."

Lily's gaze dropped to Kelsea's belly, but Kelsea stopped her before she asked. "No, I'm not pregnant. Not even trying or thinking. It's hard not to have baby fever when there's an adorable baby around."

"He was so cute, wasn't he?" Lily said.

"Who? Junior?" Pilar asked.

The others nodded.

"Holding him made me want a baby," Pilar admitted.

"Me, too," Lily and Kelsea said.

"Are we being insensitive?" Pilar asked Kyra. "I'm sorry. I feel like we are."

Kyra shook her head. "You should want what you want. It's not insensitive to want a baby just because I can't conceive."

"You can still be a mom," Lily said.

Kyra nodded. "And I will."

The topic changed to the other events of the day, and Kelsea asked if Kyra was okay.

Kyra shrugged. "It's been a crazy day. I think I'm still processing all of it."

"I don't blame you," Lily said. "You haven't really had time to let it all sink in."

Kyra nodded, some of the emotions hitting her while they talked.

"Maybe you two should get away for a few days. Go on a trip. Go see his family," Kelsea suggested.

"Take some time off," Pilar said. "You need a break."

"And agree to move in with him, because you both need it," Lily added. "He hasn't taken his eyes off of you since you walked out of the bedroom with your wet hair and wearing his clothes. Nice touch, by the way."

The others nodded with knowing grins.

"I'm not going to feel guilty for wanting that man," Kyra said, catching him watching her. "I hope I never stop."

SLADE WAS ready to kick everyone out so he could be alone with Kyra again when Jack walked over to him. Kicking everyone out seemed like an even better idea.

"I'll leave," Jack said. "It's not fair that you leave because of me."

Slade rolled his eyes. "No one's fucking leaving."

"If you can't trust me—"

"Don't be a dick, and I'll be able to trust you. Are you going to pull this shit again and make Kyra think I don't really love her?"

Jack shook his head. "No."

"Then we'll get through this. You weren't trying to hurt either of us, you were just running your mouth. Maybe you should shut it once in a while."

Jack nodded. "I've been told that my whole life."

Slade laughed. "There goes my hope."

Jack slapped him on the back and walked away. It wasn't long enough before Dex took his spot.

"Can we talk?" Dex asked.

"About?"

"I'm happy for you," Dex said.

Slade watched Kyra get up and add another slice of pizza to her plate. She went back over to where the other women were sitting and laughed at something Pilar said.

"You almost ruined it. She could have been killed today, and I never would have known where she was because she left without telling me," Slade said, his whole body tense with the knowledge he almost lost Kyra.

"I know."

"You can't pull this shit again," Slade said, turning to face Dex. "Williams almost tore us apart. He did his damn best. We came through that as a team, and that team included Lily, Pilar, Kelsea, and Ashleigh. Now it includes Kyra."

"She belongs here."

Slade nodded sharply.

"I don't just mean on the team, I mean with you. You're different with her around. She fixed something in your head, didn't she?"

Slade nodded again, more slowly. He was surprised Dex picked up on it. He wondered how much they all saw since Rocky said the same thing.

"Good."

Dex walked away, leaving Slade reeling slightly. He grabbed another beer and winked at Kyra when she looked up at him. He mouthed *are you okay?*, and she gave him a nod, then went back to her conversation.

"Glad I didn't have to patch anyone up," Rocky said when Slade took a seat next to him.

Slade chuckled. "Me, too."

"We all good now?"

Slade nodded. "We will be. I need her in my life. I need all of this."

"You have it," Rocky said, tapping his bottle against Slade's.

Howler walked over and whimpered, then rested his head on Slade's leg. One of his signs that he needed to go out.

"Come on, buddy," Slade said, standing and heading for the back door. Howler chased after him and ran out into the dark yard once the door was open.

It was quiet outside with only the sound of the team filtering through the open door. Slade stood at the edge of his patio, watching them. He was still pissed off at Jack and

Dex, but he'd get over it, eventually. It was tough to hold on to his anger when he got the girl in the end.

Speaking of... Kyra joined him on the patio, not hesitating before she slid her arm around his waist and rested her head on his shoulder.

"Hey," he said softly.

"Hey."

"You doing okay?"

She nodded. "Yeah. I think everything is catching up to me."

"It was a lot for one day," Slade said.

She nodded again. "Can I ask you something?"

"Always."

"Did you mean it when you asked me to move in?"

"Hell, yes."

"What about when you asked if I wanted to be a mom?"

"Of course. Why?"

She looked up at him with tears in her eyes. "I never thought I'd find someone like you. I've always wanted to be a mom, but I never thought it could happen."

"DNA doesn't make you a mom," he said.

Kyra nodded. "I know."

Howler came back and whimpered at them. He was getting tired, too.

"I think it's time to throw everyone out," Slade said.

"You don't have to," Kyra argued.

Slade chuckled. "I've been dying all night with you wearing my clothes. I'm barely holding myself in check. Trust me when I say I will not feel bad at all throwing them out."

Kyra turned and wrapped her arms around his neck and pulled him down for a soft kiss. She pulled back just enough to separate them and whispered, "Then I probably shouldn't tell you I'm not wearing any panties."

Slade scooped her up without hesitation, holding her thighs wide around his hips. He stalked into the house with Howler on his heels and told the room, "Let yourselves out. Do it soon. We're going to bed."

Kyra buried her face in his neck, but the others just cheered. Slade didn't care one way or another. He loved her, and he was going to take every chance he had to show her that for the rest of their lives.

He made it into the bedroom and closed the door, but when he tried to kiss her, she pulled back. He tilted his head and looked at her.

"My answer is yes," she said.

"Yes?" Slade asked, unsure what the question was. He barely had any blood left in his brain.

"To moving in and being a mom. My answer is yes."

Slade grinned and nibbled on her neck. "Then we better get in some practice."

ROCKY SAT on his couch later that night nursing a beer. Dex and he came home from Slade's, and Dex crashed, but Rocky was antsy. Like there was something he should be doing.

He stared at the TV as the movie played in front of him without seeing it. He didn't like the uneasy feeling he had. Like he'd forgotten to do something.

His phone buzzed in his pocket. When it didn't stop, he dug it out and smiled when he saw it was his mom. "Hey, Ma."

"Adrian, how are you?"

"Good. How are you? How's everything going? Do you need anything?"

His mom chuckled. "I'm the parent. I'm supposed to be asking you those things."

"I'm an adult, Ma. I can take care of myself."

"Yes, but you're still my baby. Are you dating anyone?"

Rocky snorted. "Nope. Sorry, Mom. No grandkids from me. Keep bugging Becky and Dana."

"I bug them all the time. They tell me you're the oldest so you should have that requirement."

Rocky laughed softly so he didn't bother Dex. "Yeah, well, they're the ones who are married."

His mom grew quiet for a long moment. "I miss your father. I wish he was still here."

Rocky's chest squeezed. He tried to convince himself it was all in his head, but the tone of her voice changed. Maybe it was grief, but Rocky heard blame. It was his fault his dad died. His mom and sisters blamed him. They weren't wrong.

"Me, too, Ma. Hey, uh, I need to go. It's getting late here, and I need to be up early," he lied. They had the next day off, but he wasn't going to admit that.

"Okay, sorry for calling so late. We'll talk soon."

"Love you, Ma."

"I love you, too."

Rocky pinched the bridge of his nose and tipped his head back to rest on the back of the couch. Guilt overwhelmed him. He could never bring his father back. Nothing would ever change that. If he could have traded places, he would.

Rocky was born to help people, to save them and heal them and make them whole. He'd done it for hundreds of people, but he failed his own father.

Maybe there was more he could do. Something he hadn't thought of. Or hadn't been brave enough to consider.

Rocky unlocked his phone and searched for living donors. Being an organ donor was something he signed up for as soon as he was old enough, but registering as a living donor was different. It meant taking a piece of him when he was alive. Giving to someone who needed him now.

The tightness in his chest eased as he reviewed the information online. It wasn't the only answer, but it felt like the right one. He'd survived war overseas, but there were people fighting a war that lived inside their bodies.

It was the right answer.

Rocky signed up to receive more information and turned off the TV. Even though they had the next day off, he knew he wouldn't sleep. He'd be up early, workout, and most likely go into the office, anyway. He didn't have anything else to keep him busy.

THANK **you** so much for reading Slade and Kyra's story! I enjoyed sharing them with you and writing a story less about a personal vendetta and more about two wounded characters who needed each other to heal.

The series continues with Rocky's story. He met Nikki years ago, and they spent a wild weekend together during his leave. They didn't exchange last names, and he never expected to see her again. Definitely not with a little boy who looked just like his father and needed Rocky's help in order to survive. Read Family today!

. . .

ARE YOU READY FOR MORE? Newsletter subscribers get *exclusive* bonuses like short stories, bonus scenes, and a first look at everything new. Sign up for my newsletter today so you never miss a thing!

WHAT IF YOUR book boyfriend was real? Blake is newly single and not looking for another relationship. Ian made a promise to a dying friend that he would tell Blake how he feels. Actions always speak louder than words, but Blake isn't ready to listen. Read His Curvy Friend now!

ABOUT THE AUTHOR

USA TODAY Bestselling Author Mary E Thompson spent most of her childhood wishing she had a few less curves. She hid in the pages of books because her favorite characters never cared what size her clothes were. Now, neither does Mary, and she writes stories that celebrate women like her. Real women who have curves, chase dreams, and find love, because we should all be happy, no matter our dress size.

Mary spends her non-writing time with her husband and two kids, watching too much TV, cheering for her hometown football team (Go Bills!), and hiding chocolate from her family.

Visit https://MaryEThompson.com/ to sign up for Mary's newsletter, **Romancing the Curves**. Subscribers get free ebooks and other fun stuff, like exclusive, members only content and giveaways, plus are the first to know about new releases and sales!